HEX TYPE THING

A MOONSTONE BAY COZY MYSTERY BOOK FIVE

AMANDA M. LEE

ONE

*W*hen I was a kid I dressed as a witch for Halloween one year. My father had a fit, said the neighbors would get the wrong idea and think we were pagans. Now, at the time, I was only eight so I didn't really know what that meant. In hindsight, I recognize his fear came from a different place.

It came from this. It came from Moonstone Bay.

That's where I, Hadley Hunter, witch extraordinaire, now call home. I'm a real-life witch, and Dad always knew it. However, we'd yet to discuss it over the phone. Whenever I brought it up he had an emergency that called him away from the conversation.

We were due for a reckoning. That's exactly what I was talking to my new friend June Seaver about. As the owner of the Moonstone Bay Cabana Clutch Hotel, a local business with an unfortunate name she refused to change undergoing a rather extensive renovation, she had a lot of time on her hands because she wasn't catering to guests at the moment. I was gearing up to open my own business as a psychic and tarot card reader (even though I had no experience with either), so I was happy to have someone to talk to.

"He's being a big pain," I complained, sipping my iced tea as we sat in the shade and watched the construction crew work. "I honestly think he believes if he keeps distracting me that I'll suddenly forget that I want to talk to him about this and let it go."

June was older, although not in a decrepit way or anything. She had experience on her side even though she'd never had children of her own to pass it along to, and she'd been something of a sounding board for me the past two weeks, ever since I'd unleashed a boatload of magic to save my friends from a gang of renegade cupids.

No, seriously. That totally happened.

"Well, let me ask you a question." She adopted her most pragmatic tone, which told me I was in for a bit of parenting after all. "Have you and your father ever had a serious conversation about your mother's family?"

That wasn't an easy question to answer, and not because I didn't know. The truth was, I'd never asked about my mother's family because I was afraid of the answer. All I knew was that my mother died in childbirth, leaving me with a caring if somewhat distracted father, and she'd been estranged from her parents at the time. I thought that meant I shouldn't care about them either, because I owed her some loyalty. I was the reason she was dead, after all.

The death of my grandmother May Potter changed everything for me. She left me ownership of a lighthouse on Moonstone Bay, introducing me to a world that I didn't know existed. In short order I'd found out that shifters, vampires, merfolk, cupids and even demons not only existed but essentially had the run of the island. In addition, I discovered I came from a long line of powerful witches and I had magic at my disposal. I was still getting used to the magic, but I was getting better at casting spells with each passing day.

That didn't change the fact that I felt as if I'd been denied my birthright by not learning about my witchy heritage at a young age. Now I was lagging behind and feared I would never catch up.

"I never asked," I admitted. I felt foolish, but June had been nothing but open and welcoming to me and I knew she wouldn't judge me for decisions made when I was young and dumb. "My father told me from the start that my mother didn't want anything to do with her family. He made it sound as if they had a big falling out."

"They did," June acknowledged. "Your mother wanted a break from the island and the magical destiny that she felt was being heaped upon her. She chose to walk away from this life."

"Yeah, but everything I've learned about her since tells me that she would've eventually told me the truth and let me make up my own mind about things."

"I think that's true."

"My father never gave me that option. He just cut my grandparents out of my life and didn't even give them a chance to get to know me."

"And you're bitter because you feel as if you've missed out."

"I *know* I've missed out." I heaved out a sigh and shook my head. "Wesley and I have been spending time together. He even let me name a horse. I go out there to help him take care of it sometimes. We're getting along really well."

"I've always liked your grandfather. He's a pip of a guy. He has attitude coming out of his keister."

My eyebrows inadvertently drew together as I tried to picture what that would look like. "He's a lot of fun," I said finally. "I worry about him, though. He spends all of his time with May's ghost. They play board games and hang out on the porch together, and basically live like hermits."

I almost laughed at my inadvertent joke. They couldn't live like hermits, because my grandmother was dead. Sure, her ghost remained behind to visit from time to time, but there was no future for her in the real world. My grandfather, Wesley Durham, was another story.

"I don't think you can insert yourself into that situation," June warned. "Wesley and May always had a tempestuous relationship in life. I wouldn't expect it to change in death."

That was an understatement. In life they'd gotten divorced, kept separate households and yet spent certain nights together every week. They fought constantly, bickered to the point one of them walked away, and then ended up sharing a bed despite all of that.

I didn't like to think about that aspect of their relationship too much because it weirded me out.

3

"I'm his only living relative," I reminded her. "If I don't look out for him, who will?"

"You're not his only living relative."

"I'm not?" A horrible thought crept through me. "He didn't have another family when he and May split up, did he?" I didn't like the idea of inheriting half-cousins I knew nothing about.

June chuckled at the notion. "No. You don't have to worry about that. Even when they were split up, May and Wesley were completely devoted to one another. But he has other family. He has a brother and some nieces. Maybe a nephew or two, too. I can't really remember."

"Oh." That was much better than what I was envisioning. "Do they live on the island?"

"Mainland. Tampa."

"Do they visit?"

"I think they come once a year or so. You'll have to discuss that with Wesley. He might be holding them back so as not to overwhelm you. Everyone in the family tends to come on a bit strong. You're the new element. I'm sure he wants to protect you."

He'd been protecting me since we'd met. "Yeah." I rolled my neck and made a sound halfway between a sigh and a groan, extending my legs in front of me as I readjusted. "I really am worried, though. I don't think it's healthy for him to spend all of his time with a dead woman."

"Have you spoken to him about this?"

What was with her? It was so much easier to gossip behind people's backs than to tackle things head-on. First she suggested I talk rationally with my father and now with my grandfather. I was going to stop this at the gate. "I can't talk to him about this."

"Why not?"

"Because it's none of my business."

Her lips twitched, but she otherwise managed to keep a straight face. "I see."

"Oh, I know what you're thinking." I offered up a half-hearted hand wave. "You believe I should stay out of his business and let him handle his own affairs. The thing is, I just got him. I've read stories about people who lose their life mates. If they don't have something to live for they simply give up and die. I don't want that to happen to Wesley."

"Has he given you any reason to believe he's going to give up and die?"

"No, but ... I just want to make sure it doesn't happen."

She chuckled, the sound low and throaty. "You can't control him. It would be nice if you could force him to your way of thinking — I've always had a crush on the man — but he's going to do what he's going to do. No matter how much he loves you, he won't stop being who he is just to make you feel better."

Sadly, I had a feeling that was true. Wait a second ... . "You have a crush on him?"

She wagged a finger in my face and made a tsking sound with her tongue. "Don't even think about it. You're far too old to play match-maker. Wesley made his choice a long time ago. Some people mate for life. I believe he and May were those types of people. You can't change that and you shouldn't want to."

She had a point. Still, I couldn't hide my annoyance. "If you say so." I took another sip of my iced tea. "Do you really think people are destined to mate for life?" I opted to change the subject to something happier.

She nodded. "I do. I believe in destiny, and sometimes she extends a hand and leads people to one another because the alternative means they'll never find the right fit on their own."

"Do you think it happens a lot?"

Her eyes twinkled. "Are you asking if I think you and Galen are destined to be together?"

I was totally asking that, but I didn't want her to know that's what I was hinting around about. Apparently I wasn't nearly as slick as I thought. "Of course not. Galen and I have only been together for a little bit."

"Uh-huh." June was clearly dubious. She knew Galen Blackwood, my boyfriend and sheriff of Moonstone Bay, even better than I did. She'd been keeping a close eye on him since he was a kid and she was one of the few people who could exert even a minor bit of control over him. "I'm glad you don't want to hear my opinion about that."

I frowned. "You don't think we belong together?" For some reason that hurt. "I assumed you approved of our relationship."

"Oh, I definitely approve." She snorted at my pout. "You are the worst when it comes to holding your cards close to your vest, Missy. You need to get a better poker face. I was just messing with you."

"You were?" I exhaled heavily, secretly relieved. "That's nice. I mean, I don't really care if you approve or anything, but I'm glad you do."

The laugh she let loose was raucous. "Oh, it's a good thing you didn't have your heart set on being an actress. Every emotion you feel is visible on that pretty face of yours. You would be the absolute worst actor on the stage if you had to pretend to feel something different."

"I ... ."

She barreled forward, ignoring whatever I was about to say. It didn't matter. I was feeling verbally clumsy, so it was probably best if I kept my mouth shut, something that was easier said than done. I'm one of those people who speaks before they think ... and then always regrets the outcome.

"I happen to believe you're absolutely perfect for Galen," June volunteered. "You're strong of mind, body and personality. You're also strong of spirit, which means you don't let him walk all over you. I don't know if you've noticed, but he tends to be a bossy thing when he gets up a full head of steam."

I had to laugh. He was beyond bossy.

"You also have an open heart, something he needs because he's a giving soul and he got a lot of guff as a kid for being sensitive," she continued. "He always wanted to help others. That's who he is. He also wanted to take care of animals. At one point his parents announced that he could no longer bring home stray animals."

I perked up. I loved hearing stories about Galen when he was a kid. "What kind of animals?"

"He didn't care. Cats. Dogs. Raccoons. He once brought home a wounded hermit crab. The thing was missing both claws and couldn't possibly survive, but he was determined to save it."

My lips curved at the thought. "He likes to talk big, but he's soft inside."

"Yes, and he makes you go weak and gooey at your core when he smiles." June winked to let me know that wasn't an insult. "You two are genuinely adorable together."

I happened to agree. Of course, we were newly in love — even saying the words to each other regularly despite both of us being anxious about the exchange — and we'd been living in the clouds since the big cupid fight. We hadn't as much as sniped at one another in the weeks since. "I can't disagree when you tell the truth like that."

She laughed, her eyes traveling to the beach. There was a flurry of activity down the way and she seemed interested in what she saw. "What do you know about this big festival they're setting up?"

That was a good question. Galen hadn't been miserly with the information, but he didn't exactly seem keen on sharing. "They're calling it the Skyclad Festival," I replied. "I don't know what that means. Galen isn't happy about it. He said thousands of people are flying to the island to participate. Since most of the income here comes from tourists I'm not sure why he's so upset."

When June didn't immediately respond, I turned my eyes to her and found her shoulders shaking with silent laughter. I was genuinely at a loss. "What's so funny?"

"Are you sure he said it was called the Skyclad Festival?"

"Yeah. Why?"

"Because skyclad means naked in pagan circles."

I was taken aback ... and suspicious that she was having me on. "Are you sure?"

She nodded without hesitation. "I'm sure. I might not be a witch, but I'm up on all of the paranormal shenanigans that happen on this island. Skyclad definitely means naked. In fact, there was a group of witches who lived out in the hills about twenty years ago who tried to host a skyclad festival of their own in town.

"They showed up on Main Street, doffed their robes and started dancing to music only they could hear," she continued. "Some of the tourists thought it was a real thing and joined in. And then some of the regulars, who all knew it wasn't legitimate but thought it was funny, also joined in. I believe there were three-hundred arrests that weekend."

I worked my jaw, flabbergasted. "Why would the Downtown Development Authority allow a festival that's named after a nudist activity?"

"That I don't know. I didn't realize that was the name. I've been busy with the renovations on the hotel. They're taking a long time."

"The place is going to be beautiful when you're finished," I reassured her, my mind still on the festival taking shape on the beach. "Galen has been dealing with preparations for this thing for the last week. He was hopeful a few days ago that it was going to fall apart at the last second, but that doesn't seem to be the case."

"My guess is that he well remembers the last skyclad festival. He would've been about ten years old about that time. I seem to remember him and Booker hiding in the shadows and watching the dancing. They were giggling like maniacs."

My lips quirked as I tried to picture Galen and the resident cupid lothario acting like hormonal idiots as the entire town got naked and danced without music. "I guess I'm sorry I missed it. That's another thing I have to be angry with my father about. If he'd allowed me to spend time with May and Wesley as a kid I might've been able to witness it and have a fun memory, too."

"You didn't miss much," June countered. "Not everyone should dance naked. I'm not into body shaming or anything, but there's no harm in shaving a little back hair now and then."

On that we could agree. "Well, I'm still interested in checking out this festival. Galen said there will be a lot of witches and a few other paranormal types ... although he swears up and down that no shark shifters will be present."

"Yes, he told me you're obsessed with the idea of shark shifters. There aren't many left, you know. You might never see one."

"Oh, I'm going to see one. I don't know when or how, but I'm totally going to see one. In fact ... ." I trailed off when I noticed a flurry of movement on the beach. There had been about twenty people working in different areas, all toiling away for the festival. Now they were all converging on the same spot.

"What do you think that is?" June asked, her eyes focused on the growing crowd.

"I don't know. I guess it can't hurt to wander down there and check it out."

"You read my mind."

TWO

*I*t turned out the cause of the excitement was none other than Galen. He stood in the middle of the workers, hands on hips, and glared at an older man who was gesturing wildly and relating some extravagant tale.

"Who is that?" I asked June as she came to a stop next to me, inclining my chin toward the man.

Her grimace was enough to tell me she wasn't any fonder of him than Galen appeared to be. "Alastair Herne."

That name meant absolutely nothing to me. "I'm going to need a bit more information."

She chuckled dryly. "I keep forgetting you're new to the island. You won't have known all the Alastair stories. He's something of a ... well ... twiddle pants. I guess that's the best term."

I still had nothing. "I don't know what that means."

"Oh, well, in my day that's how we referred to men who always adjusted themselves in public."

It took me a moment to grasp what she was saying. "Oh, gross." I wrinkled my nose. "You mean he puts his hands in his pants in public?"

"Oh, no." She vehemently shook her head. "He would never be that undignified. Putting your hands inside your pants is frowned upon. He's comfortable molesting himself over his pants. And he likes to stick his hands in his pockets and move them around quite often, too ... usually when he sees some pretty young thing in a bikini jiggling her rear end as she walks down the beach."

That was a bit too much information. "So, you're basically saying that he's a pervert."

"Oh, he's so much more than that. Alastair is a member of one of the island's founding families. He's rich, to the point of being able to wipe his behind with golden toilet paper, and he has real power on the island."

I eyed the man speculatively. Now that I'd learned the term "twiddle pants" I couldn't get it out of my head. "Does that mean he gets away with molesting young girls or something? Because, if so, I'm going to make him pay no matter how much money he's worth."

June snorted, amusement on full display. "No. He's never molested young girls to my knowledge. I don't think he has an eye for the underage ones. He likes them in the eighteen- to twenty-two-year-old range."

I didn't see how that was much better. "Why do you think he's down here?"

"He's heading up the festival," June replied. "I heard at the grocery store this week that he partnered with some singer to host it."

"What singer?"

"Um ... I think they said her name was Calliope."

I was floored. "Calliope? She's huge. Or she was, like, two years ago. She hasn't had a hit since then, but she has her own reality television show, so that means she's still huge."

"Oh, is she an opera singer?" June's face was blank. "I assumed it was some sort of pop sensation. I would be more excited by an opera singer."

"I didn't mean huge as in ... ." I decided not to finish the sentence. There was no graceful way for me to smooth over my answer and I wasn't keen on sounding like an idiot if I could help it. "I just meant that she's got, like, three hits in the top one-hundred in the same month and she's all over television. The young kids love her."

June smiled. "You're not all that old, my dear. I don't know that you can use the term 'young kids' when you can be considered one yourself."

"I'm referring to teenagers. I'm more of an Imagine Dragons and Mumford & Sons fan."

"Yeah. That's not real music. Try listening to the Beatles ... or Stevie Nicks."

We could agree on Stevie, although getting lost in a conversation about which generation had the better music seemed a waste of time given what was going on around us. "I'm just surprised that Calliope is involved in this. I guess it's a bigger deal than I realized."

"Well, Alastair is a millionaire fifty times over and it sounds like this singer is, too. I'm sure it will be quite the event ... whether nudity is involved or not."

I bit the inside of my cheek to keep from laughing — thus drawing attention to us, and focused on Galen. He didn't look to be in awe of Alastair like the rest of the workers. No, he looked annoyed. He was sporting a ten o'clock shadow — as a wolf shifter, he grew hair like Hagrid on steroids — and a scowl that I recognized from the few times (really, they were minor incidents and best left forgotten) we'd gotten into legitimate arguments.

"I don't think you're listening to me," he barked, hands on narrow hips. "You have people arriving for this stupid thing tomorrow. Are you ready for them? Is the beach set up? Where are the bathrooms? This is a total disaster."

I'd never much thought of Galen as the party planner sort but it made me smile to see him getting out his aggression on others. That meant any fight we were destined to engage in was still weeks away. Er, well, hopefully.

"Oh, calm down," Alastair drawled. He had that disaffected ennui that television taught me belonged only to the uber-rich. He also had really bad hair plugs. Apparently, money couldn't buy everything.

"We've been over this a hundred times in the past two weeks, Galen. I told you that I have everything under control."

"Does this look under control to you?" Galen gestured toward the beach. "This doesn't look under control to me."

Honestly, I wasn't certain what he was so worked up about. The beach looked fine. Of course, I wasn't the sheriff. Perhaps he knew something I didn't.

"You have thousands of people coming to this beach tomorrow," Galen snapped. "Thousands! There are supposed to be tents. There are supposed to be bathrooms. Do you have any idea what's going to happen if there aren't enough bathrooms? Can anybody answer that question for me?" He looked expectantly at the other workers.

No one answered, so I held up my hand. His eyes were filled with fury when they turned to me, and then they cleared.

"What are you doing here?" he asked, clearly surprised by my presence. I thought for sure he'd watched us approach, but apparently he was too busy yelling at the workers to notice. Perhaps there was an insult buried in there, but I was too amused to pay it much heed.

"Well, hello to you, too," June drawled. "I don't know that I've ever heard such a warm greeting. I feel tingly all over."

His frown only deepened. "I didn't mean ... I just ... stay right there." He extended a finger in our direction and then turned back to Alastair. "I want the bathrooms in place tonight or I'll shut you down. There are no ifs, ands or buts about it."

Alastair's mouth dropped open. "You can't shut us down. You don't have the authority."

"Oh, no? This gives me all the authority I need." Galen tapped his badge for emphasis. "If I deem any activity a danger to Moonstone Bay or its residents I have the right to act accordingly."

"You can't shut us down!" Alastair's hands landed on his hips. "I won't allow you to threaten us this way. Do you have any idea how much time and money went into this festival? We're talking my money. Millions of dollars."

The figure caused me to glance around again. I was understandably confused. "You spent millions of dollars on what?" I asked.

"This." Alastair waved his hands at the beach. "Don't you understand what this is?"

"It's the beach." My response was perfunctory. "Last time I checked, the beach was here before you even started setting up for your festival. I don't see anything around here that could've cost millions of dollars."

"Ha!" Galen jabbed a finger at Alastair. "See! I'm not the only one who has noticed you've done nothing. This place is a disaster."

"I wouldn't go that far," I countered. "I mean ... it's a beach. It looks like a beach. I don't think there's anything wrong with it."

"Ha!" Alastair mimicked Galen and gave him the finger — not *that* finger — right back. "There's nothing wrong with the beach. You need to calm down. There's no reason to get worked up."

The look Galen shot me was murderous. "Don't you think you should head back to the hotel?" He asked the question in a pleasant enough voice, but there was a hint of malice to it. "I'm not telling you what to do or anything — and you know I love it when you give your opinion on stuff you don't understand — but I think you'd be more comfortable at the hotel. I mean ... it's really hot."

I narrowed my eyes. And here I thought we were going to continue our streak of not fighting. I, apparently, was an idiot. "What don't I understand?"

"You understand everything fine, dear," Alastair responded before Galen could. "Galen is the one who seems to have bricks in his head. Do you know how I know that? I can hear nothing but the dull thud of idiocy coming out of his mouth."

Okay, he really was a twiddle pants. Even though I was annoyed with Galen's response to my well-thought-out opinion, I didn't like this guy's condescending attitude one bit. "Where are your festival guests going to go to the bathroom?" I asked, keeping my face impassive even though I wanted to sneer at him. "It won't be sanitary if they go on the beach."

"Thank you!" Galen threw his hands in the air. "I'm glad to see you were listening. I wasn't sure."

I pinned him with a dark look. "Keep it up. You're going to snap our no-fighting streak if you're not careful."

This time the look he shot me was devilish. "Yes, but then we can make up. We haven't made up in weeks. We're due."

He had a point. Wait ... what were we talking about again? Oh, right. Bodily functions. There was little more that I liked talking about more than urination and defecation. "I think the other tourists will be turned off if their kids discover buried ... um, treasure of a different sort ... while building sandcastles two weeks from now."

Alastair's expression was so dark I had to take an inadvertent step back. Mayhem etched across his features and he took on a decidedly foreboding countenance that caused my heart to skip a beat.

"Young lady, I'm curious what you have to do with this discussion," he started, his tone chilly. "I think you should listen to our esteemed sheriff and mind your own business."

"Hey!" Galen's agitation was on full display as he took a step toward Alastair. "Don't talk to her like that."

"You just did."

"Yeah, well ... that's neither here nor there." He shot me an apologetic look. "I'm serious. I'll shut this festival down tonight if the bathroom situation isn't fixed to my satisfaction. That's all there is to it."

"And if you try, I'll go to the Downtown Development Authority and tell them how you plan to cut off a huge source of revenue for the island. I'm sure they'll be thrilled about that."

I internally cringed at the threat. The Downtown Development Authority had something of a badass reputation. They were the real power on the island and everybody, including Galen, was terrified of them. Oh, he put on a good show when he was certain they were out of earshot, but it was clear that he was as leery of the nearly invisible board as everyone else. So far, I'd met only one member of the board — Morgan St. Pierre — and he was the exact opposite of pleasant.

"You'll want to be very careful about threatening me," Galen warned, his voice low. "I mean ... *very* careful."

"And you'll want to be very careful about threatening me," Alastair fired back. "I'm not going to sit back and let you ruin this festival. If you think that, then ... well ... I guess we'll have to take it to the higher authorities."

I didn't like the sound of that. I sucked in a breath, debated if I should try to pull Galen away from the confrontation, and then lost my train of thought when a blonde beauty cut across the beach in our direction. Calliope. The singer who had only one name, like Cher ... and Madonna ... and Enya. What? I have eclectic taste in music. Sue me.

"What's going on?" she called out, a friendly smile on her face. She wore a pair of the tiniest shorts I'd ever seen, the sort that allowed her butt cheeks to hang out the backside but in kind of a fashionable way. She had on a neon bra under a fishnet top, and she wore so much makeup I was convinced I would be able to run my fingernail down her cheek and leave a trail.

"Oh, Calliope, you're here." Alastair sent Galen another warning look before hurrying forward to greet the singer. "I can't tell you how great it is to see you."

I moved up to Galen's side and watched along with him as the odd duo bent their heads together in whispered conversation. It was obvious Calliope was trying to get to the bottom of the argument. Alastair, of course, would be putting his spin on the story. Galen would know that, yet he didn't look bothered in the least by the new wrinkle.

"Did you miss me today?" I asked brightly, hoping to coax a smile out of him.

The look he shot me was bland, but I swear I saw his lips quirk. "Should I have missed you? I've seen you twice since we rolled out of bed."

"I know but ... we spent the entire weekend in bed. We didn't even go out for drinks. We had food delivered. I thought you might miss spending that level of quality time with me."

This time he couldn't hide his smile. "If you play your cards right, we can do the same thing this weekend."

"Not if you're dealing with mountains of poop on the beach."

He scowled. "This was an absolutely terrible idea. I can't believe the DDA approved it. I mean ... I just can't."

"It sounds to me like they care more about dollar signs than anything else. Besides, they won't have to deal with the fallout. You will."

"That's right." His eyes were heavy-lidded when they locked with mine. "I plan to threaten Alastair two more times and then my shift is over. How do you feel about scallops and beer on the beach?"

"I think I could live with that. Although ... I thought you threatened to shut them down if they didn't have the toilet issue taken care of by the end of the night. How will you know if they follow through if you're with me?"

"I figured we would take your golf cart and then drive it down the beach on the way back. I'll be able to check then."

"Ah. Good thinking." I tapped the side of my head for emphasis. "You're more than just a pretty face."

He snorted and shook his head, his eyes traveling to Calliope as the woman plastered what could only be described as the sexiest smile known to man on her face and sauntered over.

"I don't think I've had the pleasure," she purred, extending her hand in dainty fashion. "I'm Calliope. That's one word ... and no last name."

If she expected Galen to be impressed, she was about to be disappointed.

"I'm Galen Blackwood," he supplied. "That's two words, one of which is a last name, and I don't care who you are. You're partially to blame for this fiasco. You have three hours to get the bathroom situation sorted out or I will shut you down."

"Oh, don't be a gloomy Gus." She ran her finger down his arm, causing my temper to flare. She might've been a big star, but she was trying to poach my man. "You need to relax. You're wound too tight. I know, how about we head down the beach and have a few drinks at that delightful little tiki bar?" The atmosphere sparked with more flirt than humidity. "I bet that would loosen up both of us."

I opened my mouth to tell her exactly where she could stick her invitation, but Galen was ahead of me.

"You're welcome to go wherever you want and have as many drinks as you want," he said, taking a step back so she could no longer touch him. "I don't really care what you do. What I care about is that the bathroom situation is solved.

"Now, I'm going to have dinner with my girlfriend," he continued, his head tilting toward me. "We're going to spend some time eating, drinking and then frolicking on the beach."

I wrinkled my nose. "Since when do we frolic?"

He ignored the question. "When I come back this way in three hours, if the bathroom situation isn't handled I'm going to shut you down. Plain and simple."

"Try it!" Alastair barked. "If you try to shut us down, I'll shut you down."

"You can try." Galen was matter-of-fact as he linked his fingers with mine. "You have three hours." He glanced around dubiously. "You'd better start working."

THREE

*O*ur favorite beachfront restaurant had oysters on special. Galen ordered them as an appetizer to accompany our daiquiris and mozzarella sticks. He looked relaxed as he sat at a patio table with me, but I knew him better than most and recognized the stress lining his handsome features.

"You're trying not to talk about it," I noted. The oysters hadn't yet arrived and I was nervous to admit I'd never tried them. I decided to put that off and focus on his problems rather than my own for a change. "It might make you feel better to vent."

"I don't want to vent. I want to enjoy my time with you." He rested his hand on top of mine and stared out at the ocean. "What did you do with June today? I didn't realize you two had plans."

As much as he loved June — and it was honest and true adoration with him — I could tell he was leery regarding the amount of time we'd been spending together. She knew all of his secrets, and she wasn't afraid to tell old stories that made him and Booker look ridiculous. That's only one of the reasons I loved hanging out with her.

"I needed someone to complain to and Lilac was busy at the bar getting ready for this festival — she expects to be completely packed for the next few days — and May was out visiting Wesley. I don't have many friends."

"Good. That means you can dedicate all your time to me." His grin was wolfish as he squeezed my hand. "What was bothering you that you needed someone to talk to?"

"You don't need to hear about it."

"Unless it's some female trouble thing that's going to give me nightmares, I want to hear about it. Your problems are now my problems, so lay it on me."

I wanted to point out the reverse was also true, which meant his problems — including the approaching festival — were now my problems, but I knew better than to push him before he was ready. In a short amount of time I'd learned to read his moods, and it was obvious he was trying to calm himself before we got to the main conversation of the evening.

"I talked to my Dad today," I volunteered. "I tried to pin him down on the witch stuff."

"Let me guess, he suddenly remembered something he had to do and hung up on you."

"He said goodbye before ending the call, so he didn't really hang up on me. Of course, he didn't wait for me to say it back, so ... I guess he did hang up on me."

Galen pursed his lips as he regarded me. "I'm not sure what you want me to say," he said finally. "Your father sounds like a real piece of work. I think you're better than him. But he's still your father. You can't choose your parents."

"Which is why you still haven't introduced me to your mother, right?"

He growled. His mother, who lived on the island, was a sore subject between us. He swore up and down I was better off not meeting her, but I was starting to get a complex about it. We were supposed to be in love, yet he wanted to hide me away. It wasn't a good feeling.

"Forget I said that," I offered. "I don't want to argue."

"I don't either. I'm trying to set something up so you can meet my mother ... even though I guarantee you'll regret that meeting before it's all said and done."

"I just want to know where you came from."

His smile was sweet. "I get that. I really am working on it. Give me a little time."

That had been his mantra for two straight weeks and I'd seen no forward momentum. I couldn't even get my father to talk to me for more than five minutes, though, so I had no room to judge. "Okay. You can have as much time as you need."

"Thank you."

I thought better of my previous offer. "Scratch that. You can have another two weeks and then I'm tracking her down myself."

He let loose a sigh and then nodded. "Just let me get through this festival. It's too much to deal with while trying to wrangle my mother. She's ... difficult."

"Maybe we should introduce her to my father. They can be difficult together."

"That sounds like a nightmare in the making."

He wasn't wrong. "Anyway, I want him to come out and visit me. I want him to see the lighthouse, see that I'm happy here. I want him to meet you, unless you're opposed to that for some reason. He won't even stay on the phone long enough for me to extend the invitation, though. He's driving me crazy."

"I have no problem meeting your father. I might say a few things to him that will upset you, but that can't be helped. I don't think he treats you well and I want him to correct the situation."

"He's not a bad father," I argued hurriedly. "In fact, he was a great father growing up. He never yelled or anything."

"That just means he wasn't a monster. I know you don't want to hear it, but the fact that you're afraid to talk to him means something."

I was curious. "What do you think it means?"

"That he's a jerk and he doesn't know how lucky he is to have you in his life." As if to prove it, Galen lifted my hand and pressed a kiss to the palm. It was a romantic gesture that should've made me roll my eyes. Instead, my heart stuttered and I had to work overtime to calm myself. "Me, on the other hand, I know exactly how lucky I am to have you."

My cheeks heated at his gaze. "That was really smooth," I offered when I was certain I could speak without my voice cracking and giving me away. "I take it you're bucking for adult playtime when we get home."

He chuckled and released my hand. "Why do you think I ordered the oysters?"

"Yeah, about that ... um ... I've never eaten oysters and I'm afraid they're gross."

"Why would you think that before you've eaten them?"

"Because I've known people who have ... um ... indulged, and there's a rumor they taste like snot."

"They don't."

"Maybe you have a higher tolerance for snot and don't realize they taste like snot."

"They don't taste like snot. They're good. You'll like them."

I wasn't convinced, but at least I'd lodged my discomfort on the record. There was nothing to do but wait until I could confirm the snot theory. "So ... Calliope was hot for you. I can't tell you what it did for my ego when you turned her down in favor of me."

"I would turn down anyone in favor of you."

"I think you proved that with Calliope."

"Meh." He shrugged, seemingly indifferent. "She really does nothing for me. I prefer my women dark and mysterious ... and with a touch of witchy fun."

"Well, then I'm perfect for you."

"I've thought that since the moment I met you."

When I thought back to our first meeting, he'd seemed agitated. Bringing that up now was unnecessary. I wanted to hear more about the festival. He'd been talking about it for two weeks, but in our love haze I'd tuned out most of it.

"What's the deal with the Alastair guy? June says he's richer than God and can basically buy and sell the island."

"He's not that rich. Don't get me wrong, he's well off, but there are others on this island who have more money than him."

"He seems to think he can get the DDA on his side. You have to be nervous about that possibility."

"I'm not afraid of them." He said the words with bravado, but I knew better. The members of the DDA could hurt him if they put their minds to it. I didn't know much, but I did know that.

"I'm sorry he's making things difficult for you." I meant it. "You'll be fine. Everyone in this community loves you."

"Not everyone. And, honestly, I only care about you loving me right now."

"I definitely love you."

"Right back at you." He leaned forward and pressed a soft kiss to my lips, pulling back at the sound of a wistful sigh.

There, standing next to our table with an appetizer platter in her hand, was Lola Pierce. A local woman a few years younger than Galen, obvious about her crush on him. Most of the women I'd come into contact with on the island had crushes on my boyfriend — and weren't afraid to share that little tidbit with me — so I was pretty much used to it at this point.

"Here are your appetizers." Lola didn't move her eyes from Galen's face as he leaned back and cleared room on the table for her to place the platter. "Can I get you anything else before your entrees are ready?"

"We're still working on our drinks, so we're good," he replied, offering up a friendly smile. "Thanks for the oysters, though. I plan to put them to good use."

"Oh, yeah?" For a moment, Lola looked hopeful. Then, apparently, she remembered Galen wasn't alone. The look she shot me was dour. "Well, enjoy your dinner."

I watched her go with a mixture of amusement and annoyance. "Do you know what I find interesting?"

"No, but I'm sure you're going to tell me."

"Every woman on this island would be willing to kill me for a shot at you."

His forehead wrinkled as he drew his eyebrows together. "I think that's a gross exaggeration. Most of the people on this island are incapable of murder. At most, they might be willing to pull your hair or gouge out an eye or something."

Oddly enough, that didn't make me feel better. "Well, thanks for that."

He chuckled and grabbed one of the oyster shells from the tray and handed it to me. "Bottoms up."

I eyed the slimy-looking delicacy and frowned. "I don't know. Can't I just eat the mozzarella sticks? They're more my speed."

"You have to at least try one. I won't make you eat more than one if you don't like the first, but you should always be open to new experiences. If you weren't, we wouldn't be here right now. You'd still be hiding out in the lighthouse trying to figure things out on your own.

"Instead, you opened yourself to a new experience, and it worked out well for both of us," he continued, grabbing his own oyster. In a move I never saw coming, he hooked his arm through mine and then returned the oyster to the spot in front of his mouth. "We'll do it together."

I wasn't quite ready to admit defeat. "What if you eat all the oysters? Then you'll be all riled up for tonight and I'll happily go along for the ride."

"Just try it."

I glared at the oyster. "This is going to be gross. I just know it."

I decided to attack the situation as if slamming a shot. I tipped up the shell, emptied the contents into my mouth and swallowed as quickly as possible. I couldn't keep my face even as the taste hit me.

"Good, huh?" Galen smiled as he wiped the corners of his mouth with his napkin. "Did you like it?"

"Yeah, that totally tasted like snot."

He held out his hands and offered up a lopsided grin. "You win some, you lose some."

. . .

HE DROVE MY GOLF CART ALONG the beach during the ride home. The moon was bright above the water, the breeze stiff, but welcome after the heat of the day. The golf cart had been a gift from my grandfather because vehicles — unless expressly needed for farm work, construction, taxiing guests to the various hotels or law enforcement – were strictly forbidden. I'd come to cherish the cart. Sure, it had been peach when he first gave it to me, but Booker had helped me paint it a lovely purple, and now I had plans to use it for my business ... if I ever got it up and running.

"It's a nice night," I noted, my head resting against the seat. "I never realized what I was missing by not living on an island."

He slid me a sidelong look. "You were talking about me, right?"

"Among other things."

He moved his hand over to hold mine as he drove. Luckily for both of us the beach was relatively flat and there was no worry of running into anything. I knew he would hold true to his promise and check the festival area. I also knew that he would shut down the festival, despite the damage it could do to his own career, if he felt things weren't up to snuff.

"When is the festival supposed to start?" I asked.

"Tomorrow, but my understanding is only the VIP guests arrive tomorrow. They get a private night on the beach. The other guests come in the next day."

"How many VIP guests are there?"

"I have no idea. However many idiots they could suck an extra ten grand out of, I guess."

I was flabbergasted. "What? People paid ten thousand dollars to attend this festival?"

"That's what the regular guests paid. The VIP guests paid twenty grand."

"That is ... ridiculous. You could buy a car for that."

"Yes, but we're talking about people who get off on their station in life rather than what's important. Why else do you think they're following a celebrity whose only claim to fame is a song about a diamond-encrusted thong?"

Oh, well, now we were getting somewhere. "I didn't think that was your sort of music. I'm surprised you know who she is."

"I did my research when news of the festival popped up. She essentially has three songs to her name, a reality television show that proves she's trying to cling to her fame, and nothing else. I listened to one of her songs because one of my deputy's daughters said she's 'to die for.' It was auto-tuned nonsense."

"So ... you don't like hearing about diamond thongs?"

"Unless you're wearing the thong, I genuinely don't give a crap."

"What kind of music do you like?"

"Bob Seger."

I pressed my lips together to keep from laughing. "Are you sure about that, Grandpa?"

"Go ahead and joke. The man is a legend. I also like Bon Jovi."

"You're a constant surprise."

"And don't you forget it."

We lapsed into amiable silence for the rest of the ride. He was the first to break it as we drew closer to our destination. "Well, it looks like they've made some progress," he muttered.

"Are those Porta-Potties?"

He nodded. "They belong to the city. They're kept in a warehouse outside of town. We usually don't need all of them, but in this case I think it's necessary." He killed the engine on the cart and climbed out, casting a glance back at me. "You don't have to come. I just need to check this out. I won't be long."

"I would rather stick with you." I moved to join him, frowning when I caught the look of mischief in his eyes. "What? Oh, don't tell me I have something on my face. It's probably oyster slime. My body is still rejecting it."

He laughed and shook his head. "No. That's not what I was thinking."

"What were you thinking?"

"That I can't believe a few short months ago I didn't have anyone who would rather stick with me. It's kind of ... humbling."

"It will be rewarding if you hurry up and check everything out that needs to be checked out."

"Oh, yeah?" He cocked an eyebrow. "How so?"

"I'll show you when we get back to the lighthouse."

"If that's not a way to get me moving, I don't know what is. Let's do this."

He held my hand as he led me through the rows of portable bathrooms. There looked to be about fifty, which seemed overkill, but given how many people they were expecting at the festival I couldn't be sure it was enough.

"Are they going to pass your test?" I asked after a few minutes.

"They'll get a reprieve," he replied, releasing my hand and pulling out his phone. "They need twice as many units as this, but the fact that they got these out here as fast as they did means they can do the same in the morning for the rest of them."

"Who are you texting?"

"Alastair."

"I'm sure he'll be thrilled to hear from you." I grinned as I turned away, my eyes falling on something on the ground near a beach lounger. I first thought it was a towel, probably discarded by someone taking a swim to cool down. The more I stared at it, though, the more I thought it resembled something else. "Galen?"

He didn't immediately respond because he was busy typing on his phone.

I cleared my throat to strengthen my voice and tried again. "Galen?"

"Hmm? I'll be right with you, Hadley. Then we'll head to the lighthouse and you can reward me like you promised."

I had bad news for him. Nobody was getting rewarded tonight. "I don't think that's in the cards."

"Oh, you can't back out now. You already promised. I'm revving on oysters. It's cruel and unusual for you to tease me that way."

"Yeah, I'm not the problem." I extended a shaky finger toward the lump on the ground. It was about fifteen feet away, but the distance was too great to make out any features under the limited moonlight. "I think that's a body."

"What?" He was perplexed as he shifted his eyes to the spot I indicated. Instantly, his nostrils flared and his back went ramrod straight. I remained rooted to my spot as he approached the shape. The set of his shoulders told me everything I needed to know. "Well, crap," he lamented as he lifted his chin. "I guess those oysters are going to waste."

FOUR

*G*alen kept me close as he studied the body while waiting for the medical examiner to arrive. Even though he was intent on his task, he kept flicking his gaze to me to make sure I didn't wander far. It didn't hit me until after the third time that he was worried.

"What happened to her?" I asked, focusing my full attention on him. I didn't want to look too closely at the body. I had a bad feeling about what I would find.

"She was stabbed," he replied, his eyes going between me and the golf cart. "You know, you don't have to stay here. I can call Booker to take you home and I will follow with the golf cart as soon as I'm done." He turned apologetic. "I'm sorry you ate an oyster for nothing."

I tried to muster a laugh for his benefit, but came up empty. "I'll stick with you."

"I could be here for hours."

"I guess it's good I've yet to start my job, huh? I don't have to get up tomorrow morning until I feel like it. I'll stay." I was firm this time, letting him know that there was no sense arguing because my mind was made up. "Do you know her?"

He nodded and blew out a sigh. "Her name is Salma Hershey. She's the daughter of Benton and Barbara Hershey."

It was wrong to be judgmental, but I couldn't stop myself. "There's a guy named Benton Hershey on the island?"

Galen let loose a hollow chuckle. "He's a banker. He owns a fifty-one percent stake in Hershey Banking and Trust."

I recognized the name. The banks were regional in the South, but located almost everywhere, including on Moonstone Bay, where they were the only option. "I take it that means he's rich."

"You could say." He had on rubber gloves, pulling them from his pocket after our discovery, and his fingers were busy as they moved over the woman's chest. "She's twenty-one. Lived here her whole life."

There was something about his tone that set me on edge. "Did you know her well? I mean, like, were you guys ever involved or anything?" I felt foolish asking, but he seemed to be taking the young woman's death harder than I thought he would.

"Seriously?" The look he shot me was withering. "She's twenty-one."

"So? She's been an adult for three years. I've been here only a few months. I know darned well you had an active social life before me."

"I can't seem to remember it at all. My memories of before you came into my life are so dark I can barely see them."

I managed a grin. "That was a really good lie."

"It's not a lie." He held my gaze for a moment and then sobered. "I never dated her. I preferred spending my time with actual adults. Salma might've technically been legal, but she had the mindset of a middle-school girl."

Oh, well, now we were getting somewhere. "Meaning what?"

"Meaning that she was superficial, shallow and altogether annoying. She was one of those entitled trust fund kids who think the world and everyone in it should bow at their feet simply because they were born into a family with money."

I was starting to detect a theme with Galen's disdain. "You really don't like rich people, do you?"

"Honestly, there are plenty of rich people I do like. I don't like people who think they're better than others simply because of the amount of money they have at their disposal. I have no use for people like that."

"I guess that's why you like me, huh?" I kept my eyes to the ground, looking for clues. It was dark and the area would soon be crawling with people. I didn't want Galen to inadvertently miss anything. "I'm dirt poor."

When he didn't immediately respond, I turned back and found him staring at me, bemused. "What?"

"Honey, I don't know how to break this to you but that lighthouse May left you is worth millions of dollars. You could spark a bidding war that would leave you set for life if you wanted."

I stared at him for a beat, dumbfounded. "Millions of dollars?"

He nodded. "You're one of the Moonstone Bay elite now."

"Um ... I have, like, two-thousand dollars in my checking account and that has to last me until I get this witch-on-call idea off the ground. The lighthouse might be worth something, but it's not as if that benefits me, because I have no intention of selling it."

"No, but you could take out a home equity loan if you needed money. But I don't recommend that unless you're really desperate. You have me, so you'll never be that desperate."

"Your family has money, right?" I was trying to get to the bottom of his attitude when it came to the uber-wealthy. He was something of a mystery when he wanted to be. "Do you not like these people because you knew them while growing up?"

He shrugged. "I don't like some of these people — and I stress *some* — because their attitudes stink. That's the start and end of it."

"Okay, well ... what can you tell me about Salma? I mean, other than the fact that she's beautiful." It was true. The young woman lying on the ground, her blood seeping into the sand, was lovely. She had long dark hair, as black as mine, and her emerald eyes were open. She had the sort of high cheekbones that you find only on the pages of a magazine, and her skin was the color of fresh honey.

"There isn't much to tell." Galen craned his neck and stared toward the parking lot, which remained empty. It was clear he was getting antsy while waiting for backup. "She was an empty vessel."

I waited for him to continue. When he didn't, I pushed. "Is that kind of like being a twiddle pants?"

I'd related the term to him during dinner, causing him to roar with laughter. He confirmed that Alastair really was a twiddle pants, but the joke only brought a tiny smile this time.

"No. She basically spent all her time shopping, hanging out at the beach and drinking coffee at the various shops."

"That's nice work if you can get it. What did she do for a living?"

"Nothing."

"Nothing?" That didn't sound right. "She must've done something. She was an adult. I mean ... was she going to school or anything?"

"It's impossible to get a decent degree on the island," Galen reminded me. "We have some tourist tracks that are good for most of our kids, but there aren't many options if you don't want to get involved in that field. Salma didn't want to be involved in any field. She basically wanted to be paid for doing nothing."

"That's also good work if you can get it," I teased. "How did she manage that gig?"

"Her father enabled her. He didn't make her work. She was allowed to run wild, do anything she wanted, and he funded her lifestyle."

"That sounds great in theory, but I think you'd get bored with it after a time. I know that I've been a woman of leisure for far too long. I'm looking forward to starting a business."

"That's because you're the sort of person who believes in earning your keep. That's not who Salma was. She spent all her time on the internet recommending products and taking selfies of herself. She got free stuff because of it."

I was taken aback. "Wait ... you're saying she was one of those internet influencers?"

His face was blank. "I don't know what that is."

"They're those people who spend all of their time recommending restaurants or makeup or shoes on the internet because they've amassed a bunch of followers. And they get paid for it."

"That's not a job."

"I agree, but that doesn't mean it's not happening. I read a story ... ." I trailed off and searched my memory. "Oh, right. Now I remember. There was that woman who was on that old sitcom with those freaky-looking twins. She played the aunt on the show. You know the show I'm talking about, right?"

"I don't recall watching any show with freaky-looking twins. I think I would remember that."

I ignored the sarcasm. "It doesn't matter about the show. She was married to some fashion designer and they were caught bribing their daughters' way into college."

"I vaguely remember the story," he acknowledged. "What does that have to do with Salma?"

"Nothing. But this woman's daughter was an influencer, and she lost all of her endorsements. She had some eyeshadow deal going with one of the makeup companies and was hawking dorm room decorations for another. She was literally paid to recommend stuff on the internet."

"And I'm saying that's not a job."

"It's not. But it's still a thing. Salma was doing the same thing."

"Are you suggesting there's a motive for her murder in there?"

"I don't know," I hedged. "Did she make enemies with anybody on the island? Maybe she had a rival who wanted to do the same thing she did, or maybe she wouldn't recommend something and someone lost his or her temper."

"And stabbed her seven times?"

I took an inadvertent step back. "What?" I couldn't stop myself from looking at the body, but it was dark, so I'd missed the obvious signs of trauma. A second glance told me everything I needed to know. The attack on Salma had been quick and frenzied. "I guess that notion of someone killing her over makeup seems kind of out there." I chewed my bottom lip and continued to stare.

"Don't look at her," Galen instructed, moving to obstruct my view. His expression was serious. "There's no need for you to see that."

It was too late. I couldn't unsee the trauma. "I didn't realize ... ." I trailed off, feeling like a ninny. "You said she was stabbed, but I thought that meant just once."

"Would it have mattered if it was just the one time?"

I shrugged, noncommittal. "Kind of," I hedged. "I mean ... one wound might signify that someone lashed out in a moment of anger and regretted it. Seven stab wounds seem to suggest there was a lot of rage on this beach when it went down. Do you know how long she's been out here?"

"That's for the medical examiner to decide. You have a point about the sort of attack we're dealing with, though. I hadn't really thought about it like that, but you're right. I don't think this was an accidental flash of temper."

"No." I forced my eyes back to the sky. The moon looked amazing with the rippling waves cresting beneath it. "Do you think this has something to do with your festival?"

Galen opened his mouth, perhaps to deny the idea, but he thought better of it. "That's a very good question. Why else would she be here? I bet she was one of the people who spread word about the festival. I always wondered how they got so many people in such a short amount of time. I bet they were using these influencers you've been talking about."

My eyes drifted back to her face. The look of horror reflected in her eyes would stick with me for a long time. "Do you have to notify her parents?"

He nodded solemnly. "Yeah. My offer to call Booker to get you home still stands. You don't have to stick around for this."

"I want to be with you."

"Okay. Stay out of the way but don't go too far. We don't know if our killer is still out here."

"I won't go very far. I promise."

· · ·

IT WAS ALMOST TWO BEFORE WE made it back to the lighthouse. We were both dragging when we parked the cart in the driveway. I unlocked the door, Galen made sure it was secure once we were both inside, and then we trudged up to my bedroom.

I stripped out of my clothes and crawled directly into bed. Galen held it together long enough to brush his teeth and splash cold water on his face. I could tell his mind was busy even as it whined for him to shut down.

When he climbed in next to me, he slid his arm around my waist and tugged until my head rested on his chest. He radiated heat but I didn't mind because the central air was on full blast.

"The medical examiner said it was a frenzied attack, just like what you surmised," I noted as I ordered myself to wind down. "That seems to indicate that it was a lover or someone close to her."

His eyes were closed, his breathing regular, but I knew he was still awake. "Are you bucking for an investigative position on my team?"

"No. Just giving my opinion. That's allowed."

"It's more than allowed. I like hearing what you have to say." He squeezed my shoulder. "Just out of curiosity, though, why do you believe that?"

"Because to kill someone in the way Salma was killed you have to know the victim. You either have to love them so much that your heart was shattered by something they did or hate them so much that you can taste it. There's a reason people say there's a thin line between love and hate."

"I'm not disagreeing, but have you considered that we might be dealing with a confused individual? I've seen frenzied attacks with the mentally ill. They don't mean what they're doing, but the outcome is the same."

"But in those cases something happened to cause the individual to snap ... and they're usually apologetic right away. I don't think that's what we're dealing with here."

"I agree. I think she definitely knew her killer."

"Which is why she was on the beach by herself after dark. She was expecting to see someone, but things didn't turn out as she expected."

"I agree with you there, too." He brushed his lips against my forehead. "You need to sleep. Morning is going to come soon enough."

"Except I can sleep in," I reminded him.

"Like I'm going to allow that. You need to get up and make me breakfast, send me out to face the world with a full stomach. That's what good girlfriends do."

I pinched his flank, causing him to yelp. "I know you think you're funny but I don't."

He chuckled as he snuggled close. "You think I'm a little funny. Admit it."

"I wonder if Salma thought someone was funny," I mused. "Maybe she was meeting a man out there, one she hurt — whether on accident or purpose — and he ended her to ease his own pain."

"That's a very ... soap opera ... way to look at things. I don't care how much you hurt me, I wouldn't kill you."

"That's a great relief, but I have no intention of hurting you."

I felt his lips curve against my forehead. "Right back at you."

"I don't think the majority of people have the ability to murder. But those who do can probably convince themselves of anything."

"Baby, I think your head is a little too busy tonight. You need to shut it down."

I let out a sigh. "Yeah."

"You need your rest to cook me breakfast."

I was too tired to argue. "I'll make you breakfast ... if you fix that handle that keeps coming loose on the back door. I can't find a new handle to fit it because it's so old and I don't know how to fix the old one."

"Your wish is my command."

I rested my hand on the spot above his heart. "I love you."

"I love you, too. Now ... sleep."

FIVE

*G*alen was scowling at his phone when I woke the next morning. We were still wrapped together, my head pillowed on his chest, but he was already in work mode.

"Is the shine already off our romance?"

He shifted his eyes to me, light flitting through them, and then pressed a kiss to my mouth. "Good morning."

"Good morning. Why are you so unhappy?"

"Honey, any morning I wake up with you I'm happy. Why do you assume I'm unhappy?"

His phone was still clutched in his hand and I could tell he was anxious to get back to whatever he'd been doing while I slumbered. Still, he wasn't an idiot. He was smart enough to give me his entire focus.

"You have a growly face that you use when people are irritating you. I've seen you point that face at me a time or two. It isn't pretty. You had it on when I opened my eyes."

"I think you're mistaken. I only have a happy face when you're around."

I snorted and stretched. "Right. You might as well tell me. I'll figure it out anyway."

"How will you do that?"

"There will be no breakfast for you until you tell me, and I happen to know that you're a hungry boy in the morning."

This time the grin he graced me with was warm enough to send tingles to my toes. "I am definitely hungry."

I recognized exactly where his mind had gone. "Not for that." I pinched his flank. "Just tell me. I don't understand why you're playing coy."

"I'm not. I was texting Alastair to tell him I needed to see him. He's not responding, but his assistant said I have to work around his facial and pedicure."

I pressed my lips together to keep from laughing at the dark expression that took over his features. He was a grump in the morning before he had his first shot of coffee and carbs. "I'm guessing you're not going to work on his timetable."

"Nope. But he seems to think I am."

"Well, then I pity him." I rolled to my back and stared at the ceiling. "I'm going to hit the shower and then head down to make your breakfast. I don't want to send you off on an important investigation in a bad mood."

"I can't be in a bad mood when I'm with you."

I cast him a sidelong look. "You don't have to keep saying stuff like that. I know we've been in a bit of a honeymoon period because we're both a little giddy, but we still live in the real world."

"Are you saying I'm laying it on too thick?"

"Maybe just a little."

"Then I'll rein it in." He gave me another kiss and then went back to his phone. "Honestly, it's been a little hard for me to keep coming up with romantic things to say. I think I need to watch some movies or something."

That made me laugh as I rolled out of bed. "You're fine the way you are. Not every moment has to be flowers and paper hearts. I prefer something real to anything forced."

His eyes turned serious. "Everything I've said to you is real."

"I know, but you don't have to go overboard. I like who you are on a normal day ... even if you're occasionally grumpy."

"Good to know."

I BOOTED MY COMPUTER IN THE kitchen and ran searches while futzing with pancakes and coffee. By the time Galen joined me, he was showered, shaved and looked to be in a better mood.

"There's my favorite girl in the world," he teased. "I'm surprised cartoon hearts don't shoot out of my eyes when I see you."

I merely stared at him.

"I just had to get it out of my system and annoy you a little bit along the way. How did I do?"

"You're nothing if not a consummate professional," I replied dryly.

"On that we can agree." He flipped the pancakes so I didn't have to get up and do it and then positioned himself behind me so he could look over my shoulder. He didn't seem surprised when he realized I was reviewing Salma's social media feeds. "Anything good?"

"Well, her Twitter account is one nonstop advertisement for the Skyclad Festival. I mean ... five Tweets a day. Every day for the past month."

"It's almost as if she was contracted to put out that many Tweets, huh?" Galen's eyebrows drew together as he leaned forward. "Why are you looking at the stuff she was posting before the festival?"

"I find it interesting. I mean ... look here. She's praising a new perfume, saying it smells like visiting Heaven while sitting on top of a rainbow."

"I prefer my women to smell like coconuts." He nuzzled the back of my neck and inhaled my body spray. "Seriously. You smell good enough to eat."

I ignored his attempt at romance and tapped the screen. "There are two typos in the Tweet."

He frowned and straightened when he realized I wasn't going to play his game. "So?"

AMANDA M. LEE

"So all the Tweets before the ones about the festival have typos. That seems to indicate she was doing the bare minimum or didn't actually know she was coming across as illiterate. Seriously, who doesn't know the difference between your and you're? It's not something she gets wrong once or twice either. It's every time ... like looser and loser. They have vastly different meanings. None of the Tweets about the festival contain typos, so either someone else was writing them for her ... ."

"Or she suddenly developed business ethics and good grammar," he surmised.

"I never met her, but from everything you said I have to believe someone else was sending out the Tweets."

"I bet it was her assistant, who I happen to have an interview with in an hour. I can't get ahold of Salma's parents. I'm hoping this woman will be able to help me."

"You don't want them finding out their daughter died from a news report."

"Definitely." He grabbed the spatula and started doling out the pancakes. "I'm going to have a busy day dealing with the festival and interviewing workers. What do you have planned?"

"May is coming by to give me a lesson on how to be a psychic."

"Oh, yeah?" His smile was back. "Does that mean you'll be able to read my mind when I get back?"

"I don't need to be a mind reader to know what you're thinking. I'm serious about this, though, which means I need to learn. I think May is my best bet."

"I agree. Plus, you'll be safe working here with May. What's not to like about that?"

I figured I should pick a fight with him strictly on principle for that one, but I let it go. There would be plenty of time to bicker. For now, we had other things to worry about.

AS A GHOST, MAY OBVIOUSLY DIDN'T need or use a watch. She

showed up at ten o'clock on the dot, though, and she looked ready for action.

"How are you?" she beamed at me as I drank my fourth mug of coffee. She seemed overly perky, something for which I wasn't sure I was in the mood.

"Tired," I admitted. "It was a late night."

"Oh. You and Galen?" She asked the question in a prim and proper manner, telling me her mind was clearly in the gutter.

"Murder."

Her expression shifted in an instant. "Who died? I was out at Wesley's place playing Scrabble last night. We didn't hear anything about anyone passing on."

"The news didn't break until late. Galen and I found the body on our way back after dinner last night. Someone named Salma Hershey."

May was already pale to the point of being transparent, but I swear she lost two shades of color. I didn't even know that was possible for a ghost.

"Salma? Benton and Barbara's girl?"

"Um ... I think that's what Galen said." May was obviously familiar with her, but it wasn't exactly sorrow I saw reflected on her face. "What can you tell me about her?"

"I don't know." May had kept her mannerisms from life, displaying them now as she sat on the couch. She looked shocked and saddened. "I didn't know her well."

"You obviously knew her parents."

"I did," she nodded. "We were all property owners together."

She delivered the line as if it should mean something to me. "I don't understand."

"Yes, well, you haven't gotten your first invitation to the landowners' association quarterly dinner. You would've been here for the last one, but they probably didn't invite you because you were the new element in town. I don't think you'll be lucky enough to wiggle out twice."

"Is the landowners' association like the DDA?"

"They're similar, and yet they're different. I don't want to ruin the surprise for you. You can judge the group for yourself. As for Benton and Barbara, they weren't really my cup of tea. I mean, they weren't horrible people, but they were out of touch with pretty much everything in the real world."

"Galen says they're uber-rich."

"They are. What's worse is they know it and feel the need to lord it over others."

"Galen said that, too." I shifted on my chair. "She was stabbed seven times. That seems to indicate that she knew whoever killed her. That's a lot of rage to take out on a stranger."

"It is, but I don't think it's out of the realm of possibility. Ted Bundy killed women he'd never met with enough blows to practically sever heads."

I frowned. "Why do you know Ted Bundy facts?"

"Netflix had a documentary Wesley and I watched a few weeks ago. It was fascinating. He was truly a sociopath, but one who was worried about public perception more than anything else."

"I'll have to take your word for it," I said dryly. "I've never been a big fan of serial killers ... though I do love horror movies. Maybe I should check out that documentary."

"You'll love it. Galen will find it fascinating. Did you know Bundy escaped from police custody not once but twice? He killed multiple young women at a sorority house in Florida after the second escape."

"I think that's just going to cause Galen's blood pressure to go through the roof. He's already agitated enough."

May's expression shifted to one of consternation. "What's wrong with Galen?"

"Things aren't going his way right now. Alastair Herne is threatening to call the DDA on him and there's a big festival happening on the beach this week that's supposed to draw thousands of people."

"Yes, I heard about the festival." May made a harrumphing sound and rolled her eyes to the ceiling. "I don't like talking bad about people — really, I don't — but Alastair Herne is the biggest tool in the shed. I mean ... I can't believe someone hasn't killed him yet."

It was rare for May to go off on the island denizens. They'd been her family for most of her life and she often took up for them, even if they harbored a few quirks that I found bothersome. Apparently Alastair was the exception.

"Tell me about him," I prodded.

"Have you met him?"

"Yesterday, before dinner. He was on the beach giving Galen a hard time."

"I imagine Galen didn't take that well. No blood was shed, I hope. Well, unless it was Alastair's blood. I wouldn't mind if he lost a pint ... or ten."

My mouth dropped open and a laugh escaped. "Tell me how you really feel."

"I hate Alastair Herne. He's a ridiculous, pompous, self-serving, egocentric ... moron."

"That's quite the combination. Why do you hate him?"

"He's a jerk of the highest order ... and he's the reason that my friend Rebecca Blythe is dead."

I was aghast ... and curious. "He killed her? How is he running free if he's a murderer? Galen didn't mention him being a murderer and I can't help but think he would've led with that."

May's scowl was pronounced. "He didn't kill her with his hands ... or a knife or gun, for that matter. He killed her with words."

This looked to be turning into a convoluted story. "I'll need more information than that."

"Of course you do. It happened more than thirty years ago. Galen obviously doesn't remember. Becky was gone long before he started forming memories."

"What happened to her?"

"She was a local girl, like me. Her father owned one of the hotels downtown. It has since been razed and replaced with a bigger hotel, even though the older one had more charm. Becky was younger than me by a good decade, but we got along well. We met at the landowners' association meeting when she stood in for her father one night.

"Anyway, she was the shy sort and didn't go out much, which I thought was a real shame," she continued. "She claimed that men made her nervous, but I think she spent all her time with her head in romantic clouds, something I worried you might be doing with Galen until I realized you were just high on love for a bit and would settle."

I shot her a dark look. "Let's stay on the subject, shall we?"

She chuckled, but pushed forward. "Fair enough. Becky was sweet, unassuming and in line to inherit a vast fortune. That's why Alastair started sniffing around." The disdain on her face couldn't have been clearer if she'd painted frown lines in to deepen the effect.

"He pursued her with a great zest, squired her around town, professed his love and made her believe that they were soul mates," she continued, her voice cracking. "Then Becky's father made an offhand comment about how he would have to sign a pre-nup before they got married so he couldn't touch any of the family's money.

"Well, he hemmed and hawed and kicked up a fuss, said he wanted to be a true part of the family. Becky's father held firm, though, and in the end Alastair dumped Becky because he said she didn't trust him and he couldn't live like that. In truth, he just didn't like being cut out of the money. And he had grand designs on that hotel."

"He sounds like a real douche canoe," I noted. "I still don't understand how he killed your friend."

"I'm getting to it," May tsked. "Becky was so upset about losing Alastair that she followed him to one of the town festivals and begged him to reconsider ... in front of everybody. He was already dating someone new, one of the Woodbridge morons who lost their shirts in the stock market crash of 2008. He laughed at her in front of everyone, insulted her, and then sent her on her way.

"I made a choice that night that I regret to this day," she continued. "I let her go, thinking I would track her down the following day — after she'd had herself a good cry — and help her start to heal. I never got the chance. She took a handful of sleeping pills thirty minutes after Alastair embarrassed her. She never woke up."

My heart sank at the admission. I'd suspected the story would go down that road, but it was still jarring. "I'm so sorry."

"Why? You didn't do it." May heaved out a sigh and mimed patting my hand. "I'm sorry for being so dark. It's just ... I hate that man. I mean, I truly hate him. He didn't even bother going to Becky's funeral. Ten years later, when her father died of what I'm sure was a broken heart, he tried to swoop in and buy the hotel.

"Lawrence — that was her father's name — left the decision up to me about who to sell to," she continued. "All the money was going to charity, but it was my decision who would be allowed to buy the hotel. Guess who didn't make the cut."

My lips twitched at the evil way she delivered the line. "I'm guessing that would be Alastair."

"You're darned tooting. You should've seen his face when he realized there was no way that hotel would ever get in his hands. I made the sale contingent on the fact that he could never purchase it, through personal or business finances. I completely shut him out."

"You got your revenge." I couldn't help being impressed. "That's ... pretty cool."

"No, it's bitter," May corrected. "I'm still bitter about what he did. Nobody deserves to feel how Becky felt at the end. Nobody deserves to die alone like that."

May had died alone. She'd been poisoned by her attorney because he wanted her land. Ultimately that blew up in his face — and Wesley took revenge for that deed — but she'd still been alone when she died.

As if reading my mind, May slowly turned her eyes to meet mine. "I wasn't alone. People sat vigil by my bedside at the end. I was sick but didn't realize I was dying. It happened faster than I would've thought possible. But I wasn't alone, even when others weren't in the room. I felt their love and strength all around me."

Well, that was a relief, but it sparked something in the back of my mind. "We should probably get started on our lesson. While we're doing that, there's something else I want to talk to you about."

"What's that?"

"Wesley. Well, Wesley and June Seaver. I just ... learned something yesterday and I want to talk to you about it. It's not a big deal, but I have questions."

"Lay them on me. I have all day." She chuckled hollowly at her own joke. "Actually, I have forever. I'm eager to hear what you have to say. Something tells me it's bigger than you're letting on because you're unbelievably nervous."

She wasn't wrong.

SIX

I worked harder than I expected and was mentally fatigued. At one o'clock, May let me go, but only after I promised that I would set up another lesson ... and soon. We both agreed I needed to recover. I had no idea how taxing trying to read minds could be.

"You look rough."

Booker — he claimed to only have one name, but I had my doubts — sat at a table in my friend Lilac Meadows' bar. He had a glass of iced tea in front of him. His dark hair, normally immaculate, was shoved away from his face in a haphazard manner. He appeared legitimately happy to see me, which was a bonus.

"I was just about to say the same to you," I responded as I slid into the booth seat across from him. The bar was blissfully cool because Lilac preferred keeping it that way. When I first moved to the island I assumed that was for the benefit of the customers. Now that I knew she was a demon and could make brimstone weapons appear out of thin air I was starting to think she simply ran hot and needed the chilly atmosphere to feel comfortable.

Either way, given the temperatures outside, I felt blessed to be inside with friends.

"I asked first." Booker leaned back in his seat and tipped back his iced tea, drinking long and hard until there was nothing left but ice. Something told me his day hadn't been any easier than mine, which was interesting.

"Well, for starters, I discovered a dead body last night," I offered.

Lilac, who had been breezing by with an empty tray on her way back to the bar, took an exaggerated turn and slid into the booth next to me. "You found Salma? Dish."

She looked far too excited at the prospect. "It's not something to be happy about," I chided.

"Of course not." Lilac adopted a morose expression that didn't make it all the way to her eyes, which twinkled as if she were having a grand time. "Dish with the proper respect."

Booker barked out a laugh. "I'm a little curious, too. I heard the news that she died, but I didn't realize you were the one who found her. I'm officially intrigued."

"It's not that great of a story," I lamented. "Galen and I went to dinner and he was checking on the beach on our way back when I thought I saw something weird. It turned out to be a body. End of story."

"That's pretty lame," Lilac agreed. "I was hoping for more."

"Like what?"

"Like maybe someone shaved her bald and made her wear shoes from a discount store."

It shouldn't have been funny — a woman was dead, after all — but I couldn't stop myself from laughing. "That is ... absolutely horrible," I sputtered. "It's not funny."

"I wasn't trying to be funny." Lilac was matter-of-fact. "That's simply how I always dreamed of her going. And trust me, I *have* dreamed about it ... long and hard."

I flicked my eyes to Booker, expectant. "Would you like to explain?"

"Sure." He was seemingly unbothered by Lilac's uncouth showing. "Salma tried to ruin Lilac. Our favorite bartender wants to throw a party now that she's dead."

"Um ... you're leaving out pertinent details," Lilac complained.

"My bad." Booker feigned contrition. "*We* want to throw a party now that she's dead. I didn't like her either."

I was starting to feel as if I was trapped in one of those After School specials about good kids going bad. "Let's focus on the important stuff," I suggested. "Like, for starters, what did Salma do to you, Lilac?"

"She came in here drunk one night — I want to stress she was already hammered before she walked through the door — and started causing a scene. The cops were called. Galen wasn't on that night. It was one of his deputies, and because she was underage at the time I was looking at some pretty stiff fines."

"That sucks." I felt bad for my friend. "Obviously you survived."

"She's not finished," Booker interjected, lifting his glass to shake the ice in an effort to get the passing waitress's attention. She shot him a dirty look, which he immediately brushed aside with a flirty smile and wink, and before I could even acknowledge what was happening she'd retrieved his glass and was getting him a refill. "There's more to the story."

"I'm dying to hear it," I drawled, pinning him with a dirty look. "I thought you weren't supposed to use your powers for evil."

He adopted an innocent expression. "How was that evil?"

"You don't have any interest in that woman."

"I didn't say I did. I'm doing nothing but slaking my immense thirst. Some of us were out working in the sun all day."

"Yeah, yeah, yeah." I brushed my hand at him and turned back to Lilac. "What else happened?"

"The deputy called her father to the scene," Lilac replied, her eyes darkening. I looked for signs of fire lurking in her irises and came up empty. Good. That meant she wasn't about to lose her cool and conjure a sword of flame. While cool to watch, it was utterly terrifying ... especially when her hair turned red and looked as if it had caught fire.

"He started yelling, ranting and raving, and said he was going to take some trip away from her that she'd had planned for a long time," she continued, grim. "To get herself out of trouble, Salma lied and said that I had not only served her but forced her to drink. I'm a demon, and everyone knows it, so he went to the DDA and tried to get the tiki bar taken from me."

I was absolutely horrified. "No way. How could he believe a drunk teenager over you?"

"Not everyone is comfortable with my demon lineage," Lilac argued. "Half of the town thinks I'm something to fear and the other half thinks I'm something to kill."

My mouth fell open as I looked to Booker for confirmation. He appeared unusually stoic. Normally he would be cracking jokes about now, but he didn't appear to have any to offer.

"That's heinous," I said when I regained my senses. "I can't believe you had to go through that. Obviously the DDA sided with you."

"Only after certain people argued on my behalf, including Wesley, May and Galen. All three of them went to bat for me."

"As did I," Booker reminded her. "Of course, I don't have nearly the pull with the DDA that Galen does. He's their golden boy."

I thought of the threats Alastair had spewed the night before. "Are you sure?" I related the tale to them, leaving nothing out. When I finished, I was almost as angry as I had been the previous night. "I don't think he's the golden boy you think he is."

"He's still their favorite son," Booker shot back. "As for Alastair, he's all talk. It's not as if the DDA likes him any more than the rest of us do. That guy has the top entry under the word 'tool' in the urban dictionary."

"You're the second person to use that word when talking about him with me today."

"Who was the first?"

"May."

"Well, she had more reason than most to hate him," Booker supplied. "My understanding is that he pushed her best friend to commit suicide. It was before my time, but people are still talking about that, and most of the residents of a certain age honestly can't stand that guy."

"So ... how did he get involved with the festival?" I asked. "I don't understand how something so important was put under his care. If nobody likes him, why are they rewarding him?"

"I don't think you're reading the situation correctly," Booker countered. "The town isn't hosting the festival. Alastair is. He put his money up to front the event. He pre-paid for all the food, water, clothing, souvenirs ... you name it. He's easily got several million dollars into this event."

I was stunned. "How is that possible?"

"He's rich."

"I know that. I just ... why would he do that? It makes no sense."

"Of course it does," Lilac volunteered. "For every million dollars invested in this festival he expects to make five million back. It's not as if he's an altruistic soul who wants to give out of the goodness of his heart ... or a gambler, for that matter. He thinks he's got a line on money and he's going to follow the thread for as long as he can."

That begged another question. "If he's so rich, why does he need the money from this festival? I mean ... can't he live comfortably forever without making another cent?"

"I guess in theory that's true," Booker confirmed. "The thing is, he lives a pretty fancy lifestyle. He has a private jet. He has a yacht. He has a multi-million-dollar house. He has groundskeepers, maids, personal chefs and trainers. The upkeep is exorbitant.

"My understanding is that he took a beating when the stock market fell in 2008, but he came out the other side and survived," he continued. "He's still rich. By our standards he's filthy rich. By his standards, though, he might feel he needs to add to his coffers."

That sort of made sense. "Did you know that skyclad means naked in the pagan language?"

Booker's eyes lit with amusement at the way I lowered my voice. He looked genuinely tickled, which made me distinctly uncomfortable. I hated it when I made a ninny of myself and I was starting to suspect I'd done just that.

"Technically there is no such thing as the pagan language," he started. "Most creatures have their own language. Some adhere to the languages of the countries they live in. If you run into a really preten-tious vampire he might speak Latin because he thinks that makes him sound important. But there is no such thing as a pagan language."

"Oh, well, thank you for the history lesson," I drawled.

He ignored the sarcasm. "Secondly, skyclad means naked dancing, and is less formally known as something that happens under the full moon. I think the organizers named it that as a nod to the paranormal roots of this community. While I haven't heard anything overt mentioned in the advertising that's been hitting the internet and radio stations, I wouldn't be at all surprised if there aren't whispers tearing through certain circles about this being a magical island."

I swallowed hard, surprised. "Seriously? What does that mean?" I glanced at Lilac. "Are we in trouble? Should we lay low?"

She snickered at my discomfort, which made me want to pinch her. "I don't think that's necessary. Most people who visit here do so for that specific reason. They're paranormal in nature and want a place to relax where they can be themselves and not constantly have to worry about who may be looking over their shoulders."

That brought up another question. "Does that mean those coming to the island are paranormals?" Until this moment I hadn't even considered the possibility that paranormals would outnumber the "normal" human beings. "Are we about to be invaded by witches?"

"I think witches are one of the groups that will be well represent-ed," he confirmed. "Vampires might be hanging around at night, but it's not as if they can risk sleeping in a tent on the beach. They prob-ably won't be a concern.

"Shifters, reapers, sirens and leprechauns should be well repre-sented, too," he continued. "There might even be some pixies, but I'm trying not to get my hopes up because they're fairly rare."

There was so much packed into that statement I didn't know where to start. "Leprechauns are real?"

Lilac giggled at my incredulous response. "Yes, but they don't look like they do on television. They're not little or anything. They're regu-lar-sized and only turn green when they're ... you know."

It took me a moment to understand what she was saying. "Oh, gross! I'll have to take your word for that. I mean ... they turn green?"

Her grin widened. "They're magically delicious."

Booker laughed so hard I thought he might spit into his fresh iced tea. The waitress had delivered it, loitered at the side of the table for a full ten seconds to see if he would say something to her, and then stalked away in a snit. He really did have a "special" way with people.

"I don't understand how I didn't realize this was going to be a festival full of paranormals," I admitted after a moment's consideration. "I mean ... it makes sense. In hindsight, that should've been my first inclination. I just assumed it was going to be a festival of mostly normal people with the occasional paranormal thrown in for good measure."

"There's no such thing as normal people," Booker countered. "Everyone has their own freak flag to fly. We just happen to be more open about it here. As for the festival, it's turning into a righteous pain. I was down there all morning and things are about to get rough."

My interest was officially piqued. "How so?"

"Alastair's assistant is freaking out because Galen is demanding twice the number of Porta-Potties. I think that number is still low and they're just begging for trouble, but nobody asked me. He's also making noise about Salma's death and wants answers on why she was down there, but he doesn't seem to be getting much cooperation."

"Did she have anything to do with the festival?"

He held out his hands and shrugged. "I don't know. I'm only helping because the money is good. I'm working in a freelance capacity, though, and the second that stupid assistant says something to annoy me I'm out of there. He knows it, too. I warned him."

"But the festival is still on, right?" I pressed.

He nodded. "It's on. There's too much publicity surrounding the event to cancel it now. Golden boy or not, Galen won't be able to wrangle the support he needs to shut it down if it becomes necessary. He'll be hung out to dry, expected to maintain law and order, and blamed if things go wrong."

My heart gave a little jolt. "Will things go wrong?"

The look he shot me was amused. "What do you think? We're dealing with thousands of paranormals — or humans who want to hang around with paranormals — and there aren't enough bathrooms. There's going to be a steady stream of alcohol, and Galen has, like, six cops ... and that includes his two weekend warriors. There's no way this thing isn't getting out of control."

That wasn't what I wanted to hear. "Well ... crap." I pressed the heel of my hand to my forehead. "I was hoping you would give me good news."

"I have no good news to give you. Sorry."

"Ugh." I rubbed at the tension starting to build in my sinuses. "And I was having such a good day. I mean ... finding the dead body last night was jolting and there are better ways to spend an evening. Before that, though, I tried an oyster and it tasted like snot. Despite that, I didn't die. Galen and I had plans for romance that the body derailed, but it wasn't the end of the world."

"When don't you and Galen have plans for romance these days?" Lilac asked dryly.

"You're just jealous," I teased, wagging a finger in front of her face.

"I am jealous," she agreed. "I'm on the dry spell to end all dry spells."

"I think you're just picky. I wasn't done telling you about my day, though. I had a lesson with May this morning and guess what."

"It's too hot to guess," Booker replied.

I wasn't really expecting him to guess anyway, so I pretended I didn't hear him. "I learned to read minds this morning. She taught me. It's my first step to opening my own business."

Lilac blinked several times. "You learned to read minds? In one morning, to boot."

"I did."

"Give it a try," Booker suggested, exchanging a quick look with Lilac that wasn't lost on me. They didn't think I could do it.

"Fine. Make sure your mind is empty of anything you don't want me to know, though. Booker, if you have any deviant sexual fantasies it would probably be best to bury them deep. I'm only going after surface thoughts. Just a simple message to start things off."

"I promise you won't see any dirty thoughts in my head," he said dryly.

"Great. I ... ." It didn't work. I'd barely begun my descent into his mind when I ran into a brick wall. It wasn't a metaphorical brick wall. The thing that I smacked into looked like a real brick wall. "Hey!"

Booker smirked when I pinned him with a dark look. "What's wrong?" He adopted an air of innocence. "I thought you were going to yell at me for those dirty fantasies."

I was legitimately confused. "Why can't I see inside your head?"

"Because I'm a cupid."

I glanced at Lilac. "Will I have the same issue if I try to see inside your head?"

She nodded. "Booker and I are paranormals. We can shutter. Not all paranormals are as adept as we are, but there's no getting inside our heads if we don't want you in there. I guess, if we were drunk enough and incapable of shuttering, you might have a chance of slipping inside. But if we're aware and present, you're fresh out, honey."

Well, that was disturbing. "What good is this ability if I can't use it?" I felt deflated, as if I'd just wasted a monumental amount of time and hope. "This really sucks."

"It's still a good ability," Lilac countered. "You can't use it on us because we're strong paranormals. Like you, we sprang from the original elementals. You're not going to have much luck with us. As for other paranormals, there's always hope. You're probably powerful enough to steamroll some of the others even if they try to stop you."

Oh, well, that was encouraging. "I need to find some of them to practice on."

"I would start with a standard human," Booker supplied. "Very few of them have good mental blocks. You need to build from the bottom up. There's no such thing as mastering mind reading in a single morning."

"Thank you. You've already rained on my parade. There's no need to keep harping on it."

"I was just voicing an observation."

"Yeah, well ... ." I trailed off, an idea popping into my head. "A normal human, huh? I think I know just where to go to practice."

SEVEN

*I*nvading the minds of those I was close to seemed a bad way to practice. Galen would've let me try — although I predicted that game would've turned dirty really fast — but Wesley was likely to shut me down right out of the gate. He loved me, but we were still getting to know one another. Reading his mind held certain risks.

I could've asked June. She was a "normal" human. That also seemed dicey, especially because I knew about her crush on Wesley. That was something I brought up to May during our training session. She didn't seem surprised by the admission. In fact, she appeared tickled. When I brought up that I was worried about Wesley spending all of his time with a ghost she took me completely by surprise and said she would broach the subject of him dating June. I wasn't expecting that response, but she said she was mildly worried about him, too. Of course, she also warned me not to get my hopes up. Wesley was set in his ways and unlikely to change. If May really was heading out to whisper in his ear about June, that probably meant he would be in a foul mood the next time I saw him. I didn't want to risk that today.

What did that leave? The docks, of course. Ships were due to arrive throughout the day. Thousands of people from all walks of life

AMANDA M. LEE

would be arriving in a steady stream. They would be so focused on the festival they would have no time for me, which meant I could practice without drawing attention.

With that in mind, I bought an iced tea from one of the vendors and picked a spot in the shade. It was a corner table, a nice breeze billowing in from the water and ruffling my hair. There, I pretended to be relaxing even as I practiced invading people's minds.

The first time I successfully managed it was with a woman named Minx Martin. I doubted that was her real name, even though it was the one on the surface. I dug deeper and found that her parents named her Mary and she'd always fancied herself a sexy witch. So, when she was an adult and sick of their crap, she changed her name to Minx. She was looking forward to the Skyclad Festival because she was convinced she would find a coven. She'd spent her entire life savings to come ... and I couldn't help thinking she was going to be disappointed.

Up next was Rance Maynard. Unfortunately that was his real name. His parents were farmers and thought he would work the land in Idaho and keep up family traditions for a whole new generation. They were sadly mistaken. Rance was a grifter. It was the only word that seemed to fit him. He pretended to be psychic, read tarot cards and palms, but was actually simply observant. He could read people well and told them what they wanted to hear. He was on the island because he thought he could make a small fortune offering his services. He also believed, if he hit it just right, he would be able to parlay this appearance into a job as a psychic to the stars. He seemed like someone who should be watched, so I jotted down his name and made a mental note to turn it over to Galen later.

I continued rifling through the minds of the new arrivals. Most of them were simply so excited to be on the island they could think of nothing else. A few had plans to monetize their appearances. Others just wanted to get stoned and were eagerly scanning faces to see if they could find a local connection.

I was so lost in what I was doing I didn't notice when a shadow fell over me. When I finally did register it I almost jolted out of my chair.

58

"You scared the crap out of me, Galen!" I lightly slapped his arm as I caught my breath. "Make a noise next time."

"I said your name." He looked amused, and also curious. He dropped a kiss on my forehead before sitting in the chair next to me. "What are you doing here? I thought you were spending the day taking lessons with May."

"I already finished my first lesson." That was true. "Reading minds is easier than I thought it would be. May taught me a neat trick. I went to Lilac's bar to practice on her and Booker — I heard some interesting stories about Salma there, for the record — but apparently I can't practice on them because they can shutter."

"Ah." Understanding dawned on his face and his grin widened. "I think it's best you don't venture into Booker's mind anyway. That's a dangerous place to visit."

"He says it's a perverted place."

"That's another reason I don't want you visiting." He collected my hand and flipped it over so he could idly trace the lines on my palm. He seemed distracted, as if he was grappling with something and trying to work it out in his head. "Did you come down here to try to read the tourists' minds?"

I nodded, sheepish. "Yeah. You probably think that's invasive, huh?"

"On the contrary. I think it's a good idea. Here you're going in without any preconceived notions. Anything you dig up is bound to be real. With Lilac and Booker, you might've assumed things even though the facts didn't back it up."

"That's pretty smart."

"I'm more than a pretty face." He leaned closer so he could kiss me. "I missed you this morning."

That was an odd thing to say. "You saw me a few hours ago."

"I know, but it's been a long few hours — it feels like days — and I really wish I had stayed in bed with you this morning."

I sensed trouble, which wasn't saying much because the truth of his emotions was written all over his face. "What happened? Did Alastair threaten you again? May told me a story about him, by the way, and I hate him on principle. I can try to invade his mind and get you some dirt to work with ... if you're interested, I mean."

His lips curved into a legitimate smile. "That's a nice offer. I'll consider it later. For now ... I don't want you worrying about Alastair. He's a pain in the ass, but he's not a threat to me."

"Is that because you're the golden boy?"

His eyes narrowed speculatively. "How much time did you spend with Booker this afternoon?"

That was a thorny question. Booker and Galen had known each other most of their lives. They'd been pitted against one another competitively the older they got and, even though they were willing to work together on big projects, they were still at war in some ways. It honestly made me laugh. Testosterone is an odd, odd thing.

"I was there a grand total of twenty minutes," I replied. "When I found out I couldn't test my new toy on him he became odious to me."

"He should've already been odious to you," Galen grumbled, flicking his eyes to a group of women heading in our direction. They were young, pretty and exuded a hint of power that made me sit straighter in my chair.

"Witches," I muttered, pursing my lips. "Interesting."

He cast me a sidelong look. "How do you know? Did you read their minds that fast? If so, I have to say, that's really impressive."

"I haven't even tried to read their minds. I can tell because they remind me of that movie *The Craft*. There are four of them, which means they cast to the four corners. They're each wearing an emblem on their shirts. Those emblems stand for the elements."

"Earth, air, fire and water," he mused. "That's very good. I didn't initially pick up on that. You're getting good, Hadley." He grinned. "You're very smart."

"Compliments will get you anything you want ... later tonight." I patted his hand and turned back to the witches. "I've been doing some research on the elements since I found out about the elementals. Witch elementals are different. As a group, they're one elemental, but they call to all four elements."

"I think that's a way to harness the power they think they lost during the great split," Galen explained. "I don't know that it makes them more powerful than they already are, but you're right, it is interesting to think about."

"Yeah."

We lapsed into silence for a moment, our attention drawn to the witches. They commanded a certain amount of awe as they cut through the crowd. They were clad in robes, the sort that would've made sense in a Harry Potter movie. They were open, though, and they wore street clothes beneath.

"See if you can read their minds," Galen suggested after a beat.

"What?" I felt uncomfortable, put on the spot. "I don't know that I think that's a good idea. What if they know I'm in their heads?"

"Just give it a try. I'm curious about whether they're the real deal or all show."

I had a feeling I already knew the answer to that question, but I obliged, narrowing my eyes as I surveyed the women. "Which one do you think I should go after?"

"The blonde in the center."

I looked to him and tried to tamp down my agitation. "How did I know you would pick her?"

His grin was quick and full of adoration, so much so that it defeated whatever argument I'd planned to mount. "I already told you I have the perfect woman, so there's no reason to get ... whatever it is you're doing. Territorial, I guess. I already belong to you."

That was sort of cute ... and codependent. Still, he was right. I had no doubts about his devotion. Being jealous — especially because I'd noticed the striking witch, too, and I wasn't attracted to her in the least — was a wasted emotion.

"Okay. Give me a second." I exhaled heavily and let loose the pent-up magic. May's first lesson had been about control, and I was surprisingly good when it came to controlling my magic. I couldn't see the wisps of power I sent out, but I sensed when they invaded her mind. Once inside, they began to crawl, and the information they discovered was transmitted back to me.

"Her name is Bronwen Beasley and she's definitely a witch."

"Bronwen?" Galen arched an eyebrow, amusement lighting his features. "That's a little on the nose, huh? I bet her real name is Betty."

"A lot of the people here are going by aliases."

He straightened in his chair. "What do you mean by that?"

"Just that witches tend to want to name themselves and most of them trend toward the flamboyant. I guess I'm glad I like my name, because otherwise I might have had to change it to Sunny Skies or something."

"You definitely have a pretty name." He turned back to Bronwen, who was busy looking over a transportation brochure. "What else can you tell me about her?"

His interest was starting to make me distinctly uncomfortable. "Why? Do you like her or something?"

Exasperation, hot and fast, clawed across his face. "We've been over this. That's not what I'm interested in here."

"Then what are you interested in?"

"I want to know if these people are here because of Salma. I'm dying to know if the things she posted actually had an effect on attendance. If so, I want to know what it was about her that caused people to listen ... and if any of those people were infatuated enough to kill her."

Oh, well, crap. He was actually trying to dig for important information on a murder. I probably should've figured that out myself. "Um ... ."

He held my gaze, practically daring me to argue.

"I'm kind of sorry," I hedged after a beat. "I didn't mean that the way it came out. It's not that I don't trust you. I do. I've never trusted anyone as much as I trust you. It's just ... she looks like she should be wearing black lingerie on the cover of Witch Quarterly or something."

Instead of reacting out of anger, he chuckled and shook his head. "Is it any wonder I fell head over heels for you the moment we met? I mean ... seriously. Who else could be so oblivious to her own appeal?"

My cheeks colored as I pursed my lips. He had a way of making me feel like an idiot. In this particular case, I was an idiot. Still, though ... . "Um ... what were we talking about again?"

He grinned, delight evident, and dipped in for a kiss. "Your new talent is intriguing. You're doing really well for this being your first day. You can practice on me later. We'll make a game of it."

"I knew you would say that."

"I'm nothing if not predictable," he agreed. "In fact ... ." He sat up straighter, his attention drifting to a spot over my shoulder.

When I turned to get a look at what had caused him to lose his train of thought I found Bronwen staring directly at us ... and she didn't look happy.

"Uh-oh," I hissed.

"Don't say that." Galen shifted on his chair. "What is there to 'uh-oh' about?"

"I think ... um ... don't freak out."

"That's a great way to open a sentence," he drawled.

"I think I might have left the link between her mind and mine open when you and I started flirting. There's every chance she saw something ... um ... sweaty in my head."

His eyes widened. "Seriously?"

"I didn't mean to do it," I whined. "Sometimes these images just jump in my head when you're around. I can't always help it."

"That's both flattering and troublesome," he said. "Just ... let me do the talking." He rested his hand on top of mine and fixed Bronwen with a welcoming, and yet somehow remote, smile. "Welcome to Moonstone Bay. I'm Sheriff Blackwood. How may I be of assistance?"

Ah. He was going official right off the bat. That was smart. She would be more likely to back down once she realized he was a law enforcement representative. Even innocent people are often afraid of the police.

"That's cute," Bronwen drawled, looking him up and down. "That thing you do where you growl while rolling around naked is cute, too. I know because this one shoved the memory into my head ... though I don't think she meant to do it." Her gaze was pointed when it landed on me.

I swallowed hard. Double uh-oh. "Um ... I don't know what you're talking about." The words sounded feeble as they escaped my mouth, but I didn't know what else to say.

"Oh, don't do that." Bronwen tsked with her tongue. Up close, I realized she might've been a little older than I realized. The lines on her face sometimes looked deep depending on how the sunshine hit her face. "Own what you are, what you did. It's quite remarkable really. I didn't feel you in there until you made the mistake with the memory. You are quite gifted, sheriff." She winked at Galen before turning back to me. "Who are you?"

I felt uncomfortable with her full attention on me, but I knew better than to avoid the question. If she thought I was afraid she might take advantage. "Hadley Hunter."

"Well, Hadley Hunter, it's nice to meet you." She stuck out her hand for me to shake. I considered not doing it, perhaps playing germophobic or something, but that would undoubtedly come across as rude and I was already on shaky ground.

"Nice to meet you, too, Bronwen Beasley."

Her eyebrows practically hit her hairline. "I didn't tell you my name."

Well, crud on toast with a jelly chaser. What was wrong with me today? Apparently I couldn't keep my head out of my behind. When I risked a glance at Galen, I found his shoulders shaking with silent laughter. He looked to be having a good time.

"It's not funny," I hissed, elbowing him in the stomach.

"It's a little funny," he countered, ruefully rubbing the spot I hit. "It's not my fault you lost track of what you were doing. But I think it was a valuable lesson, and I bet you don't make that mistake again."

He was right. Still, this was a sticky situation. "I apologize," I offered lamely. "I was trying to practice. It's a new skill and I wasn't going to go for anything other than surface thoughts. I didn't mean to shove that picture of Galen into your head. That's his fault because he was flirting with me when I was trying to work."

"Of course it's his fault," Bronwen readily agreed. "It's always the man's fault. As for you, I'm willing to forgive ... this one time. You're obviously new at this. Strong, but definitely new. You can do me a favor and we'll forget all about it."

That sounded convenient ... and possibly like a trap. "What favor?"

"We were supposed to have a driver meet us here to take us to our hotel, but I just got a text that he can't make it. I need someone to transport me to my hotel."

"I only have a golf cart."

"Well, we can load all the luggage on the cart and the other girls can walk. It won't kill them, despite the fact that it's beastly hot. You can drive me and the luggage. How does that sound?"

"I guess it's okay." I squirmed and looked at Galen, who merely shrugged. "What hotel are you staying at?"

"The Moonstone Bay Cabana Clutch Hotel."

I frowned. "That's closed for renovations."

"Yes, but I know the owner. She's made an exception for us. In fact, she's waiting for us as we speak. Do we have a deal?"

I didn't see where I had much choice after being caught. "Sure. I can take you to the hotel. It won't be a problem."

"Great."

EIGHT

*G*alen walked me to the cart, helping with Bronwen's luggage, as the other women trailed behind. He didn't say much, but the rigid set of his shoulders told me he wasn't thrilled with the turn of events.

"Text me when you get there," he instructed in a low voice as we stood next to the driver's side of the cart. Bronwen seated herself without invitation. The luggage was loaded, and the other witches had already set out walking. "I don't think there's anything to worry about, but I'll feel better knowing that you're okay."

"I think the only thing we have to worry about is me sticking my foot in my mouth ... again."

He grinned and dipped down for a kiss. "That's only one of the reasons I love you," he whispered, giving me a friendly pat on the behind before sliding his gaze to Bronwen. "I hope you enjoy your stay at the Cabana Clutch."

She returned the smile in blinding fashion. "Oh, you don't have to worry about me. I have fun wherever I go. Thank you for the mental picture of you naked. I'll carry it with me for the rest of the week. I'm sure it will come in handy."

He frowned but didn't say anything as he stepped back. Really, what else was there to say? I'd made a mistake and now I would have to deal with it. He was right about the regret forcing me to think better the next go-around. I didn't ever want to deal with a situation like this again.

"Ready?" I forced a smile that I didn't really feel and slid behind the wheel. Traffic in Moonstone Bay was basically non-existent for the most part, so it wouldn't take me long to make the trek. Then I would drop her off and beat a hasty retreat ... and hopefully never see her again.

I expected to make the drive in uncomfortable silence. Bronwen apparently had other ideas.

"So, tell me about yourself," she insisted as I cut out of the parking lot.

"There's not much to tell," I replied uneasily. I didn't really feel the need to bond over shared secrets. "I live on the island and I date the sheriff. That's my life in a nutshell."

"There must be more than that."

"Not really."

"You're also a witch," she pointed out. "We have that in common."

"Yeah, well ... it's sort of a new thing for me." I took a deep, bracing breath. Apparently we were going to get into the nitty-gritty of my life after all. "I didn't even know I was a witch until a few months ago when I moved to Moonstone Bay."

"Oh?" Bronwen's perfectly arched eyebrows migrated higher. "You didn't grow up here?"

"I moved here after I inherited the lighthouse from my grandmother."

"You inherited a lighthouse?" Intrigue lit Bronwen's features as she leaned forward. "That's interesting. I don't think I've ever met anyone who lived in a lighthouse."

"Oh, well ... it's just like living anywhere else." That was a bald-faced lie. Living in the lighthouse was one adventure after another ... and the view was spectacular. I was afraid if I played it up, though, she would try to finagle an invitation, and I was keen to cut ties with her as soon as possible.

"I don't believe that. Perhaps I'll stop by and you can show me around."

Crap! It was as if she was reading my mind and punishing me for earlier events in the process. "Maybe." I kept my tone light and airy. "What about you? What kind of witch are you?"

"I'm a hodgepodge of beliefs and powers. I don't ascribe to any one set tenet."

"But you wear the air witch symbol." I gestured toward the emblem on her robe. "That means you're adept at air magic, right?"

Her smile was benign. "I'm adept at many things. Which element are you strongest with?"

That was a good question. "I have no idea. I've done a few things, but I'm still a work in progress. I think what I'll be able to do is yet to be determined."

"Your mind powers seem strong," Bronwen noted. "Perhaps that will be your forte."

"Maybe. I guess we'll have to wait and see." I took the curve that led to June's hotel more sharply than necessary and Bronwen had to grip her seat tightly to keep from flying out. She looked amused rather than testy once she recovered.

"I make you nervous," she noted sagely. "I wish I didn't. You're clearly uncomfortable around me."

"It's more that I'm uncomfortable with what I did," I hedged. "I really didn't mean any harm. I was just trying to practice. You wouldn't have known I was there if Galen hadn't distracted me."

"I can see why he so easily distracts you. He's ... very pretty."

"Yeah, well ... he has a few attributes that I like." My lips raised, unbidden, into a smile. "Why are you staying at June's hotel when it's closed? I would think you would want to stay at one of the full-service resorts."

"I didn't plan on coming to the festival when it was first announced, so I didn't reserve a room. I have no interest in staying on the beach, because ... well ... I feel too old to sleep on the ground."

"It will probably be filled with drunks and loudmouths, too," I noted.

"That was also a concern," she conceded. "Upon calling around to find lodging, I was told the hotel would be under construction but it wasn't expected to be terrible. I called June personally and we struck a deal."

"That's cool. June is great, by the way. She's a lot of fun. Even if the hotel isn't a well-oiled machine right now, you'll still have a great time."

"I'm certain I will. But ... I wasn't aware you knew June. How well do you know her? What can you tell me about her life?"

The shift in topic was a welcome one. Talking about someone else — anybody else really — was less stressful than trying to explain my current situation. "I met her a few weeks ago. She's really tight with Galen and another friend of mine. She kind of looked over them when they were boys, made them behave when no one else would. They're devoted to her."

"From the looks of it, Galen at least, is devoted to you, too."

My cheeks heated from a mixture of pleasure and embarrassment. "He's a good man. He's also great at his job. This festival is a big deal and he's been working night and day to make sure everything is perfect. He's amazing."

"It's clear you think so." She smiled as we pulled to a stop in front of the hotel. "Well, this doesn't look so bad. I was expecting scaffolding everywhere."

"It's a cute space," I offered as I started unloading suitcases from the back. "The patio area is absolutely to die for and she's not changing that at all."

"Well, that's good. Perhaps we'll get some tea out there and talk about her heritage. I'm absolutely fascinated by it."

"The pirate thing? It's a pretty cool story."

"The pirate story is mildly entertaining. I'm talking about her matriarchal lines, though. It's rare to have a witch family that goes back as many generations as hers."

I stilled, surprised. "What?" The single-word question escaped before I could think better of it. I was legitimately astonished, though.

Amusement flashed in the depths of Bronwen's eyes, which looked more gray than green in this lighting. "I thought you knew her."

"I ... do."

"Then why didn't you know she was a witch?"

That was a very good question. "Um ... I'm not sure. Are you sure you have the right person? I've never heard June mention being a witch."

"I'm positive. I'm looking forward to partaking in a few rituals with her. You're invited, of course. You can bring your sheriff body-guard if you're feeling nervous. He just needs to promise not to get naked until after the ritual is complete. He might serve as too much of a distraction for my coven otherwise."

There was so much information wrapped in that statement I didn't even know where to begin when starting to unpack it. "Um ... ."

"Just a thought." Bronwen's smile was kind as she grabbed the handles on two of the suitcases. "You don't have to help with the luggage. I've got it from here."

"Are you sure?" I felt like a bit of a villain for leaving her to wrangle that many suitcases on her own, but I was desperate to escape.

"I'm sure."

"Okay, well ... bye."

I hopped behind the wheel of the cart and turned the key. Bronwen was already at the front door when she called out once more.

"Tell Galen I said hello. I look forward to seeing more of him, too."

"I'll do that." Or not. Seriously, could she be any weirder?

GALEN WAS BACK AT HIS OFFICE when I passed by so, on a whim, I parked next to his truck and sauntered through the front door as if I had a clear purpose. His secretary was the nosy sort — she was also bossy and mildly terrifying — and I didn't want her to question me too hard about what I was doing bothering the sheriff in the middle of the afternoon. There were certain rules I was supposed to follow — all created by her — and she melted down when I broke from the schedule.

Thankfully today she was on the phone and could only pin me with a dark look as I waved and slipped behind the counter, heading directly for his office.

Galen looked to be going through a file when I pushed open his door. Irritation flashed across his face ... and then he realized it was me. The annoyance was quickly replaced by a smile.

"I said you should text, not stop in. But I'm not going to complain about the visit."

That was only one of the things I liked about him. He was always happy to see me. Legitimately so. He did wonders for my ego.

"I didn't actually come to visit. I came for some information."

"Oh, geez." He made a face. "I know that expression. You're up to something. How is that even possible? I saw you just fifteen minutes ago."

"I'm not up to anything ... and that's a horrible thing to say about your significant other. I got up and cooked you breakfast this morning despite the fact that we only got a few hours sleep. You should be worshipping me for that alone."

His face lit with amusement. "Fair enough. What sort of information are you looking for? Be forewarned, if I don't like where this conversation is going I'll refuse to answer your question. I just want to make you aware of that."

It was difficult to refrain from rolling my eyes, but I managed it ... barely. "Is June a witch?"

Whatever question he was expecting, that wasn't it. He leaned back in his chair, his brow furrowed. "That's what you want to know?"

"Yeah. What did you think I was going to ask?"

"I thought we were playing a dirty game after the image you shoved in Bronwen's head. I'll have to readjust my expectations. Give me a second."

The look I shot him was withering. "Not every conversation we share needs to revolve around sex. I'm serious."

"As am I." His eyes twinkled and he sighed. "Apparently your sense

71

of humor disappeared with the new witch. I don't know what to tell you. I believe June has some witch in her lineage, but if it was ever prominent it's not any longer. I've never seen her perform magic."

"See, that's what I thought, but that Bronwen chick said she was looking forward to performing rituals with June and it confused me. She also invited us to said rituals, but insisted you stay dressed until after the spells were completed because you would serve as too much of a distraction."

He smirked. "I am quite distracting."

"You are." I was silent for a beat and then remembered he had work to do. "Anything new on Salma's death?"

"No, but her three best friends are due any second. I'm supposed to interview them."

"Do you think they'll have information?"

"Probably not. They're all idiots, as far as I can tell. In fact ... ." He trailed off at the sound of someone — a female someone — clearing her throat by the door.

I turned to see who was joining us and frowned when I found three overly-dressed women, all looking to be in their early twenties. They glared at Galen with overt hostility.

Apparently I wasn't the only one prone to sticking a foot in a mouth.

"Sheriff Blackwood," the brunette at the front of the group drawled, disdain practically dripping from her tongue. "We're here as requested."

Yup. Galen was in for a battle.

"Hello, Cissy," Galen replied calmly. "It's good to see you."

"That's not what you were saying a second ago."

"I wasn't talking about you. I was talking about Salma's other friends, the ones who aren't as smart as you."

Cissy brightened considerably. "Oh, well, that's cool."

"Great." Galen's smile was calm, but I could tell he was on edge. "Why don't you ladies have a seat?"

"Is she going to be here for the interview?" Cissy asked, inclining her head in my direction. She didn't look excited by the possibility.

"She is," he replied, taking me by surprise. I thought he would shoo me out now that he had actual work to do, but he obviously felt otherwise. "Hadley Hunter, this is Cissy Hilton, Lindsey Murphy and Bette Durham. They were friends with Salma."

"Best friends," Bette stressed. She had short-cropped hair that was perfectly styled and a set of fake fingernails long enough to gouge eyes out if so inclined. She carried a Prada purse and wore Louis Vuitton pumps that were impractical given the uneven sidewalks in town.

"Best friends," Galen agreed. "Salma was obviously close with all of you. That's why I asked you to come in. Given what happened to her, I obviously have questions."

I felt out of place hovering next to his desk so I sat in the chair in the corner. I was largely removed from the conversation but could hear without straining, which was good enough for me. I was invested in finding Salma's killer, if only to put my mind at ease that no one else was in danger.

"We have questions, too," Lindsey shot back. Her hair was a soft flaxen, but her eyebrows were dark brown. "We want to know what you're going to do to the animal who killed our friend. We want swift justice."

"I think we would all like swift justice," Galen supplied. "I need clues to track down the guilty party. That's why I called you here. Was Salma seeing anyone?"

"No one serious," Cissy replied. "She was dating here and there, but I don't think she'd gone out with anyone in the past three weeks. She was too wrapped up in this festival to worry about anything else."

Since they'd given him the opening, Galen took it. "I noticed her social media feeds were completely taken up with this festival. Was she looking forward to going?"

Bette made a ridiculous face. "Oh, she wasn't going."

"And yet she talked about the festival nonstop on social media," Galen noted.

"Yeah, but that was her job."

"I didn't realize she had a job."

"Of course she had a job." Bette rolled her eyes so dramatically I

AMANDA M. LEE

was surprised she didn't fall over. "Her job was to promote things on the internet. It's a real thing. We all do it." She gestured toward the other women, who all bobbed their heads.

"We're good at it, too," Cissy enthused.

"This is that influencer thing you were talking about, right?" he asked me, clearly confused.

"I believe so," I replied. "I don't know that they use that word, though."

"We most definitely don't," Lindsey sniffed, her eyes dark when they locked with mine. "That's an extremely rude term, and we don't like it."

She'd directed the statement toward me, so I felt the need to respond. "Hey. I was just repeating what I read on the internet."

"Well, you should be careful what you read on the internet. Everything out there is fake."

"Including what Salma wrote about the festival?" Galen asked, dragging the conversation back on track. "Was anything she wrote truthful?"

The women exchanged quick looks, and then Cissy cleared her throat, as if she was going to say something important.

"Here's the thing," she started, her eyes darting back and forth. I had the distinct impression she was searching for the right words, something that would make Salma look good. "This job isn't without its quirks. To get a foothold in this business, you have to have three things going for you."

"Looks, brains and boobs," Bette volunteered with a smile.

I pressed my lips together to keep from laughing at the expression on Galen's face. He looked as if he was about to pull his hair out in frustration.

"I'm not making it up," Bette reassured him when Galen didn't immediately respond. "You need other things, like fast fingers and an ability to pretend you like stuff you really don't, but those are the three biggies. Very few people are qualified to do what we do."

"Yes, well ... how fabulous for you," Galen drawled, his incredulous eyes briefly locking with mine before he asked the obvious question.

"That still doesn't answer my question. Why would she promote the festival if she wasn't planning on going?"

"Because it didn't matter if she was there," Cissy replied simply. "She just needed people to believe it was important for them to be there. She never had any intention of going."

"She hated sand," Bette volunteered.

"And bugs," Lindsey added. "She hated bugs, too. She was never going."

"I see. Do you know how much she was paid to promote the festival?"

"I don't, but I know it was a lot, because she was practically squealing when she told us about it," Cissy answered. "I think you'll have to talk to Alastair Herne. He hired her."

"Yeah." Galen rubbed his chin, obviously annoyed. "I think I'm going to have to talk to Alastair, too. And I'm not looking forward to it."

NINE

"*How* can you live on an island and hate sand?"

That was the thing bothering me most once the empty-headed trio left Galen's office an hour later. He took them round and round, asking them a multitude of questions about Salma and her "job," but they really didn't expand on anything. He got frustrated and basically kicked them out once he deemed they were of no further use.

It had been quiet in the office for a good ten minutes before I asked the question. I thought maybe there was a chance he'd forgotten I was there, still sitting in the corner, and wanted to remind him of my presence.

He sighed as he shifted his eyes from his computer to me. He looked tired.

"I don't know," he replied after a beat. "I happen to love sand."

"Because you like to make sandcastles, right? You look like the type."

His grin was wide enough it practically swallowed his entire face. "More like I enjoy rolling around in it. If you play your cards right, we can take a walk on the beach by the lighthouse tonight and I'll show you."

That seemed like a bad idea. "We can't do that."

"Even if I promise to stop talking about sex so much? I know it's driving you crazy."

"I don't mind the sex talk. I was just feeling vulnerable earlier when I said that because of what happened with Bronwen. That's not why we can't go for a walk."

He leaned back in his chair, steepled his fingers on his washboard stomach and arched an eyebrow. "I'm listening."

"We can't play in the surf because of the festival."

"They're on a completely different section of the beach."

"Yeah, but when have you known drunken people to pay attention to boundaries?"

"That's a fair point, but there are signs warning them off your property. I made sure my deputies put them up this afternoon."

That was news to me. "You did?" I couldn't shutter my surprise. "I didn't know that. Why?"

"Because, like you, I sense trouble coming from this festival. I think some very bad things are going to happen, and I don't want them happening on your property."

"Aw, that's kind of sweet."

He rolled his eyes. "It's practical is what it is. We like sitting out on your back patio and ... playing games. I don't want anyone spying from the bushes when you make the water dance because you're excited."

My mouth dropped open. "That happened one time!"

"That's happened one time that I pointed out to you," he corrected. "It happened another time before we even started dating, and for an entirely different reason, that still managed to be sensuous. It has happened a few more times. I didn't tell you because I was afraid you would freak out."

Well, that was humbling ... and maybe a little frightening. "That's why you always want to drink wine on the back patio, isn't it?"

He shrugged. "There are multiple reasons why I like to drink wine on the patio. The first is that you look ridiculously hot under the moonlight. I also happen to love the smell of the ocean. I think you do, too, because it makes you frisky. That's another reason I love the patio. The water thing you do is just an added bonus."

I pursed my lips. "I think I should be angry that you've been holding out on me."

"And I think that's a waste of effort. Besides, I have an idea I'd like to broach with you."

"Does it have something to do with making the water dance?"

He shook his head, somber. "No. It has to do with Salma."

"Oh. I ... this is a serious conversation. I'm sorry. I got used to us spending every hour of the day for two straight weeks flirting because nothing was breaking on the island and that seemed to be what both of us wanted. It's going to take me a bit to return to reality."

"I don't want you to return to reality," he countered. "I don't want either of us to ever return to reality. But we have to deal with Salma's death.

"What do you want me to do? Do you want me to go down to the beach and infiltrate all the witches and warlocks down there to see if anyone had a motive? Oh, I know! I can use my new power. That will allow me to practice while helping you at the same time."

"Most of those people didn't arrive until today, so I think that would be a waste of your talent."

I was starting to grow suspicious. "You want a favor from me. I can tell, so just spit it out."

"Did you read my mind to figure that out?"

"I don't need to read your mind. I know you."

"You do." His smile was mischievous. "The thing is, I've been trying to sort through all these social media posts, but they all look alike to me. On top of that, they're all bleeding together, to the point I can't even remember what I read on what account."

That's when things started to make sense. "You want me to wade through the social media posts."

"I do."

"Because you don't want to or you think I would be good at it?"

"Are you going to be angry if I say both? Honestly, I don't know what I'm reading and I hate being on the computer like this. I would prefer being out in the field or going over reports, doing anything but reading this stuff. You're good at it. You can do it in a quarter of the time. Also, we'll be working together, which will bring us closer and make our love grow."

I choked on a snort. "You could've stopped before the last bit. That was a step too far."

"I sensed that as I was saying it, but it was too late."

"I'll help you with the posts," I volunteered. "I actually find it fascinating. We can work together instead of fighting about me finding trouble for a change."

"There you go." He blew me an air kiss. "I think this is going to work out fabulously."

He was being naive, but who was I to burst his bubble?

TWO HOURS LATER, I WAS BEGINNING TO seriously regret my decision. Following the thread of Tweets on the festival was like falling down a rabbit hole and talking to a mushroom with a face. In other words, it was making me doubt my sanity.

"This is ridiculous," I practically exploded when I found yet another clump of Tweets. "Do you have any idea how many Tweets have been issued over this festival?"

Galen, who had been working quietly at his desk the entire time I'd descended into the bowels of Twitter hell, glanced up. "No, but I'm legitimately curious."

So was I. That's why I tried to add them up. "More than a million."

"No way." He shifted in his chair. "How is that even possible? We're talking about a small festival. Sure, it's big by Moonstone Bay standards, but we're still talking a few thousand people. I think the limit was five-thousand, and supposedly all those slots were sold."

"True. But there are millions of Tweets. For example, one of the earliest Tweets I can find is from Salma. She mentioned the idea of having a cool beach party, how she always thought it was a grand idea, and then links to an article in the Moonstone Bay newsletter announcing the festival. The Tweet just happened to go out the day after the article was written."

"Do you know who wrote the article?"

"Um ... someone named Donna Hanover."

Galen scowled. "That figures. She's my least favorite person on that staff. She can be bought to give out free publicity. Everybody knows it, but no one ever calls her on it."

"I don't think her participation in this farce is what we should be worried about," I countered. "It's the trail of retweets that matters."

"What's a retweet?"

"Oh, you need to join the technology age, baby," I teased. "A retweet is what happens when one person Tweets something and another basically hits a button to copy that exact Tweet onto their page. By doing that, it expands the number of eyes that see it."

"Ah. I do know what a retweet is. I just don't care. I was hoping you might be able to track down someone who issued a threat or something over Twitter in regard to the Tweet. That's what I'm looking for."

He couldn't be serious. "No one is going to issue a death threat over the internet ... unless he or she is mentally ill or looking for attention. Our killer would have to be an idiot to do that, and given the way you're spinning your wheels, I don't think that's what we're dealing with."

His lips curved down. "So ... what are we dealing with?"

"A very-well-thought-out plan of attack. Salma and her little cohorts manufactured an event completely on their own, which is probably why Alastair hired her in the first place. He must've known what she could do. Has he returned your phone call, by the way?"

Galen's scowl grew more pronounced. "No. The little ferret is hiding. I think he's screening my call."

"Of course he's screening your call. He doesn't want to talk to you. He knows it's going to get ugly, and now that there's been a murder you have a lot more leverage if you want to shut things down."

"I also have people on the beach," he reminded me. "It would've been easier to put up signs and stop things before that happened.

Now, they've taken over and I don't have enough men to control things if they decide to get rowdy."

I hadn't thought of that. He really was in a pickle. "I'll protect you," I volunteered. "I'll make the water dance to distract them and we'll make a run for it if things get out of control."

He snickered and shook his head. "I'll keep that in mind. Have you found anything else in the social media stuff?"

"There's a lot to dig through."

"That's why I turned it over to you, my diligent, hard-working, witchy queen."

"Oh, that was way over-the-top."

"I knew I would finally get there." His grin eased. "I can't help but think there's an answer here, or at least a direction to look that I'm not seeing because I don't pay attention to the technology. I don't even have a Facebook profile."

"No, but you're all over my profile."

His eyebrows hopped. "I am?"

I nodded. "I call you my beefcake beauty and post photos of you shirtless on the beach to make all the women I went to high school with jealous. They don't believe we're dating, but I keep posting photos to torture them."

He laughed so hard he almost choked. "That's absolutely lovely, sweetheart. I can't tell you how much that inflates my ego."

"Glad to be of service."

"What's your next step with the accounts?"

"I need to figure out a way to sort them. I might have to give that some thought before tackling it again. There has to be a way to do it that I'm not seeing."

"Well, the department appreciates your help no matter how you get things done."

"And I appreciate the department."

His eyes grew heavy-lidded and I thought he was going to say something sexy, but the phone on his desk rang, ruining the moment and causing both of us to jolt.

"Hello," he growled into the receiver, his eyes holding mine. He listened for a full minute before sighing and pressing the heel of his hand to his forehead. "I'll head out there right now. Just try to keep things in line until I get there."

I watched him expectantly as he hung up.

"Come on," he said, holding out his hand to help me stand. "If we're going to be partners on this one we need to do everything as a unit. That includes heading out to the beach together."

Oh, well, now we were talking. "Do you want me to read minds?"

"No. I want you to make the water dance in case things get out of control and we have to run. Apparently the guests are getting restless and there's some sort of mutiny afoot. We need to check it out."

Who doesn't love a mutiny? "Absolutely. I'm sort of anxious to see what's going down."

"You and me both."

WE TOOK MY GOLF CART BECAUSE it was small enough that we could drive on the sidewalks. It was also sturdy enough to navigate the choppy sand of the beach. This way we had an escape hatch should things get ugly.

I thought he was probably expecting the worst for no good reason, but I figured it was wise to keep my opinion to myself. I was glad I followed that route when I got a gander at what was going down, because it turned out I was the one who was wrong ... and Goddess, do I hate being wrong.

"I want to speak to the president of this island right now!" A woman, her skirt long and flowing, stood in the center of a huge crowd and screamed demands at one of Galen's deputies. The man, who I recognized as Tom Stickney, looked as if he would prefer finding a hole to crawl into.

"We don't have a president, ma'am," Tom replied calmly. I had to give him credit, he didn't as much as raise his voice a note as he regarded the demanding woman. "That's not how things operate here."

"No? Then I want to talk to whoever is in charge."

Before Tom could answer, Galen inserted himself in the conversation.

"As far as you're concerned, that would be me," he called out. "What seems to be the trouble, ma'am?"

"Eleanor Torkelson." She stuck out her limp-at-the-wrist hand and I thought for a moment she expected him to kiss it. "And who might you be?"

"Sheriff Galen Blackwood. What can I do for you?"

"You're awfully young to be a sheriff," Eleanor muttered, briefly shifting her eyes to me before turning back to him. It was obvious she figured he had more authority than me.

"Have you looked around?" she challenged, hands landing on ample hips. "This place is an absolute mess. There aren't enough bathrooms. The food that was promised to us in the form of carts and trucks isn't present. There's a man down the way selling bottles of water for five dollars each — and we're talking teeny, tiny bottles of water — and there's no access to showers."

Galen scrubbed his cheek and frowned. "I don't understand. Why did you think you would have access to showers?"

"That's what the festival brochure says."

He slid his eyes to me, uncertain. "Um ... I don't suppose you have one of those brochures?"

"I do." She preened as she handed over the item in question.

I was curious enough that I moved closer so I could read with him. What I found on the shiny pages was troubling. "That says there will be grills located around the beach and ample access to seafood for crab leg feasts."

"That's another thing," Eleanor snapped. "I haven't seen a single crab."

"I'm sure there will be lots of crabs spread about the beach before this is all said and done," I quipped, earning a stern glare from Eleanor for my effort. "Of course, those aren't the crabs you're interested in."

Galen's lips quirked but he managed to hold it together ... just barely. "Ma'am, I don't know what to tell you about this. I mean ...

very little promised in this brochure is feasible. Who here from the festival is in charge?"

Her expression was incredulous. "Um ... I think that would be you."

"And I think you're dreaming," he shot back. "I'm not in charge of this festival. It's not an official Moonstone Bay event. There's a festival team in charge of things. Where are they?"

Her face was blank. "How should I know? You're the one in charge. You're the one who needs to figure it out."

He worked his jaw and swung his eyes to me. "Well, this is just great."

"What about the hotels?" I asked. "Can we move some of the people there?"

"The hotels are sold out," Eleanor replied. "Trust me. Once I saw the setup here, I started calling around. There's not a room to be had for anyone."

That didn't bode well.

"I bet you're glad I put signs up on your beach now," Galen muttered, dragging a frustrated hand through his hair. "If I didn't, you would've had people sleeping on your patio."

"I'm forever in your debt," I drawled. "What are we going to do about this situation, though? This is ... bad."

"I knew it was going to be bad before anybody else."

"Yes, that's the thing to focus on. You were right and everybody else was wrong. Poof. The situation is fixed."

He growled. "I don't know what to do. I don't even know who to call."

"I think you'd better figure it out before there's a riot."

TEN

"Wat are you going to do?" I asked Galen after we managed to put a little distance between ourselves and the angry festival attendees. He looked as lost as I felt.

"I'm going to find Alastair." He was firm. "This is his mess."

"Yeah, well ... good luck with that." I plucked the brochure out of his hand and gave it a better look. They spared no expense on the printed product. The festival, however, looked nothing like what was advertised. "Will you look at this? There's even a page for villas here. If you're willing to pay fifty grand for the week you get access to a twenty-thousand-foot villa. Whose villa are they using?"

Galen frowned as he snatched back the brochure. "That place isn't on this island. I don't know where it's at, but ... I would recognize this house if it were on Moonstone Bay."

"Which probably means that it's a stock photo." My mind was going a mile a minute. "The hotels are sold out. There are thousands of people on the beach and there aren't enough tents or bathrooms. This is going to be bad."

"Oh, really? What was your first clue?" Sarcasm rolled off him in waves. I understood his frustration, and what it stemmed from — he did warn everybody about this, after all — so I didn't hold the snarky

AMANDA M. LEE

response against him. That didn't mean I was willing to sit back and serve as his verbal punching bag. Luckily, he realized he was out of control right away.

"I'm sorry." He held up his hands in capitulation. "I didn't mean to snap at you that way. It's not fair to you. Not even a little. I just ... what am I going to do?"

He looked bewildered and I felt genuinely sorry for him. "You're going to find Alastair and Calliope," I replied without hesitation. "They're the only people who can fix this."

He was incredulous. "How are they going to fix this? They promised things that don't exist."

"At the very least they can refund the money ... though that's not going to help people who spent a lot on airfare. At least refunding the festival money is a start. It might be enough to placate some of the guests. I don't know the flight situation going out of here, though. Something tells me they can't fit all of these people on one plane."

"Not even close." Galen was grim as he rolled his neck and stared at the water. "There are no boats due for at least three days. This is a nightmare."

We needed to find solutions. "Find Alastair and Calliope. I'll see if I can calm down the people here."

He balked. "I'm not leaving you with these people. They're angry ... and they'll see you as a person of authority because you were with me and they assumed I was in charge. I'm not risking you getting hurt."

That was sweet, but I wasn't worried about the group turning into a mob just yet. "If you're really worried, assign me some backup ... like maybe Booker. He might be able to rein in the women at least."

Galen extended a finger, his eyes flashing. "That, baby, is a very smart idea." He dug in his pocket for his phone. "Booker can control emotions. He can handle the women. That leaves the men, but if the women are happy, the men will be happy, too ... at least for a few hours."

I tilted my head to the side, considering. "Are you happy when I'm happy?"

"Um, yeah. You make the water dance. What's not to like about that?"

He had a point.

BOOKER ARRIVED TEN MINUTES LATER. Galen refused to leave my side until he was reasonably certain I wouldn't be alone in case of an emergency.

"Watch her," he instructed Booker, grave. "These people are losing their heads."

"Oh, and here I thought you didn't care," Booker drawled. "It's gratifying to know that you love me enough to put me in charge of your girlfriend in case an angry mob attacks."

Galen's expression was withering. "If something happens to her I'll do the same to you. That's a promise."

"Got it." Booker waved off the threat, apparently unbothered. His eyes were busy as he scanned the crowd. "They don't look happy."

"They're ticked," Galen corrected. "I need to track down Alastair and Calliope. This is their mess. Until I do, try to help as best you can. I know there's very little you can do, but a lot of these people just want someone to listen to them vent."

"Fair enough." Booker's hands landed on his narrow hips as two women, who looked to be in their early twenties and sporting some of the tiniest bikini tops I'd ever seen, starting giggling and winking at him. "It might not be so bad."

I rolled my eyes. "Well, great. Now I get to watch all the women fall all over him. This is turning into a great day."

Galen snickered. "You'll be fine. He'll take care of you." He leaned over and gave me a kiss. "If things get hairy, don't hesitate to run. I'm leaving you the golf cart just in case and walking back to get my truck. If you feel something bad is about to happen, I want you to head home and lock yourself inside. I'll catch up with you eventually."

I didn't have to be a mind reader to take the temperature of the crowd. "They're not quite there yet. They haven't roughed it on the beach overnight yet. Things aren't going to get really bad until tomorrow."

"Well, here's hoping I can find Alastair and beat him until he agrees to give these people what they need. That's the only thing we have to offer."

"Then you'd best get to it." I flashed a smile and watched as he took off at a jog in the direction of the police station. He set a brisk pace, which meant he was serious about finding Alastair. I hoped he wasn't serious about hurting him.

"How do you want to handle this?" Booker asked.

When I turned back to him, I found he was looking over a buxom blonde who had caught his eye. "Knock that off," I ordered, elbowing him in the stomach. "Now is not the time for you to hunt for a new conquest. We have serious problems."

Booker rubbed his stomach. "Okay. There's no need to be vicious. What exactly are we dealing with here?"

I handed him the brochure and watched as he flipped through it.

"Well, this isn't good," he said finally. "I can't believe Alastair promised them villas ... and trampolines, though this photo of women in string bikinis bouncing on trampolines is genius."

"It's disgusting is what it is." I snatched back the brochure. "These people were sold something that was impossible to deliver. It's not as if Alastair actually thought he would be able to provide these things and somehow fell behind through no fault of his own. This was impossible to deliver from the start."

"So ... why did he promise it?" Booker mused. "It's worrisome, isn't it?"

I could think of a few other words to describe it. "It's a scam."

"Shh." Booker's eyes filled with fire as he glanced around to see who was listening. Thankfully, even though quite a few people were staring no one was invading our space to eavesdrop. "You need to be very careful using that word," he admonished. "If the tourists hear you use it they'll start using it ... and that will be bad."

"How could things possibly get worse?"

"Oh, things can always get worse." He exhaled heavily and straightened his back. "Well, first things first. I think we should tackle the things we actually can help them with."

"And what would that be? You don't happen to have a villa stashed in your back pocket, do you?"

He snorted. "No, but I do have a contact in the city who can get the rest of those Porta-Potties here."

Relief flooded through me. "Really? That actually will help."

"What will also help is food," he said. "Do me a favor and call Lilac. Tell her that we need some food trucks down here or things are going to get ugly. She'll know who to call."

I was dubious, but game. "Okay. What do we do after that?"

"Pray that's enough to placate most of these people and hope that Galen finds Alastair. We need someone to throw to the wolves. The inept festival organizer seems a good bet."

TRUE TO HIS WORD, BOOKER HAD A team delivering Porta-Potties within thirty minutes. A cheer went up from the crowd when they saw what was happening, which seemed like a sad commentary on this particular event.

Lilac also came through, arranging for no less than thirty food trucks to arrive at the beach. She followed soon after, leaving the bar in the capable hands of her workers and joining us in an effort to keep the crowd calm.

"This is a mess," she noted as she glanced around.

"No, this is a dream vacation," Booker countered.

Lilac elbowed him sharply. "Sarcasm isn't necessary."

"If I don't have sarcasm to use as a crutch I have absolutely nothing."

My lips twitched as I glanced around. The festival-goers were still in foul moods as they lined up to order food, but nobody looked to be melting down. That was a good thing, which I believed ... right up until I saw Eleanor heading in our direction. "This isn't going to be good."

Booker shifted his gaze to study the incoming complaint missile and then offered up a genuine smile. He didn't look bothered in the least by the potential for mayhem. "I've got her. Don't you worry one little bit."

I knew exactly what he meant by "I've got her" and I was mildly disgusted. Of course, we needed to keep things in check until Galen returned, so I was willing to use whatever tools we had in our arsenal.

"Hello," Booker purred, stepping in front of me to intercept the angry woman. "You look like a woman who knows how to have a good time. How would you like to get some food with me from one of the trucks?"

Eleanor was obviously taken aback and the look she shot Booker was full of suspicion. "Thanks, but I can feed myself when it's time." She furrowed her brow. "Who are you? Where did the sheriff go?"

"Galen is searching for the festival organizers," I volunteered quickly. "He's trying to get them out here so they can address your concerns."

"Why isn't he addressing them?"

"Because he didn't set up this festival," I replied. "He's not the one who screwed things up." I felt the need to stand up for my boyfriend even though it might inflame the woman. "He's not the one who lied to you."

Eleanor's eyes narrowed. "Lied about what? Are you suggesting someone lied about this entire festival?"

I sensed danger. Before I could smooth things over Booker stepped in.

"Ma'am, we're not saying anything of the sort," he replied. "We're simply trying to make things better until the festival organizers get here with the things that were promised to you."

It was impossible to provide the things that were promised to them, so I was incredulous at Booker's gumption. Still, his words had the desired effect and Eleanor calmed down ... if only marginally.

"I understand that you're not personally responsible for what's happening here," she said, her eyes trained on me. "This isn't your fault. It's just ... some of these people spent their life savings on this festival because they were promised certain amenities."

That sparked something in the back of my mind. "Were you promised things that weren't in the brochure?"

"Well ... ." Eleanor shifted from one foot to the other, distinctly uncomfortable. "I don't know that 'promised' is the right word," she said finally. "It's more that expectations were voiced and verbal agreements were struck."

That seemed a vague way to describe whatever went down. "We'll need more information than that," I pressed. "What verbal agreements?"

"I'm not sure I should share that information with you. You're not an island official."

"But I am," Booker offered calmly. "I'm the head of the tourism board and hospitality services committee. I need to know everything that was agreed upon if I'm to make sure you have the vacation of a lifetime."

"I ... can you really deliver on what was promised?" Eleanor didn't look convinced. "You don't look like an island official."

"I like to go incognito because that allows me to mingle with the tourists without standing out and making them uncomfortable," he lied. "I prefer hearing true opinions rather than what people think I want to hear."

"That's actually pretty smart." Eleanor beamed at him and I knew Booker was using his influence to calm her. There was no other explanation. "Well, because you asked so nicely and I truly think you're trying to help, I'll tell you. We were promised a group ritual to bolster our power. That's the only reason some of us came."

I was baffled. "Bolster your power?" I looked to Lilac for an explanation. "What does that even mean?"

"I think I know." Lilac was grim. "There are certain pagan rituals that have fallen out of favor that were known to give a large group of people a magical boost if certain things – dark things – were carried out. Last time I checked, those rituals were forbidden on this island."

"Well, that's a disappointment." Eleanor's scowl returned. "I'm starting to get the feeling that we were lied to about everything. That won't go over well when everybody finds out."

I'd pretty much figured that out myself. Still, I was intrigued. "What things are necessary for this big spell?"

"Ritual sacrifices," Lilac replied, her eyes flashing. "Trust me. There's a reason these rituals were banned."

"It's not as if we were going to sacrifice a person," Eleanor sniffed. "It's more like we were going to sacrifice a chicken."

"Yeah, that's not allowed either." Lilac shook her head and turned at the sound of a vehicle door slamming.

I looked in the same direction, my heart giving a little leap when I saw Galen appear out of the encroaching darkness. He was alone, and from the slouch of his shoulders I could tell that his search hadn't gone well.

"That doesn't look good." Lilac made a clucking sound with her tongue.

Galen lifted his eyes, as if sensing me watching, and he offered a wan smile when we locked gazes. He didn't speak until he was directly on top of us. "We have a problem."

"Those are words I never like hearing," Booker supplied. "What's the problem?"

"I can't find Alastair."

"He's probably hiding from you," Lilac replied. "I'm guessing he knows you're ticked and is afraid of what you'll do to him."

"That's one possibility," he agreed, rubbing the back of his neck and lowering his voice. "The other possibility is that he took the money these people paid for the festival and took off."

"You mean left the island?" I was dumbfounded. "How would he manage that?"

"The ship that landed today," Booker replied. "Hundreds of people got off. Once it was cleared and cleaned, people got on to leave. We had a group of tourists who left. I know because I transported quite a few of them to the docks."

"Alastair could've been with the group," Galen volunteered. "He could've had this planned from the start and fled before it hit the fan. I mean ... he would've had to give up his station here and everything he's come to cherish, but it's possible."

"He might have even more money than we realized," I added, explaining about the ritual and magical things promised the guests. "Some of these people paid even more money because of the promise of a magical boost."

"Well, that's just great!" Galen's anger was on full display. "I can't tell you how happy I am to hear that. I just ... could this get any worse?" He slapped his hand over his forehead and began to rub. He looked to have a vicious headache brewing.

"What about Calliope?" I asked, grasping at straws. "She's one of the co-organizers. She should be down here handling this."

"She's missing, too," Galen replied. "She hasn't checked out of her hotel room, but the staff hasn't seen her all day. There was a 'do not disturb' sign on her door. I went in anyway ... and there was no sign of her."

"What about her suitcase?" Lilac asked. "Was that still there?"

"Yes."

"Then she hasn't left." I forced myself to remain upbeat. "She's still here. Maybe she was screwed by Alastair, too, and is figuring it out. She might be afraid."

"Maybe, but she's nowhere to be found right now. We have a real problem." He was grave as he leaned closer so only the three of us could hear him. "Things are going to get rowdy here tonight and these people are already bitter about what's going down. What do you think is going to happen when alcohol is added to the mix?"

That was a frightening thought. "What do we do?"

"I'm calling in my auxiliary men to patrol the beach tonight and keep things in hand. Other than that, I don't know what to do. I'm going to have to get a meeting with the DDA tomorrow and let them handle this. I think I'm in over my head."

I couldn't help believing the same thing. "What a mess. I'm so sorry this happened to you."

He slung an arm around my shoulders and pulled me close so he could kiss my temple. "You didn't do this ... and it is a mess. Ah, well. I can only do what I can do. That means calling for reinforcements. We'll figure out the rest as we go along."

ELEVEN

*I*t took Galen two hours to secure the beach. Apparently he had more auxiliary deputies than I realized, because the place was absolutely packed when we left. Despite his best efforts, he couldn't secure an emergency meeting with the DDA and he was grouchy. Still, he picked a small, out-of-the-way restaurant that I'd never been to for dinner and I was looking forward to a bit of quiet.

"Do you really think that Alastair fled the island?" I asked as I broke a breadstick in half and dunked it in marinara sauce. I was starving, to the point I would've willingly eaten oysters to take the edge off my hunger.

"I think it's a possibility." Galen leaned back in his seat and regarded me with a soft smile. "I'm sorry you got dragged into this. I had every intention of keeping you out of situations like this for the foreseeable future. That didn't go so well."

I frowned. "Why do you want to keep me out of situations like this?"

"It's not your job."

"And I annoy you when I'm involved?"

He made a face that would've been funny under different circumstances. Tonight, though, it proved that we were both feeling out of sorts. "I like it when you're involved. After what happened with the cupids, though ... ." He didn't finish the statement, but I knew what he was thinking.

"You were the one who was injured when the cupids came to the island," I reminded him, frowning at the memory. I'd sat vigil next to him the entire night as he recovered from being attacked. He put up a vicious fight when they took him, but mostly because he was determined to get back to me. In the end, I had to fight them on my own ... until I could get a few of my magically-inclined friends to join in and really put them in their place.

"I'm well aware, but I heal quickly," he said. "I was fine the next day."

That wasn't exactly true. Even weeks later he still needed more sleep than he normally would. "Then why did you make me act as your naughty nurse?"

"That was simply to bolster my spirits." His lips curved as he pressed his feet on either side of mine. It was a way for us to touch without being ridiculous with our flirting. "I don't want you worrying about what happened. I'm perfectly fine."

"And I like to think I handled myself well during that situation."

"You did."

"So ... why do you want to cut me out of this one?"

The sigh he let loose was long and drawn out. "You just can't let it go, can you?"

"I want to know why you don't want me involved. I'm guessing there's some sexist reason, but I want to hear it from you."

He wagged a finger. "I'm not sexist. I'm ... practical. It's not that I don't want you involved because you're a woman. It's more that I want you safe because you're my woman."

My mouth dropped open. "How is that not sexist?"

"Because I love you and it's impossible to be sexist when you're protecting the woman you love."

"I'm pretty sure that's nonsense."

"No. It's a fact ... that I just made up." He leaned over the table until his face was directly in front of mine. "I'm not going to pretend that I don't want to keep you safe. That would be a lie, and I have no intention of lying to you.

"That doesn't mean that I don't think you're strong ... and brave ... and capable of taking on the entire world," he continued. "It simply means that I'm afraid of losing you. I want to keep you with me forever."

Oh, geez. How was I supposed to be angry when he said stuff like that? I would give it my best shot. "You can't keep me locked up." I adopted my most reasonable tone. "I know it's difficult for you, but we need to come to a happy meeting of the minds here.

"I love you, too, but I know better than to try to get you to give up your job and take on something safe," I continued. "I'm not saying that getting involved in this stuff will be my job, but I can't just look away when I see things happening. That's not who I am.

"I just found out I'm a witch and I have powers. I want to use those powers for good. I don't think that's an unreasonable request."

"It's not," he agreed. "I don't want to change who you are. I was attracted to that spark inside of you from the beginning. I just ... it would gut me if something happened to you. I don't think I would ever get over it."

That was a sweet sentiment ... and a load of hogwash. "I could be killed falling down the stairs. I could cut my foot on the beach and get that flesh-eating bacteria thing and die. There's no way to ensure that I'll always be safe short of wrapping me in cotton and forcing me to sit on the couch all day while you're at work."

"And I'm assuming you're against that?"

"Pretty much."

"Well ... then we're at an impasse. No matter how much you complain, I'll always want to keep you safe. That's simply how I'm built."

I didn't like the word "impasse." It made me nervous. "What does that mean?"

As if reading my mind, he grabbed my hand and gave it a squeeze. "It means that we're going to have to agree to disagree and occasionally argue. I can't change the way I feel any more than you can. That doesn't mean we'll break up or fall apart. It simply means that, occasionally, we'll disagree."

I considered the statement and then smiled. "That's not so bad. We're good at bickering, but we're even better at making up."

"And that right there is a true story." He grinned, laced his fingers with mine, and then leaned back as the waitress arrived with an appetizer plate. She was a pretty woman who obviously recognized him, and she gave him a series of smiles as she explained about the appetizers we ordered.

"I think we know how to eat stuffed mushrooms and mozzarella sticks," I said dryly.

She pretended she didn't hear me and remained focused on Galen. "Anything else?"

"I'm good," he replied. "Hadley, do you need another drink?"

Getting drunk sounded like a fine idea, but I knew better than to risk that given everything that was going on. "I'm fine." I flashed a cheesy smile toward the waitress, who didn't look as if she liked me one bit, and waited until she was gone to speak. "What is it with you and women? It's annoying to watch random chicks throw themselves at you every time I turn around."

"We've been over this. I only care about you throwing yourself at me."

"Oh, this isn't about you." We were finally getting to the heart of the matter. It was something I'd realized when I'd watched Booker schmooze Eleanor. "This is about the women. It's as if they have no self-control or self-respect. It's a little depressing when you look at it as a statement on the female gender."

His eyes lit with amusement. "Oh, well, here we go." He grabbed a mozzarella stick and dipped it in sauce. "Please explain the female gender to me as it relates to this statement."

He was teasing, but I was raring to go. "Gladly." I transferred several mushroom caps to my plate. "These women who stare at you in restaurants ... and on the beach ... and whenever we go to the park or a festival are wrapping all their self-worth in what a man can provide them," I explained. "The most important thing to them is what a man can do to make their lives better. They never worry about making their own lives better."

Galen furrowed his brow. "That's a pretty deep thought for what could be some random flirting. You know it's entirely possible they simply think I'm hot."

"Maybe. I think you're hot, so I get it. But I didn't completely lose my head when we first met simply because you're hot."

"That's true. You played hard to get."

I snorted. "Oh, I did not. You're just used to women throwing themselves at your feet and begging you to love them. I was slightly leery because this was a new world to me and I wasn't sure I was going to stay. Part of me thought I might try it for six months, hate it, and pick up and leave."

"I take it you've ruled out that possibility." His grin was wolfish. "Did I have something to do with that?"

"Yeah ... but, most importantly, I had something to do with that." I lightly tapped my chest. "When I got here, something inside clicked. It was as if I'd always belonged here and the reason I struggled in other places was because they simply couldn't measure up to this place.

"You're definitely part of it, but if we'd never hooked up I would still want to call this my home," I continued. "What I see when these women react to you sometimes — and Booker, too, although I think he helps cause it because he likes being the center of attention — is that these women lose all rational thought and all they think about is how they're going to get you to notice them.

"Take the waitress." I daintily cut one of my mushrooms despite the cheese flowing in every direction. "Do you know what she was thinking when she saw you?"

"Yeah. She was thinking that if she flirted with me enough I would leave a big tip."

"I'm pretty sure she wants a different sort of tip from you, and that if you suggested it she would totally walk off the job for the chance to walk on the beach with you."

He gaped. "That's crap. There's no way."

"It's true."

"Did you read that in her head?"

"No, but I could try doing that if you want."

"I would prefer you didn't." He was thoughtful as he cocked his head and regarded me. "You seem to have given this a lot of thought."

"I like to think of myself as a student of the human condition. I like to analyze people, figure out their motivations. I was like that long before I found out I was a witch."

"Well, it's an interesting hobby." He rested his fingers on top of mine. "You don't have to worry about me wanting to walk on the beach with the waitress. You're the only one I want to walk on the beach with."

"I know that. I'm not worried you're going to cheat on me. That's not how you're built. If you ever change your mind about how you feel, you'll be upfront and tell me."

"I will," he nodded. "The odds of me changing my mind regarding how I feel about you are slim to none. You're ... magical. I can't imagine ever feeling any differently about you. I think it's impossible."

He was romantic when he wanted to be, which I liked. "Thank you for saying that."

"You're welcome."

"You don't have to lay it on so thick, though. I'm already yours. You make me cause water to dance with simple looks. I think we're good. In fact ... ." I trailed off when I noticed two people sitting in the far corner of the restaurant. I wasn't sure how I'd missed them, but I was stunned when I realized who it was. "It's June ... and that Bronwen person."

"What?" Galen was clearly caught off guard by the information and when he turned to look in the direction I indicated he didn't appear nearly as surprised by the intimate dinner date. "Maybe they had things to discuss. The restaurant at June's hotel isn't open. She's as familiar with this place as I am. It's where the locals go, not the tourists."

That was all well and good, but it had nothing to do with the motivation behind the odd pairing. "Do you think they know each other? I mean ... outside of this festival. When I brought up June to Bronwen she seemed excited at the prospect of spending time with her. I'd assumed they'd never met. Perhaps I was wrong."

Galen shrugged. "I guess it's possible. Does it matter? Maybe they just enjoy hanging out."

I cast him a sidelong look. Was he hiding something? There was an evasive tinge to his words, but I couldn't quite put my finger on why I thought that. "Do you know something I don't?"

He took a long drink from his iced tea before answering. "And what is it you think I could possibly know? I met that woman at the same time you did this afternoon. You spent a lot more time with her than I did."

That was true. Still ... . "What about June? Do you know something about her?"

"I know a great many somethings about June. She's a woman who likes tall tales, and I've heard more than a few stories."

That wasn't really an answer. "Maybe we should go over there, say hi."

"I think they're fine."

"Maybe we should join them," I pressed. "We might be able to learn something."

"Absolutely not." He was firm when he shook his head, catching me off guard. "We're not going over there to bug them. They're obviously having a conversation that has nothing to do with us. I refuse to interrupt that."

Agitation bubbled up. "I don't want to interrupt them. For all you know they might be happy to see us."

"I doubt it, and I don't want to spend the entire night talking about the festival and what's going on. That's all they'll want to talk about. I need time to think."

Guilt rolled through me. Of course they would be interested in digging up information about the festival. "I'm sorry." I meant it. "I didn't mean to suggest putting yourself on the spot."

He absently waved his hand. "No, I'm sorry. I didn't mean to snap at you. It would be best if you minded your own business when it comes to June, though. If she wants to tell you something, she'll volunteer it on her own. Don't go snooping behind her back. That's not what a friend would do."

I felt like a chastised child. "I'll try to restrain myself."

Instead of coddling me, he merely nodded. "That would be best."

I WAS STILL FEELING SORRY FOR MYSELF when we returned to the lighthouse. Dinner had been a quiet affair, although the food was good and the ambiance nice. If Galen noticed that I'd grown quiet after he admonished me not to be a busybody he didn't say anything.

He took a moment to study the night sky when we reached the lighthouse and I left him there to stare at ... well, nothing ... as I made my way to the door. I was tired and more than a little crabby. What I really wanted to do was go to sleep and forget about this day.

He caught me before I reached the halfway point and wrapped his arms around me from behind. "I'm sorry," he whispered, kissing the ridge of my ear, causing shudders to run up my spine. "I didn't mean to upset you."

I bit back a sigh, suddenly feeling foolish. What did I have to complain about? He was right. I was obsessed with the fact that June might be a witch. I had no idea why, even though he told me he believed any magic she might have was minimal. Moonstone Bay was an island filled with paranormal creatures. The fact that June had some witch in her bloodline shouldn't have been a surprise.

"I'm not angry." I turned in his arms and lifted my chin, finding an amused smile waiting for me. "Okay, I'm not all that angry," I conceded. "I just ... I think I got a little excited at the prospect of her being able to help me with this witch thing. May is a great help, but she's not alive. Having a real person I trust to help would be great."

"You trust me, right? I'll help you."

"But you can only do so much. You're an expert on shifting ... and Lilac is an expert on being a demon ... and Booker is an expert on being a cupid. Sometimes I feel as if I've stepped into an alternate universe and I'll never catch up. I don't think that's something you can help me with. I'm not sure, even if she had magic at her fingertips, that June could. I hate feeling left behind."

His fingers were gentle when they brushed the hair from my forehead. "I won't ever leave you behind. As for learning about being a witch, do you have any idea how fast you're churning through stuff? You practically took out an entire cadre of cupids on your own. You learned how to read minds in one day."

"Yeah, but I screwed it up."

"You made a mistake, and it's one you won't make again. You're still doing remarkably well."

His words bolstered me. "I guess I'm just being a baby. I don't mean to be so whiny. I just ... sometimes it's overwhelming."

"And that's normal. The thing is, the times you feel overwhelmed, that's when you have to come to me. I want to help you even if it's only to serve as a sounding board while you vent. That's why I'm here."

It was the exact right thing to say. "Thanks." I threw my arms around his neck and pressed myself to him, relishing the way his hands moved over my back. I briefly shut my eyes, inhaled his scent and then stared out at the ocean. "Do you want to make the water dance?" I growled.

He tightened his grip on me and chuckled. "I thought you'd never ask. There's little more I want than to make the water dance."

"Then let's do it. The night is young and you need a mental break. I think I know exactly how to give it to you."

"Bring it on."

TWELVE

*W*e both slept hard. The lack of sleep the previous evening had us passing out wrapped around one another. When I woke the next morning, we were still in the same position, and this time Galen wasn't distracted by his phone.

"Morning," I murmured.

He smiled and stretched. "Good morning?"

There was something off about his smile. "What? Do I have food on my face or something?" I immediately reached up to wipe, but he caught my wrist.

"There's no food on your face. Your hair is a different story."

"How did I get food in my hair?" I sat up to look at myself in the mirror across the room, cringing when I saw the odd angles of my hair. "Ugh. I shouldn't have slept on it wet."

"I like it," Galen countered. "I think it has ... charm." He laughed at my murderous expression. "What? You made the water dance and we had an absolutely lovely time. Nobody cares about your hair."

"I care about my hair." I gave it another look and then flopped back. "I guess it doesn't matter. I'll shower before leaving the house."

"My thoughts exactly." He automatically reached for his phone. "I need to make sure that nobody killed anyone at the festival last night.

I also need to request another meeting with the DDA since they shot down my last one."

I was confused. "I thought they turned you down last night but agreed to meet you today."

"No, they agreed to hear another request for a meeting today. That doesn't mean I'm in."

This DDA sounded like a real nightmare. "How did these people get so much control? I don't understand why they haven't been ousted yet."

"Because everybody is afraid of them."

"I've noticed, but why?"

"I don't have an answer for you. The DDA was set up more than one-hundred years ago, back before Moonstone Bay was a tourist destination. Farming was the way the islanders made a living back then, but they knew it wouldn't last because transporting goods to the mainland was often cumbersome, contingent on storms, and expensive. We needed something else to base the economy on and tourism became that thing."

My understanding was, in the days when manufacturing and agriculture could support an island the size of Moonstone Bay there wouldn't have been a need to entice outsiders. That's probably how it became a hotbed of paranormal activity. It was isolated and those magically inclined felt safe here.

"So ... you're saying the DDA became a thing when you decided to switch over to tourism."

He nodded. "The switch didn't happen immediately. It took a lot of planning. Thankfully most of the town elders at the time had made good money in previous businesses, because they were expected to fund the bulk of the transition."

"And they own the land to this day?"

He nodded, sliding his eyes to me. "Why? What are you thinking?"

"Nothing about the festival," I reassured him. "I was just thinking about what you told me after I first arrived. Property here is at a premium because there's nowhere to expand and it can be a cutthroat game. The story May told me about Rebecca Blythe was heartbreaking. Alastair only dated her because he wanted her father's property."

"Yeah, he's a real jerk," Galen agreed. "When I find him — and mark my words, I will track down that little ferret — he'll wish he never met me."

Something niggled at the back of my brain. "Yeah, but it doesn't make sense. You told me Alastair is one of the richest guys on the island."

"He's well to do. I wouldn't call him one of the richest."

"It still doesn't make sense." I couldn't let it go. "If he was so rich, why would he be so desperate to make money? And if property on Moonstone Bay was so important to him, which he proved when he went after Becky, why would he leave the island after swindling a bunch of people, knowing he could never return? He still has a huge mansion, right?"

Galen nodded, his expression hard to read. "That's true. I need to run a financial probe on him. I guess it's possible he's buried in debt to the point he's losing the house, and nobody knows about it."

"In a community this small?" That didn't make much sense. "That doesn't feel right."

"It doesn't," he agreed. "But I have to chase the possibility. For all we know, Alastair took a reverse mortgage on the house because he knew he was going to pull this and ran."

"But ... why? If he has money he shouldn't be in such dire straits. If he doesn't, what happened to the money he had?"

"That right there is a very good question." Galen tapped his finger against the end of my nose. "You're a little a genius sometimes. I'm not sure what's going on with Alastair, but I'm definitely going to find out. I have to focus on Salma first."

"Unless she's part of this."

He stilled, surprised. "What do you mean? Why would she be part of this?"

"It's awfully coincidental that she died on the beach where the party she'd been touting for a month — but refused to go to because she didn't like sand — was being held. I don't think that's an accident."

AMANDA M. LEE

"Are you thinking that Alastair killed her because she figured out what he was doing?"

"I don't know, but that's definitely a possibility. I mean ... everything I've learned about Salma seems to indicate she's the sort of person who wouldn't blink at blackmailing someone. That's simply who she was."

"She liked the popularity that came with the job. I don't think it was the money fueling her as much as the fame."

"I think you're probably right, but that doesn't mean she didn't get greedy. Perhaps she demanded something else of Alastair, like a prime spot in the festival lineup or something. He never had any plans to put together a proper lineup, so he couldn't give her what she wanted and she threatened to out him."

"Or perhaps she figured out the entire thing was a sham from the start," Galen countered. "Salma was annoying, but she wasn't an idiot. She was smarter than most people gave her credit for, which is why she rose faster than those other three idiots in the influencer circles."

"So ... what are you thinking?" I asked. "Do you think she figured out the truth and tried to extort Alastair, causing him to snap?"

"I think there are multiple possibilities." He started ticking them off on his fingers. "One, she found out the truth and threatened to expose him to the cops. He wasn't ready to run yet — he needed time to plot his escape on the boat — so he killed her to shut her up. Two, she found out and extorted money from him, which put him under so much pressure he snapped. Her death was violent and seems to suggest a frenzy. It doesn't strike me as something that was well thought out."

"That's true." I rolled my neck. "Any other possibilities?"

"Just one more. The third possibility is that he didn't kill her. Maybe he's not on the run. Maybe he hired someone to handle this festival, someone who got in over his or her head and couldn't deliver what was promised, and that individual, when confronted, lost it and killed Alastair."

"If so, where is his body?"

"It could be hidden anywhere. There are a lot of wooded areas on the island. If animals find the body there won't be much left within a few days. There's also the ocean. If our killer has access to a boat maybe he was dumped at sea. The sharks and fish would take care of it out there."

I shuddered at the thought. "How does that explain what happened to Salma?"

"Maybe she saw the killer putting Alastair's body on a boat. Maybe she saw the murder. Maybe she ran and the killer caught up with her on the beach."

"But why not dump her body in the same place?"

"Perhaps that was the original plan. Maybe the killer left to get something to wrap the body in and upon returning found us. The only one who knew we were coming back was Alastair. Once we arrived there was nothing that could be done about the body."

I hated to admit it, but it was possible. "That's a lot to think about."

"It is," he agreed. "We have a lot of possibilities and absolutely zero answers."

"And Alastair."

"If he's still alive I will find him. Today I need to focus on Calliope. It wouldn't be as easy for her to sneak on or off the island without anyone seeing. I need to find her first because she's either a victim in all of this or another predator."

"So ... showers and then breakfast before planning our day? We are partners, after all."

He smirked. "How about one shower, to conserve water, and then I'll cook breakfast?"

"I could live with that."

"I was hoping you would say that."

GALEN OPTED FOR FRENCH TOAST. It was one of his favorite breakfasts and I wasn't surprised when the scent assailed my nose as I hit the main floor. I smiled to myself as I headed toward the kitchen, the sound of someone knocking on the front door catching my attention before I could make much progress.

My grandfather met me with expectant eyes when I opened the door. He was up early — especially since it took him a good twenty minutes to get into town — and he didn't look happy.

"Did you look through the peephole before you answered the door?" His tone was accusatory.

"Yes," I lied.

"You did not." He rolled his eyes. "I was watching your shadow under the door. You just walked right up and let me inside. It was reckless."

"If you knew I didn't look why did you ask?"

"I wanted to know what you would say. It turns out, you didn't say anything smart."

"Oh, geez." I turned on my heel and headed for the kitchen. "It's awfully early for a lecture," I called out. "How about we table that and I'll pour you a mug of coffee?"

"I've had worse offers," he said. I didn't miss the distinct sound of him double-checking the front door to make sure it was locked. Apparently it was going to be one of those days.

"Hey, Wesley," Galen called out in greeting from behind the stove. "I'm making French toast. Do you want some?"

Wesley didn't immediately answer. Instead, he tattled on me. "She didn't look through the peephole before answering the door. Are you going to do something about it?"

"I'll spank her later," Galen shot back. "I'll spank her until her little bottom is black and blue and then I'll make her dress like a maid and clean the lighthouse."

Wesley worked his jaw. "You're an extra-special pervert, aren't you?"

Galen chuckled and finally shifted his eyes to my grandfather. "She'll do what she's going to do. I can't order her around. She knows to check the peephole. If she doesn't follow through it's on her."

I was under attack from all sides. "I forgot," I complained. "I was up early this morning and I'm still waking up."

"We slept for ten hours," Galen reminded me. "We were in bed by nine."

"Because you're a pervert," Wesley challenged, his eyes dark. "I always knew you had an overactive libido."

"Hey, don't blame this on me." Galen waved his spatula. "It's not my fault she made the water dance. She knows it drives me crazy."

"Is that a euphemism for something?"

The conversation was starting to make me excessively uncomfortable. "No, it's not. I think we should table this discussion. You're here early, Wesley, so I'm assuming that means you need something."

"I definitely need something," Wesley agreed. "I needed to know that you were all right. I heard someone died on the beach the other day — a young woman with dark hair — and I wanted to make sure it wasn't you."

I frowned. "You could've called."

"If it was her I would've called you," Galen pointed out. "I wouldn't have just left you twisting in the wind."

"If it was her I expect you wouldn't be able to remember how to operate a phone," Wesley countered. "I was just making sure because nobody bothered to call me and say she was okay."

Ugh. This family stuff was getting complicated. "I apologize. I didn't really think about it, especially since the story made the news."

"I didn't see that," he countered. "I just heard from one of my workers that a young woman was dead and Hadley's cart was seen on the beach that night. I was worried."

"Oh." Realization dawned. "I'm sorry." I really was. "The cart was out there because Galen and I took it to dinner. We stopped at the beach on the way back to make sure things were progressing for the festival. We found the body."

"Well, that explains that." Wesley climbed onto one of the counter stools and inclined his head toward the coffee pot. I automatically headed in that direction to pour him a mug. "May said you were fine, but I'm mad at her so I didn't believe her."

"Why are you mad at her?" Galen asked.

"She made an absolutely ridiculous suggestion," Wesley replied. "I've never heard anything so stupid in my entire life."

I swallowed hard. "Um ... that suggestion didn't have anything to do with June, did it?"

Wesley's eyes narrowed to dangerous slits. "How do you know that?"

"The suggestion might've come from me." I felt put on the spot. "I didn't think there was any harm in making the request. I just ... don't want you to be alone, and June mentioned that she'd always had a crush on you. I thought dinner and a movie might be good for both of you."

Wesley immediately started shaking his head. "Kid, I'm glad you're in my life and I'm enjoying getting to know you, but stay out of my personal life."

"But I'm worried about you."

"Don't. I'm capable of taking care of myself. And while June might be a nice woman, she's not my type."

"Who is your type?"

"Your grandmother, who I was angry with because I thought she was making the suggestion because she was tired of me. Turns out she made it because you're a pain in the butt. Now I have to apologize. I hate apologizing."

I wrinkled my nose and flicked my eyes to Galen, who looked to be thinking hard. About what, though? Normally he would find a situation like this funny. Apparently that was not true today. "Well, I'm sorry," I said finally. "The suggestion came from a place of love. I won't do it again."

"Fair enough." Wesley awkwardly patted my hand. "Don't get worked up about it. It's not the end of the world. What else is going on around here? Any other gossip to spread?"

"Just that the festival on the beach is a total disaster," I replied. "Alastair Herne is in the wind. He's either dead or took a bunch of money and fled. We're not sure which, but we're fairly certain his disappearance ties in with Salma's death. I think that's it."

"I think that's enough."

"Oh, and that singer is missing, too. Calliope. We can't find her even though her belongings are still in her hotel room."

"Maybe she's out at her cabin," he suggested.

"What cabin?"

Galen looked up from the stove. "Yeah. What cabin?"

"You're talking about the blond singer with the song about the thong, right?"

I was horrified. "How do you know about the thong song?"

"I know things ... and my men mentioned it. Apparently she wore a diamond thong in the video or something. They were all excited when she arrived on the island. They were even more excited when she bought the old Ingalls cabin out by the lake."

That meant absolutely nothing to me. Apparently it was of interest to Galen, though.

"I didn't know she bought that cabin," Galen said. "When?"

"She closed, like, two weeks ago. I've seen her out there a few times since. I think she's just been cleaning up and making some plans for renovations or something. I haven't seen her out there after dark or anything."

"Still." Galen's eyes were thoughtful when they locked with mine. "Do you want to go for a ride after breakfast?"

"Are we going on a pop star hunt?"

"Absolutely."

"Then I'm in."

"I figured as much." He started doling out slices of French toast onto plates. "Are we all good here? Everybody has made up and is happy, right?"

"Nobody was fighting," Wesley countered. "I just feel I'm old enough to figure out my own romantic entanglements."

"On that we can agree. Okay, breakfast is ready. Everybody dig in. It's going to be another long day."

THIRTEEN

J brooded over Wesley's gentle slapdown as Galen drove to the cabin. He seemed to know where he was headed.

"You need to let it go," Galen advised, his eyes on the road. He obviously wasn't a big fan of my pouting. "Wesley is an adult. He's allowed to make decisions for himself."

"Did I say he wasn't?" I challenged. "It's just ... I don't want him to be lonely. I just found him and I read this article about people who lose long-term partners. Sometimes they lose the will to live in the process. I don't want that to happen to him."

"I get that. The thing is, he didn't really lose May. They're still hanging out together."

"But how fulfilling can that possibly be? They can't touch ... or hold one another ... or hang out in public. I don't want Wesley to become some hermit who never leaves his house because the ghost of his dead wife is there."

Galen snorted. "I bet that's a sentence you never thought you'd say."

"You have no idea. I'm being serious."

"I know you are. I think it's kind of cute."

"I'm not trying to be cute."

"For some, it's effortless." He winked at me, but when I continued to scowl he heaved out a sigh. "Listen, I get that you're worried about him. You don't know him all that well. Your bond is growing, which is great, but you still don't know all the Wesley stories. He was never that social, even when May was alive."

"I still don't like it." I stubbornly folded my arms over my chest and stared out the window, watching as the foliage blurred. "I don't think it's unreasonable to want my grandfather to be happy. I mean ... if something happens to me, I don't want you to spend the rest of your life hanging out with my ghost."

He didn't immediately respond, and when I looked to him I found him watching me with unreadable eyes. "What?"

"I don't like you making jokes about dying," he said finally, turning to watch the road. "I don't happen to find it funny."

"It wasn't a joke. It's not as if I plan on being reckless or anything. I don't want to die. But if the unthinkable happens I want you to be happy."

"And what if I say there is no happiness without you?"

"I would say that's sweet but impractical. I don't want you to be alone."

He worked his jaw, a muscle ticking. "Listen, I don't like this conversation. Nothing is going to happen to you. I won't let it. We should just drop it."

That wasn't in my nature. "Are you saying that you would want me to pine over you for the rest of my life if something terrible happened and I lost you?" Even as I said the words my heart filled with a sick sense of dread. I didn't want to even think of a scenario in which he wouldn't be a part of my life. That's how much I'd come to rely on him.

"I would definitely want you to pine," he said without hesitation. "I would want you to become a shell of a person, someone who locks herself in the lighthouse and shuts out the rest of the world while eating ice cream from a cardboard container and not washing your hair for two weeks straight."

I rolled my eyes. "You talk big, but that's not what you would want."

"It is. I would also want you to shoot Booker when he inevitably comes sniffing around after what he deems a proper time of mourning ... because I guarantee that would happen. Wait, shooting him is too kind. You should curse him so his penis falls off, maybe as a memorial to me so I know you'll always love me."

I didn't want to encourage him, but I couldn't stop from laughing. "I see you've given this some thought."

"Actually, it just came to me. I guess I'm gifted when it comes to thinking of retribution for Booker."

"I guess so." I groaned as I went back to staring out the window, my lips curving when I felt Galen's hand creep over the console so he could link his fingers with mine. "Would you come back as a ghost to be with me?"

"Yes."

"Is that because you would want to spend time with me or torture Booker?"

"I can multi-task."

I squeezed his hand. This talk of death was starting to depress me. It was time to change the subject. "Do you think we'll find Calliope at this cabin?"

"I don't know." He turned serious. "I didn't even realize she'd purchased the cabin. It doesn't strike me as the sort of place a star would want to live in."

"Why?"

"I wouldn't say it's run down, but it's not a fancy space with a lot of amenities. The electrical system is old and needs a total upgrade. On top of that, it's surrounded by woods. The nearest store is in town. It's not convenient for someone like her."

"That sounds a little judgmental. I think you're just prejudiced against diamond thongs."

"I have no problem with diamond thongs. In fact, if you want to parade around in one twenty-four hours a day that would be the greatest thing ever."

"I think that would chafe."

"That's your problem. I'm just suspicious about Calliope's motivations for buying this place. Even if she really did want to purchase a vacation home here — which seems unlikely given the fact that she doesn't know anyone on the island other than Alastair — why would she want to live out in the middle of nowhere? Wouldn't it make sense to purchase one of those timeshare rentals at one of the hotels?"

"Maybe she likes privacy. Maybe the woods make her want to write music. Maybe she's deeper than we thought."

"Yes. The diamond thong song clearly speaks to depth."

I pressed my lips together to keep from laughing. "We don't know anything about her. Besides, I'm not entirely convinced we're going to find a vain and shallow woman hanging around in the woods."

"No?" He arched an eyebrow. "What do you think we'll find?"

"Maybe a dead woman. I mean ... if Alastair really is covering his tracks before running Calliope might be someone who needs to be silenced."

Galen's mouth flattened into a grimace. "I'm a little worried about that myself. When we get there, I want you to stay in the truck until I make sure things are safe. Are we clear?"

"Yeah." I agreed even though I had no intention of staying behind. If he was going in hot, so was I. He simply didn't need to know that until it was too late for him to do anything about it.

IT TOOK US TWENTY MINUTES TO get to the cabin. It was off the main highway, buried deep on a winding dirt road. When we pulled to a stop in front we found the area quiet.

"It looks empty," I said as I unfastened my seatbelt.

"Yeah." Galen tilted his head and stared into the trees behind the cabin. "Stay here. Keep the doors locked." He pressed the keys into my hand. "If something happens, head straight to Wesley's place. It's only five miles from here."

I stared at the keys for an extended beat, my face blank. "Are you saying you want me to abandon you if something attacks?"

"That's exactly what I'm saying."

"Well, that won't happen." I slapped the keys back in his hand and reached for the door handle. "If there's something out there we'll fight it together. That's what being partners means."

His eyes flashed with annoyance. "You said that you would wait here until I cleared the scene."

"No, I agreed we were clear when you were issuing orders. I didn't agree to follow orders."

"Listen here ... ." He lifted a finger, probably to start shaking it, but his attention was diverted to the opening front door. There, her hair disheveled and her top hanging off a bare shoulder, stood Calliope.

She looked a little worse for wear.

"Well, at least she's not dead," I offered, smiling brightly.

"You're a pain," Galen muttered as he pushed open his door and hopped out. He was in official mode now, which meant the argument would have to wait until we were alone. I was fine with that. I was becoming a master of distracting him when he wanted to bicker. Sometimes I believed he knew what I was doing and simply didn't care. "Hello, Calliope," he called out, his eyes returning to scan the foliage. Eventually content that we were alone, he took a step in her direction. "I'm Sheriff Galen Blackwood. We met the other night. Do you remember?"

"Um ... ." Calliope looked genuinely confused. Her makeup was smeared under her eyes, which were puffy and red-rimmed, and she clearly wasn't wearing a bra because her assets were on display as she bent over to rub her hands on her knees, giving Galen a clear view of everything she had to offer.

"She's a total slut," I hissed as I moved to his side. "Like ... a complete and total slut."

This time the look he shot me was full of amusement. He shuttered it quickly. "We have some things to talk about, Calliope." He was firm. "We need you to get it together."

"Do you have coffee in there?" I asked.

"Coffee?" Calliope furrowed her brow. "Oh, yeah. I have coffee. I was just about to make some."

I flashed a smile that I didn't really feel and started toward the cabin. "How about I make that coffee? You should run into the bathroom and splash some cold water on your face." And put on a bra, I silently added. "You're going to need to be more coherent for this conversation."

"Okay," she replied dumbly, her eyes on me. "Have we met?"

"You met me the same night you met Sheriff Blackwood."

"I don't remember you."

"Do you remember him?"

"Yeah." She bobbed her head. "He's hard to forget."

Yup. I should've seen that coming.

CALLIOPE TOOK MUCH LONGER THAN should've been necessary in the bathroom. Galen and I had started arguing about which of us was going to check on her.

"It has to be you." He was adamant. "You have the same parts as her so you're used to seeing them."

That was the most ludicrous argument I'd ever heard. "You've seen my parts and you seem comfortable enough with them."

"Yes, but those are your parts. I don't want to see her parts."

That was both a comfort and annoying. "Fine." I made a face as I moved to stand from the table. "If she's dead in there I'll never forgive you."

"Fair enough. I ... ."

The door opened and Calliope strolled out. She'd washed her face, changed her clothes and applied a whole new mask of makeup. I was dumbfounded.

"It took you long enough," Galen complained, his eyes flashing. "We're here on official business. We have a schedule to keep to, and you've thrown that into disarray."

Calliope didn't look bothered by the assessment. "I apologize. I'm a night owl. I was up late last night and I just needed to freshen up." The look she shot Galen was sultry ... and despite the work she'd done on her face to erase the dregs of a long night she still wasn't wearing a bra. "You're the sheriff? That sounds like an interesting job. I've been considering writing a song about law enforcement. Perhaps we should put our heads together. You would make a fabulous star for the video."

"Yeah, I'm good." Galen inclined his chin toward the chair across from him. "Please sit down. We have some things to discuss."

"So serious." Calliope blew him an air kiss, which caused me to grit my teeth, and then sat. She was putting on a good show, but the momentary flash of pain that invaded her eyes told me she was feeling nothing but discomfort this morning. "Hangover?" I queried.

"I'm pure of body and soul," she countered. "I don't drink."

I ran my tongue over my teeth as I glanced at the counter, where three empty wine bottles rested. She noticed and frowned.

"Wine isn't liquor. It's natural ... and it's good for you."

"If you say so."

Galen cleared his throat to get her attention. "I don't really care how much you had to drink last night. As long as you weren't out driving, it doesn't matter to me. We're here on a different matter. I need to know when you last talked to Alastair."

Calliope's eyebrows drew together. "Why do you want to know about Alastair? If you have questions for him, you should ask him."

"I would like to but he's disappeared," Galen replied. "We're not sure where he is, whether he left voluntarily or was killed by the same individual who took out Salma. All we know is that he's left a mess with that festival, and it's officially become your responsibility to clean it up."

Calliope's mouth dropped open. "You can't be serious."

"Oh, I'm serious." Galen refused to back down. "You're listed as a co-organizer on all the documents. That means what's happening on that beach — and, trust me, it's not good — is now yours to deal with."

"But ... ." She looked like a guppy trying to gulp air when she turned to me. "This isn't my fault. I had no idea this was going to happen. You can't expect me to fix this. I don't even know where to start."

"You should've thought about that before you went into business with Alastair," Galen snapped. "We need to know where he is. When was the last time you talked to him?"

"I ... don't know. It wasn't yesterday. I didn't see him yesterday." She screwed up her face in concentration. "It was the night before, on the beach."

"When I saw you."

"Right." Her smile was back. "That moment is seared into my memory."

"Oh, knock it off," I groused. "Nobody is buying your act, and he's already taken. Besides, he doesn't like the diamond thong song."

Calliope's gaze was withering. "I don't believe I was talking to you."

"And yet she's not wrong," Galen supplied. "I am taken ... by her. Now cut the crap. This is a serious situation. Salma Hershey is dead. None of the things promised to the festival guests have been delivered and they're threatening to riot. Alastair is gone and you're left holding the bag."

She blinked several times, making me think she was trying to work up some tears, and then she took me by surprise when she broke into a hissy fit.

"I just knew this was a terrible idea," she complained, smacking her hands against the table and lifting her eyes to the ceiling. "I don't know why I let him talk me into this. I knew it would backfire. He said it would be easy money. It turns out he was right. Of course, it was easy money ... for him."

"I need more information than that," Galen responded calmly. "How about you start from the beginning?"

"I don't know what you want me to say." Calliope was bordering on belligerent. "I got sucked into this thing when he contacted my management company. He heard I was looking for entertainment investments to expand my repertoire and thought I might be interested. I was ... at first ... but then I started to realize that some of the things he was offering weren't possible.

"I questioned him on it and he told me to shut my mouth," she continued. "He swore up and down that everything would be fine and that we were going to make quadruple our money. He seemed to know what he was talking about, so I let him handle things.

"Then, the night before last, Salma approached him on the beach. She was angry. Said that she knew he was scamming everyone and that she was going to go to the newspapers and entertainment shows. I was worried, but Alastair said it would be fine. Then he sent me to the bar with a pat on the head. It was condescending, but it was better than dealing with things myself. He wanted to be in charge and I let him be in charge."

Galen shifted his eyes to me and I could see fury lurking there. "Well, that's just ... lovely. I guess we know that none of this happened by accident. Did he kill Salma?"

"How should I know?" Calliope held her hands out and shrugged. "I told you he sent me to the bar. I was happy to go. They were still arguing when I left."

"And you didn't think to call me when news spread that Salma was dead?"

"Not really. Why would I call you?"

"Because Alastair is a suspect in her death, you ninny," I snapped. "She was murdered. It's not as if she fell and hit her head."

"I had nothing to do with that." She suddenly found something on her fingernails to study. "Is that all? I'm really feeling the need for a nap."

"That's pretty far from all," Galen growled. "You need to get it together, because you're coming into town with us. Somebody needs to placate that crowd and it's going to be you."

She made a series of protesting sounds. "But ... I don't know what to do."

"I guess you'll have to figure it out."

"Why can't you do it?"

"I have to find Alastair."

"When you do, tell him I still want my cut of the money. If he tries to bolt with it I'll send people after him. I don't know who, but I'll find people ... and send them after him."

As far as threats went, it wasn't very creative. Still, she kind of made me laugh ... when I wasn't envisioning throttling her. "We should head back now so we can start the search. The longer we go without finding him, the easier it will be for him to hide. We need to track him down now."

"Agreed." Galen got to his feet. "I want you with me. You might be able to help."

"That's what I'm here for."

"That and so many other things." He rested his hand on my shoulder and glared at Calliope. "Get dressed in something you can wear in public. You have a long day in front of you."

"You should probably pick something that requires a bra," I added.

Calliope stomped, whined and cried, but to no avail. Galen was firm. She was heading to the beach, and we were starting an official search.

FOURTEEN

$\mathcal{C}$alliope tried to take the front seat for the ride back to town, but Galen ordered her in the back and then told her to sit on my side of the truck so he wouldn't accidentally catch a glimpse of her pouting in the backseat. He then proceeded to give her instructions on what he expected from her as we drove.

Even though I had things to say, I was amused enough to sit back and let him run the show. He wasn't about to put up with Calliope's crap.

"You don't have to yell at me," the pop singer groused as we pulled into the lot across from the beach. Galen had texted his men to meet us there. He didn't want to garner the attention of festival-goers, which is why he made sure to stay out of their line of sight.

"How are things going?" he asked Deputy Michael Briggs as he opened Calliope's door and instructed her to climb out.

"Nobody died during the night," Michael said dryly. "That's about the only thing I can say."

"Were things bad?"

"They weren't good. Most of the people behaved themselves, but there are some who need to be watched."

"Keep your eyes on them," Galen insisted. "Don't let this get out of hand. Aurora and a few of the sirens will be patrolling the water when they can manage for additional help. If you need more than that ... I'm not sure what I'll do, but I'll think of something."

"We're okay right now." Michael was calm, focused. "I think the overnight hours are what we need to worry about. People are less likely to act up during the day."

"Then I'll find more help for the overnight hours." Galen flicked his eyes to Calliope, who looked as if she wanted to be anywhere else but heading to the beach. "I've made her aware of her duties. In case she forgets and needs a reminder from you, though, she is to pitch in and calm the festival attendees. She's to make right what's gone so wrong. She's also to provide entertainment.

"If she tries to flee, restrain her — and do it publicly," he continued, causing Calliope to make dramatic protesting sounds as she shifted from one foot to the other. "Make sure someone takes photos to send to the newspapers and broadcast entertainment shows. We can sell the photos and make money to give back to the people who have been ripped off."

"You're mean," Calliope whined, adopting a voice I knew would grate on Galen. "I can't believe how mean you are ... and I can't believe I thought you were hot. Mean people are not hot."

"I'm fine with that." Galen was blasé. "I'm not joking with you. If you don't calm these people down I'll make your life a living hell."

"My life is already a living hell," she shot back. "Alastair ran off with my money. I don't have anything to give these people."

"Well, you'd better figure it out." Galen hopped back in the truck. "You won't like what happens if you don't fix this. You can whine, stomp your foot and bat your eyelashes all you want. It won't matter if you don't get it together."

"I don't know what to do," Calliope complained. "This wasn't supposed to be my responsibility."

"Figure it out."

"How?"

"I don't know. That's up to you. If you don't figure it out, you won't like the consequences." He turned to Michael. "I'm serious. Cuff her and lock her up if she tries to leave."

"Yes, sir." Michael almost looked amused at the prospect, but he held it together. "Where are you going?"

"We're heading to Alastair's house. I'm going to turn that place inside out until I find a clue as to where he's gone."

"Maybe you'll find my money while you're there," Calliope suggested, brightening.

Galen rolled his eyes. "Any money seized will not be going to you. It will be going to the people who were screwed, the ones out on the beach, the ones who are going to be trying to grab your throat when they see you."

Calliope swallowed hard. "You really are mean."

"I'm fine with that." Galen remained silent until we were on the highway and heading toward the north end of the island. He seemed focused on the road, but I could practically hear the gears in his mind working.

"You're not going to be mean to me, are you?" I asked after a beat. "I know that you're warming to your new persona, but I happen to like it when you're nice."

The smile he slid me was sly. "I'll be nice to you later."

"Okay. Just checking."

IT TOOK US TWENTY MINUTES TO reach Alastair's house. When we pulled into the driveway, I openly gaped. The house standing before us was a mega-mansion. My entire lighthouse could've fit into a corner of the yard and still not hurt the view of the tennis courts, pool or putting green.

"I guess this is what it's like to have money," I said as I climbed out of the truck. "Wow."

Galen slid his eyes to me. "I prefer the lighthouse. It has personality. This place is ... too much."

"Yeah, but ... it's like something out of a movie."

"And I still prefer the real deal," Galen said. "This isn't real. It's a facade."

He was serious enough that I had to pull my gaze away from the grounds and focus on him. "What are you worried about?"

"There are so many things to worry about that I don't even know where to start. The big one is obviously those people on the beach. We don't have the means to get them off this island before their scheduled departures. Even if we could, most have already made their travel arrangements. We can't mess with them."

"It's going to be okay." It was obvious that he needed reassurance. I wanted to give it to him ... if I could swing it. I wasn't certain that was in my wheelhouse, but I was going to give it a try. "We'll figure this out. The people on the beach are inconvenienced. Nobody has gotten hurt. We can keep it that way."

"Salma was hurt."

I stilled. "She was." I studied his strong profile as he looked over Alastair's island paradise. "You can't blame yourself for that. What happened was ... terrible, but you couldn't have stopped it."

"No?" He didn't look convinced. "What would've happened if I'd stayed on the beach that night? What if I'd overseen everything? Then Salma would still be alive and Alastair wouldn't have had the opportunity to run."

"Except that's not what happened. You can't go back in time and change things. I get that you're upset. That's who you are. Guilt is a useless emotion, though. It will eat you alive if you allow it. Please ... don't allow it. It won't do you or me any good."

He heaved out a sigh and dragged his hand through his hair. "I know you're right." He leaned over and gave me a kiss. "I love you. What we have isn't a facade, like this place. I much prefer what we have, and that's never going to change."

He seemed ridiculously serious. "Okay." I stroked my finger down his cheek. "I prefer what we have, too. That doesn't mean I'm not going to enjoy going through the rich guy's house. Do you think he has golden toilets? I heard that there was some rapper who was famous back in the day who had golden toilets."

Galen's eyebrows drew together. "What would you do with a golden toilet?"

"The same thing you do with a regular toilet."

"That seems a waste."

"Opulence is always a waste. That doesn't mean it's not fun to look at."

THE FRONT DOOR WAS LOCKED, BUT that didn't deter Galen. He had a lock pick in his pocket and immediately set to work to open the door.

"Is that legal?" I asked as I watched him work. "I mean ... aren't you supposed to have a warrant before entering a home? If television has taught me anything, it's that."

His lips curved but his focus remained on the lock. "Moonstone Bay doesn't operate under the same rules as the mainland."

"How is that possible? Certain rules are fixed no matter where you live, as long as it's in the United States."

"I think that's true of most places but, remember, Moonstone Bay isn't a state. It's a territory. We have travel treaties in place with the United States. This is technically American soil. We're not bound by the same rules, though. That was established hundreds of years ago because the island forefathers didn't want conquerors coming in and trying to boss us around.

"We agreed to be part of the United States, but we also held onto our own rules and autonomy," he continued. "I work under the auspices of the DDA and can basically do whatever I want. Of course, the opposite is also true. The DDA can boss me around and force me to do things I don't like if they decide it needs to be done."

The more I heard about this DDA, the more I didn't like them. "They sound like little despots," I complained. "Why don't you guys overthrow them?"

Amusement lit his features as the lock clicked and he pushed open the door. "I don't think it's quite as dire as that. Besides, they're not going to simply sit back and cede their power base. They could do a lot of damage, kill a lot of people, on their way down. You have to remember, these are some of the most powerful entities on the island. We can't simply walk in, tell them their reign is over and expect them to leave quietly."

That only made me feel worse. "I think they're freaks."

"They have issues," he agreed, putting his hand to the small of my back and prodding me inside. "Now, let's invade Alastair's privacy and find out where he went."

"Okay, but I'm totally drooling over whatever cool decorations he has in here. You've been warned."

Galen chuckled as he closed the door behind us. "If you see anything you like, make note of it. All this stuff will be seized to sell at auction given what's happened. You might get a good deal on something."

"Oh, good idea. I ... ." Something immediately caught my eye and my mouth dropped open as I swiveled. In the center of the foyer — which was the size of a train station — stood a fountain. It was ornate, garish and kind of cool. The best part about it was the figure in the center of the action. It was a huge fish. Er, well, slightly better than a fish. "Is that what I think it is?" I was transfixed.

Galen snorted as he moved behind me. He didn't seem as impressed by the fountain. "If you mean a half-man, half-shark, then yes. That's what you think it is."

"It's a shark shifter." I was desperate to see a shark shifter. Once I found out they were real I could focus on little else. Galen claimed they were rare, but I knew I would see one ... some day. "He has a fountain of a shark shifter. It's just ... so weird. How much do you think this will go for at auction?"

"More than you have," he replied. He was already heading out of the room. "You don't want that anyway. It's ostentatious and you don't have room. Where would you put it?"

"The back patio, where any passing shark shifter could see it and want to come and pray." On a sigh, I moved away from the fountain and followed him. "One day I'm going to have enough money to buy something that impractical. Just you wait."

"Money isn't everything." Galen was flipping through a stack of documents on a table in what could laughingly be described as a living room ... if living rooms were the size of small libraries. "There are more important things in life than money."

"I know." That was true. I wasn't obsessed with money. I didn't like the idea of being poor, either. I wanted a happy balance. "I would never pretend that money was the be-all and end-all of everything. That said, I would like a fountain with a shark shifter in it. I can't say why, and know it's not possible. I still want it. It's ... neat."

Galen sighed and shook his head. "I don't mean to take away your joy. I really don't. It's just ... this island has always been ruled by money. As far back as when pirates used it as a way to avoid the authorities. Money always talks here, and I don't particularly like it."

From his perspective, I could see how that would be bothersome. "I'm sorry. I shouldn't get all worked up over material possessions. It's just ... it's a freaking shark shifter."

He smirked. "It's cool. We need to focus on important stuff now. That means finding anything that could lead us to Alastair ... dead or alive."

"Where do you want to start?"

"He has to have an office in this place. I say we start there."

FINDING THE OFFICE WASN'T DIFFICULT once we adjusted to the size of the house. There was a method to the madness of how it was laid out, but the method wasn't exactly linear.

"I found something," I announced, holding up a stack of papers I'd discovered in the trash bin under Alastair's desk. We'd been searching the office for a good hour and I'd only just found the trash bin because it was secured so far under the ornate mahogany desk that I had to get on my knees to look.

"What did you find?" Galen sat on the floor several feet away, his eyes keen as he went through file after file. "Do you know where he is?"

"No, but there's a bunch of correspondence here."

"Correspondence?" He furrowed his brow. "I don't know what that means."

"They're emails that he printed out, exchanges between him and several witches. It was the witches who requested the festival. The correspondence started almost two years ago."

Galen abandoned what he was looking at and crawled over to join me. His hand automatically went to my back to start rubbing as he read over my shoulder. "Is there any mention of why they wanted the festival here?"

"Just that they consider this place a nexus of power. I can see that. All the paranormal creatures that live here definitely make it feel magical. That's on top of the fact that you have a cemetery where the dead rise and walk around every night. There's nothing about this place that is 'normal.'"

"I've always thought normal was highly overrated."

"And I always thought I was normal until I came here," I mused, thoughtful. "I was a pretty boring individual before I got that letter from May's attorney. Then I came here and suddenly I was interesting."

Galen's gaze was keen. "I think you were always interesting and you didn't allow yourself to believe it."

"No, I was pretty boring."

"I don't believe that." He pressed his lips to my cheek. "It doesn't matter. You're the most interesting person I know now. Do you recognize any of the witches in this correspondence?"

"Just one." I handed over a sheet of paper. "I think maybe we should talk to her first."

"Bronwen," Galen read from the paper. "That's ... interesting."

"I don't know that I would use that word, but I think it's definitely worth checking out. Also, I found this." I shook a different piece of paper. "This is an email exchange between Alastair and his accountant. Two weeks ago, he asked that all the money from the festival escrow account be moved to his personal account.

"The accountant argues that's not a good idea, that he could get in trouble over it if he's not careful, but Alastair refuses to back down and demands the transfer," I continued. "I don't know about you, but to me, that seems to indicate that he always planned to run with the money. He was never going to try to create an event that people wanted to attend. He lied, did the absolute bare minimum so people would believe he was working on it, and then fled with the money."

Galen plucked the sheet of paper from my hand, his scowl growing more pronounced with each word he read. "Well ... that slimy bastard."

"We're going with twiddle pants."

He ignored me. "He definitely had this planned. The question is: Was it a scam right from the start or did he realize at a certain point he couldn't deliver what he'd promised and came up with the idea then?"

"Does it matter?"

"It might. For our purposes now, it doesn't matter. He's gone. I think we have to assume that he fled of his own volition. No one took him. He was covering his tracks and he's in the wind."

"So ... how do we find him?"

"First we have to ascertain how he got off this island. That means contacting the cruise line to find out if he got on the ship that left the night we found Salma's body. Another ship arrived and left the day after, when I thought he was just dodging my calls. In addition to that, I think we need to talk to Bronwen. I want to know why she pitched this festival to him."

"It wasn't just her. Others were involved. She was just one of several."

"We'll start with her because she's the one we know."

I wanted to clap I was so excited. "Can I go with you to question her? I promise not to be too much of a badass during the interrogation."

He shook his head and sighed. "We're not at interrogation level yet. This will just be standard questions."

"Can I go with you?"

He nodded. "Yeah, but I want you to let me handle the questions.

You get a little too enthusiastic sometimes when it comes to pinning people on details."

He wasn't wrong. "I'm just happy to be part of the team."

"You're the most important member of my team."

"Oh, so sweet." I smacked a loud kiss against his lips. "We need to go out the same way we came in. I want to see the shark shifter fountain one more time."

"Ugh. I knew you were going to say that. The thing is tacky."

"It's awesome."

"I guess we'll have to agree to disagree."

"Sometimes I think that might be the story of our lives."

FIFTEEN

*J*une was on the patio when we arrived, drinking her morning tea and reading the newspaper. She smiled and waved when she saw us, seemingly not a care in the world, and insisted we join her for breakfast.

"I'm having doughnuts delivered," she volunteered when Galen started shaking his head. "They're from the bakery ... and they'll still be warm."

He groaned. "You know exactly how to get to me, don't you?" He pulled out a chair so I could sit before settling between June and me. "I guess one doughnut couldn't hurt."

"I'm having two," I announced, causing his eyebrows to wing up. "Hey, all that breaking and entering made me hungry."

"You broke into someone's house?" June leaned forward, intrigued.

"Alastair Herne's place," Galen replied, leaning back in his chair. "He's missing."

"Missing?" June didn't look surprised. "Maybe he fell into the volcano. If anyone deserves to roast to death in the fiery pits of hell, it's Alastair. Of course, we probably won't get that lucky."

Wait ... . "There's a volcano?"

June nodded. "That mountain you see in the distance. What did you think it was?"

"I just thought it was a mountain." My stomach twisted with mild unease. "How often does it erupt?"

"It hasn't erupted in more than two-hundred years," Galen reassured me. "It's dormant. Don't get worked up about it."

That was easy for him to say. I'd seen enough movies to know that volcanoes could be unpredictable. "But ... can a volcano really be dormant?"

"The witches on the island keep it in check," June replied, grinning. "Perhaps you'll be part of that team when you get a better handle on your powers. For now, you don't have to worry. You really are safe."

Well, that at least was something. "I guess."

The arrival of the doughnut delivery derailed the conversation for the next five minutes. After that, all I could hear were a variety of yummy noises as we enjoyed our fresh doughnuts. I didn't speak again until I'd inhaled one and was about to start on my second.

"How are your witches doing?"

"My witches?" June shrugged. "I don't know that I would call them my witches, but they seem fine. I barely see three of them. They've been down at the festival during the day. Bronwen is in and out, but she's pretty self-sufficient. I warned them when they called for accommodations that the hotel would be under construction and they would be on their own for food. They seemed fine with that ... and I couldn't exactly turn down the money they offered."

"Have they said anything about the festival?" Galen asked. He had powdered sugar around the edges of his mouth, which only served to make him even more adorable.

"They've said it's not what it was billed to be. Why?" June's eyebrows drew together. "Is that why you're looking for Alastair? Has he done something?"

"All manner of things," Galen replied, his eyes briefly traveling to me as I licked my fingers. "Is it any wonder I fell head over heels for you? That is so ... classy."

I shot him a dirty look. "There aren't any napkins."

He grabbed a stack from the other side of the doughnut box. I hadn't seen them resting there, but wasn't bothered by his continued stare.

"Oh. Thanks." I licked one more finger, the middle one, for his benefit and then grabbed two napkins. "Tell her about Alastair and stop staring at me. It's making me uncomfortable."

He chuckled in response. "Yes, dear." When he turned back to June, he was all business. "There are some things going on you should probably be made aware of. In fact ... if it was an emergency, how many people could we get into your hotel?"

June looked taken aback by the question. "The hotel is a mess, Galen. It's not open for business."

"I know that. Things are going to start deteriorating on that beach very quickly. If we can get some of those people into rooms, even if the restaurant isn't open, that might defuse some of the problem."

"I don't have a full staff," June reminded him. "They're off on paid vacation while the hotel is under renovation. I can't call them back. That's not fair."

"Why do you need the staff?" He sounded frustrated. "They can clean up their own rooms. Most of them won't be able to pay anyway."

"Hold up." June held up her hand, annoyance flashing in the depths of her eyes. "Are you saying you want me to open my hotel and not get any money out of the deal?"

"Well, when you put it like that ... ." He shifted on his chair. "We're in a real pickle here, June. Alastair lied about what he could deliver and the people on that beach paid thousands of dollars to be here. We can't get them off that beach because there's nowhere to put them, and the transport doesn't return for days.

"I tried calling the cruise line company yesterday to ask if they could get a ship back here before the next scheduled arrival and they pretty much laughed at me," he continued. "They said that's not how it works, they don't just have ships hanging around to be called like taxis."

"Well, you can hardly expect them to voluntarily take a loss," June argued. "That's what you're asking of me, too."

Galen didn't immediately respond, instead shifting his eyes to the ocean. I decided now was the time for me to swoop in ... even though it would probably anger him.

"Galen's under the gun," I explained, refusing to meet the murderous gaze he swung in my direction. "The DDA is going to blame him if something bad happens ... and we're already dealing with Salma's death. We have reason to believe that Alastair killed her, and now he's missing. He's the only one who can make things right financially with these people."

"I see." June worked her jaw as she stared at Galen. "What is the DDA threatening you with?"

"They haven't come right out and threatened me just yet," he said. "They're playing it coy. Morgan St. Pierre is salivating to come after me. He's still upset about what happened with the hotel, how his plans to take it over were thwarted when you found that treasure. Now there's no chance he'll ever get this place because you've paid everything off and are turning it into a premier destination."

"And you're afraid he might be looking for payback," June surmised. "You're definitely in a mess." She mustered a wan smile. "I'm fond of you, Galen. You know that. You've been one of my pets since you were a child. You and Booker are like my own children."

"But you can't help," Galen finished. "I get it. I shouldn't have asked."

"You didn't ask," June reminded him. "You insinuated, and you didn't tell me how serious the situation is. Of course I'll help you."

"You will?"

"Don't be ridiculous." Annoyance crested on a wave and cascaded over her features. "Look at all the things you've done for me over the years. Just recently you put yourself in the line of fire with the DDA to protect me. The only reason St. Pierre is even acting like this is because he's put out. He's an extremely poor loser.

"I'll help because it's you," she continued. "I would never turn my back on you, no matter what. I would think you'd know that by now."

Galen was sheepish. "I do. I just ... this is a mess. I don't even know what to do. We're spinning our wheels. I'm trying to confirm that

135

Alastair left the island on the ship the night before the festival started — or the one that arrived the next afternoon, although we were already looking for him by then. It's feasible that he somehow managed it. The cruise line keeps citing privacy issues, so I have the prosecutor chasing it.

"Salma is dead and from everything I've been able to uncover Alastair makes the most sense as her killer," he continued. "She apparently knew that he was lying and was trying to gouge him for money. He needed to buy time, so he killed her. It's possible that he planned to remove her body from the beach but ran out of time because he wasn't expecting Hadley and me to return so quickly."

"It sounds like you're dealing with a lot," June said. "I'm sorry. That's very ... weird. Alastair is a jerk — I would never say otherwise — and I'm pretty sure he doesn't have a conscience. That said, I also don't think he has the stomach to murder someone.

"According to the article in the newspaper, Salma was stabbed multiple times. Can you actually imagine Alastair risking getting dirty with someone else's blood? I just ... that seems unlikely. He's a total weenie when it comes to stuff like that."

"That's true." Galen rolled his neck until it cracked and absently reached for another doughnut. He was a stress eater. Unfortunately, he was under a lot of stress at the moment and there was very little any of us could do to fix that for him ... unless we could find Alastair. That was the key. "He's our best suspect right now. Who else would've killed her?"

"She was an unpleasant girl," June replied, her gaze drifting to the hotel doorway, where Bronwen had appeared. I'd sensed the witch an instant before the hotel proprietress looked in that direction. "Come join us. I have warm doughnuts."

Bronwen beamed at the invitation and headed in our direction. She looked happy, sunny even, and the look she graced me with was enough to make me squirm. "Ah. It's the intrepid witch with the hunky boyfriend. Are you back to try to invade my mind again?"

My cheeks burned as I stared down at my doughnut. "I already apologized for that."

"What am I missing?" June asked, glancing between faces. "Is there a problem?"

"No problem," Bronwen replied, snagging the open chair between June and me. "I'm just teasing your friend. There was an incident at the docks when I arrived that was ... mildly entertaining."

Bronwen launched into the tale, causing me to make a series of faces as she breezed through it. When she was finished, June was laughing so hard I thought she might cry and Galen looked decidedly amused. I wasn't happy with either reaction.

"First, I was just testing my powers," I argued. "I wasn't trying to be invasive. Secondly ... ." I trailed off. In truth, there was no secondly.

"I would think that entering someone's mind without invitation is invasive no matter how you look at it," Bronwen pointed out. "As I said, I'm not angry. I appreciated the sexy look at your boyfriend. He's a lovely specimen of the male form."

Now it was Galen's turn to squirm with embarrassment. "Oh, good grief. Do we have to talk about it?"

Bronwen ignored the whining. "You should be proud. You put a smile on her face. That's all that matters."

"Ugh." He slapped his hand to his forehead and snuck a glance at me. "I blame you for this."

Of course he did. That was his way. "You're the one who likes to play that particular game. But there's no need to dwell on it. I believe there are other things to dwell on ... like certain correspondence." I tilted my head in Bronwen's direction. "That's why we're here, right?"

He shot me a dirty look. "Smooth. That wasn't obnoxious at all." He shook his head and then forced a smile for Bronwen's benefit. "So ... there's this thing."

"So I ascertained." Bronwen didn't appear bothered by the shift in topic. "What 'thing' are we referring to?"

"Well, we're looking for Alastair Herne. He's disappeared and things aren't going well at the festival."

"I've noticed," Bronwen said dryly. "Let me guess: He took off with the festival money and is on the run."

"Yeah," Galen nodded. "That's exactly what happened, and it's a problem for multiple reasons, not the least of which is that he's a suspect in a murder. We went to his house this morning, sorted through his things and found some copies of emails that were sent between you and him."

"So?" Bronwen didn't look bothered by the revelation. "I didn't realize it was against the law to write back and forth with a festival organizer."

"I'm not saying it's against the law," Galen countered. "The thing is, you were the one pitching the festival to him. Hadley told me that you only came at the last minute, but these emails were from almost two years ago."

Bronwen picked at her doughnut for a moment, anger flashing, and then sighed. "I don't know what to tell you. I am the one who had the idea for the festival years ago. I contacted June first to see if she could help organize it, but she was buried at the time."

"You contacted June?" Galen shifted on his chair. "I don't understand. Why would you contact June? I was under the impression you'd just met."

"That's not true. I've been to the hotel before and interacted with June at various times. I've always been a fan of Moonstone Bay. I've considered moving here. June and I became close friends because of my visits. She's kept up on my career. She's a witch herself and always interested in the craft."

I glanced at June and found her smiling. "I didn't know you were a witch," I said. "I kind of wish I had. You might've been helpful."

"I'm not a strong witch," she said hurriedly. "I'm not even a mediocre witch. I'm basically a kitchen witch who can't cook, which means I'm virtually useless."

"Don't say that," Bronwen snapped. "You have a strong witch heart and mind. Those are the most important things."

"I've always been interested in magic even though I don't have any," June explained. "Bronwen explains things to me and we talk regularly. I consider her a good friend."

At the word "friend," Bronwen and June exchanged looks that were almost mischievous in nature, as if they were hiding something. I was intrigued enough to consider trying to look in Bronwen's head again. I would never dig in June's mind because that would be rude. I didn't care about Bronwen enough to worry about it, though. Was it a risk? Yes. She hadn't known I was there the first time until I got distracted and showed her the image of Galen. I would be more careful this go-around.

"I'm interested in why you pitched the festival and then only confirmed at the last minute," Galen prodded. "If the festival was your idea, why weren't you involved from the start?"

"That's simple. I contacted Alastair — and a number of other people, I should point out — about acting as backers for the festival. I envisioned it as something smaller, something that would bring witches from across the world together for a magical ritual and coven of togetherness. Alastair wasn't interested. He wanted to monetize it from the start.

"I understood that he needed to make a profit for his investment," she continued. "I was naive enough to think he would be happy with a modest profit. When I realized otherwise, I told him to forget it and moved on.

"I didn't hear anything from him again and assumed the festival was dead in the water ... until about three months ago. Then I heard whispers and started doing some digging. Apparently he stole my idea, tweaked it and decided to charge exorbitant amounts of money. That is not what I envisioned."

As she spoke, I started poking around in her brain. I simply couldn't stop myself. There was something odd going on between her and June, and I was desperate to know what it was.

"You still came," Galen persisted. "If this isn't the festival that you wanted, why come at all?"

"Two reasons. The first is that I wanted to see what he was doing. Powerful people were going to attend. I saw some of them talking about it online. I didn't want to miss out on meeting some of them because there was every chance a similar opportunity would never roll around again. You probably think that makes me shallow, but there it is.

"The second reason is that someone from Calliope's office contacted us and offered money if we would attend," she continued. "They were doling out appearance fees to get anyone in the business who had a name to show up. I didn't know about the payments, but that explained why so many big names were attending. Even though I don't like paying for someone to show up somewhere, that didn't mean I wanted to give up this opportunity."

"I see." Galen stroked his chin as I dug deeper into Bronwen's mind. I could hear June's voice whispering from somewhere, which is where I assumed the secret lived. A brick wall appeared and an image of Bronwen materialized in front of it. She didn't look happy.

"I warned you about this." She sounded like a scolding mother. "You can't just climb into people's heads. It's rude ... and you're not dealing with some garden-variety witch who can't keep you out. The only reason you managed to get in on the docks is because I was distracted. I won't let that happen when you're around again. You need to learn a lesson."

She lifted her hands and I scented magic in the air. I wasn't sure what she was going to do, but I reacted out of instinct, raising a shield. The moment the mind image of Bronwen unleashed her magic, mine flared to life. The spell she cast ricocheted against the wall I'd created and spiraled toward her.

She couldn't move fast enough to avoid it. Her eyes went wide and she was knocked backward, through the wall. I knew better than to try to walk through it and find my secrets. Instead, I beat a hasty retreat.

When I focused on Bronwen in the real world, I found that she was on her back, the chair upended, and she was staring at the sky.

"What happened?" June asked frantically, dropping to her knees. "Are you okay? What is it?"

"I'll call for an ambulance," Galen offered, digging in his pocket for his phone.

Those words were enough to stir Bronwen. "Don't bother," she said, shifting to stare at me. There was wonder in her expression. "I'm dazed, but mostly fine. As for you ... you're all kinds of interesting, aren't you?"

I had no idea how to respond.

"What's going on?" Galen barked. "Did something happen?"

"Something definitely happened," Bronwen replied. "Your girl-friend invaded my mind again and I was going to teach her a lesson. Instead, she unleashed a protection spell like I've never seen and my spell blew back on me so hard it hit me in the real world. It was ... very interesting."

She didn't look angry as much as mystified. Still, I was uncomfortable.

"Thank you for your time," I said, hastily hopping to my feet. "We appreciate your cooperation. You have a good day now." With those words, I practically leaped over the hedges that bordered the parking lot. I didn't bother looking over my shoulder to see if Galen followed. I had to escape, so that's what I did.

SIXTEEN

"What was that?"

Galen waited until we were in his truck to ask the obvious question.

"Where are we going next?" I asked, hoping he would let it go. I knew he wouldn't, but was desperate for a bit of breathing room.

"Don't even." His expression was dark. "Did you try invading her mind again?"

"Maybe." I was distinctly uncomfortable and shifted on the seat so I could look anywhere but his accusatory eyes. "It's a nice day. We should get lunch at one of the restaurants on the beach. I'll buy."

"You just ate two doughnuts."

"Yes, but I'm always up for a good lunch. I'm thinking scallops."

"Hadley." His tone was no-nonsense. "We're not leaving until you tell me exactly what you did … and why."

I could've gotten out and walked back to the lighthouse. It would've sent a strong message that … well, I don't know what. I just didn't want to admit what I'd done. Unfortunately, it was blazing hot and I didn't want to walk. I was still feeling mildly lightheaded. "At least start the truck and get the air conditioning going," I muttered. "I'm hot."

He blinked several times and then did as I instructed, watching as I lowered my face directly in front of the vents. I felt as if I was on fire.

"Are you okay?" he asked finally, moving his hand to my forehead. "You're hot."

"Thank you. You're hot, too, baby."

"I'm not in the mood for this." He was firm. "Tell me what you did."

There was no way out of this conversation. I knew that and yet pushed all the same. I had no idea what was wrong with me, but it was best to get it over with. "I thought I sensed something about the way June and Bronwen looked at each other when they said they were friends, like there was more there. I just wanted to take a look, and I didn't want to invade June's mind because that seemed rude."

"And invading Bronwen's wasn't rude?"

"Hey, it was your idea for me to invade her mind in the first place."

"When did I say that?"

"On the docks. You expressly pointed her out, but at the time I thought it was because you thought she was hot."

"Oh, geez. You're just ... I can't even."

"Don't give me grief," I snapped. "I was curious. I thought I could get in and out without her noticing. She only realized I was there on the docks because you distracted me and my mind went to a dirty place. That didn't happen today."

"And yet she knew you were there."

"Yeah." I rubbed my forehead as I related the story to him. When I finished, his expression was hard to read. "I'm really not in the mood for you to yell, so if that's your plan can we hold off until ... never? That works best for me."

He didn't immediately respond, instead placing his hand on the back of my neck and pushing my head down so I could get a full dose of the air conditioner. His fingers were gentle as they rubbed there. When he finally did speak, it was in measured tones.

"Whatever you did with the protection spell was impressive. She was surprised ... and a little awed."

"It was instinct. I just reacted."

"Well, I'm glad your instincts are good ... most of the time. The

143

AMANDA M. LEE

thing is, you can't just wander around invading people's brains. One day it might get you into trouble you can't get out of."

"I thought it would be okay."

"I know, but ... I'm pretty attached to you. Losing you isn't an option. You need to be more careful."

I didn't like that he was right. "I'll be better about it next time."

"How about you don't invade anyone's mind until this festival is over and I can give you my full attention?" he suggested. "Then I'll act as your bodyguard when you practice ... on people less likely to try to smite you for the effort."

I laughed. "She wasn't going to smite me. She doesn't have the power. I mean ... she's good, but she's not nearly as powerful as she pretends."

"Yeah, but I think you're more powerful than she envisioned, and that's going to make her curious. Just ... promise me. I can only take one catastrophe at a time."

I heaved out a sigh. "I'll think about it. That's the best I can do. I can promise not to do it for the rest of the day. That's the best I can give you."

He didn't look happy, but he nodded. "Fine. Let's get through the day. After that, we'll play it by ear."

"Good enough." I straightened. The heat was starting to drain from my body. "What's our next stop?"

"There were other witches mentioned in those emails you found. They weren't from the same time period, but if we can track them down they might have insight into where Alastair might've run. The thing is, I have no power to find him if he's off the island. I need a place to look all the same. If I can call in a tip to other law enforcement organizations they might be able to find him for us and extradite him back here."

"Do you remember the names of the witches?"

"Yeah, and they're booked at one of the hotels instead of on the beach. I just got confirmation. That seems to indicate they knew something might be going down."

"It can't hurt to ask."

"Yeah." He leaned over and I thought he was going to kiss me. Instead, he pinned me with a pointed look. "You need to be careful with this magic stuff. I know it's new to you and you're excited, but you're in over your head. You need to learn safety protocols before you run off half-cocked."

"Is that an order, sheriff?"

"It's a request. I can take a lot. Losing you isn't on that list. I know I've said it before – numerous times – but I need you to be more careful for me."

His earnest nature caused me to sigh. "You're not going to lose me. I promise. I'll be more careful."

"Okay." He gave me a hard kiss. "If you're not, we're going to continue fighting."

At least he warned me. Still ... . "If we fight, we get to make up."

"There is always that."

THE TROPICANA CABANA (SERIOUSLY, HOTEL names are often ridiculous) was two blocks from Lilac's bar. I'd yet to go inside but, from the street it looked like a tacky beach nightmare.

"This is ... weird," I announced as we strolled into the lobby. Galen had called ahead and the two witches staying at this location were waiting for us in the bar.

"What's weird?" he asked, sliding me a glance.

"Everything in here is pink ... and there are flamingos ... and that's a really weird fountain." I inclined my head. "The mermaid is naked."

"Yes, the owner is a total pervert. He loves naked mermaids. He and Aurora have gone around a few times because he likes to take his mornings on the beach and often lands at whatever place she happens to be skinny dipping that day. She believes he's stalking her."

"Is he?"

Galen shrugged. "As I've told Aurora, if she continues to swim naked in public she has to put up with creepers. That's on her. If she'd wear a bathing suit like a normal person she wouldn't have this problem."

"I think she likes to feel the water on her bits," I explained. "Who doesn't love skinny dipping?"

He arched an eyebrow. "Is that an invitation?"

"Maybe. We'll have to see if we're fighting later."

"Oh, that was low." He squeezed my hand before releasing it and leading me toward the bar. As much as he loved flirting, his mind was clearly on other things.

"What are their names?" I asked, forcing myself to focus on the task at hand. "Who are we looking for?"

"Thalia Thompson and Luster Light."

I pulled up short. "I'm sorry, but ... Luster Light?"

His grin was quick. "I know. I almost choked when I saw it, too. It's more of a porn star name than anything else."

"Or a meteorologist. Were Misty Fields and Sunny Skies already taken?"

He laughed loudly, drawing a few sets of eyes. "See. I can't stay angry at you even when I'm determined to put my foot down. You have a strange power over me ... but don't go climbing inside my head unless I agree to it. I think that has to be a rule."

"That's fair," I agreed. "I don't think it's a good idea for me to be in your head under any circumstances. I might see something I can't unsee and ... I don't want to ruin things. They're really good."

"They are. You won't find anything in there that'll ruin things, just for the record. Unless ... you won't be offended if I have images of you dancing naked under the full moon running on a loop throughout the day, will you?"

I frowned. "I've never danced naked under the full moon."

"Maybe not in real life, but you do it constantly in my head."

"Ugh. You're such a pervert."

"We're all over the island." He was markedly more relaxed as he scanned the tables until he found the one he was looking for. It was early in the day so there weren't many people drinking. It wasn't difficult to identify the witches. One was brunette with dark makeup smeared under her eyes and a sterling silver moon charm hanging from a light chain around her neck. The other was sunny and blond ... and giggling nonstop.

"The blonde is Luster Light," I volunteered as we started moving in that direction.

"Did you pick that out of her head?"

"It's just common sense."

It turned out I was right. Luster was ... well, lustrous, and she knew it. She was a laughing, eye-lash-batting, giggler extraordinaire, and I could practically feel the sex vibes rolling off her when she got a load of Galen.

"Are you the sheriff?" She extended her hand before he answered, tilting her head in a playful way as she tugged on the sun charm on her necklace. "Wow! If I'd known the cops on this island looked like you I would've made more of an effort to get arrested."

Thalia and I rolled our eyes in unison.

"I'm Sheriff Blackwood," Galen confirmed, pulling out a chair for me. "This is Hadley Hunter. She works as a consultant with my department."

That was a bit of an exaggeration, but I understood why he wanted my presence to be official.

"She's a witch," Thalia countered, eyes narrowing as she looked me up and down. "She's a powerful witch."

I kept my face neutral. "I'm an expert consultant."

"Oh, she's definitely a witch," Luster enthused. "I can feel the magic." She extended her fingers in my direction and only pulled them back when I glared. "You're a born witch. You didn't make yourself. That's ... very rare."

"I'm a born witch," Thalia countered. "It's not that rare. Not everybody likes putting on a show."

Sensing trouble, I decided to change the subject. "We're actually here for a reason. Sheriff Blackwood has some questions to ask you."

He stared at me a moment, his lips twitching, and then focused on the two witches. "I do have questions ... about the festival."

"It's a mess," Thalia replied, her eyes darkening. "It's an embarrassment to pagan festivals everywhere. News will spread and people won't want to return to the island if you're not careful. You should do something about it."

"The festival isn't my responsibility," Galen argued. "Moonstone Bay allowed Alastair Herne to pull a festival license. He's responsible for what's happening on that beach right now. We can't do anything to fix his mess."

"Uh-huh." Thalia didn't look convinced. "If you say so."

"It's the truth." Galen was firm. "Alastair is in charge. That said, I've sent Calliope down to start fixing things. She's one of the event organizers, but Alastair's name is on all the contracts."

"And where is Alastair?" Thalia asked. "Why isn't he down there?"

"We can't find him." Galen didn't mince words. "He's either been taken against his will or voluntarily fled ... somewhere. He's not at his house and he doesn't return calls. He's the reason we're here talking to you."

Luster's hand flew to her mouth, sparkly acrylic nails on display. "You think we did something to him? How could you possibly believe that? We're beacons of the light, purveyors of hope and holders of the magical chalice."

That entire final sentence sounded like nonsense. "What's the magical chalice?"

Thalia shook her head. "Oh, ignore her. She's full of it. She makes stuff up all the time. She can't seem to help herself. There is no magical chalice."

"There is." Luster was solemn. "It's here." She tapped the spot above her heart. "It's here in all of us ... if we choose to embrace it."

"Oh, shut up," Thalia growled. "As for Alastair, we don't know where he is. Why would you assume we did?"

"Before the festival, you were in regular contact with him," Galen replied without hesitation. "I know because he printed the conversations."

Neither Luster nor Thalia responded right away. Instead, they were the picture of stoic disinterest. Luster, of course, couldn't keep up the facade very long.

"We didn't hurt him. If you think we did, you're crazy. That's not who we are."

"Yes, the magical chalice won't let them hurt anyone," I drawled.

Luster ignored me. "We were only in touch with him about the festival because ... well ... we're big names in the witch world and he wanted us to attend. He made it worth our while to come all the way out here ... at least that's what we thought when we first struck our deals."

"Oh, shut your mouth, you idiot," Thalia groused. She hadn't as much as smiled since we sat down. I had the feeling she wasn't exactly a people person. "I'm sure they already know that. Why else would they be here?"

"The documents indicate you were paid for your presence," Galen agreed. "What I want to know is why. Why would Alastair care enough to pay you to come?"

"Because, as annoying as I find this idiot, she was right when she said we have reputations," Thalia replied, jerking her thumb in Luster's direction. "We have followings on the internet, and those are the types of people Alastair went after."

That made sense. "He went for Salma first, because she was an influencer. She had friends and they helped spread the word. Still, he would've needed an online presence in the supernatural world. That's why he went after specific witches ... and I'm betting part of the payment you received stipulated you had to mention the festival so many times a day."

Thalia nodded stiffly. "Yeah, and I'm not proud of what I did. But the money was good and the festival sounded out of this world."

"And yet you have a hotel room," Galen noted. "You're safely ensconced here while the people who drained their accounts to attend are crammed together on a beach that doesn't have proper amenities."

Thalia shrugged. "That's just one of life's little mysteries."

She was good, but I could tell she was lying. Luster, on the other hand, had turned into a nervous wreck.

"We heard through the grapevine that things might not be like he was promoting and didn't want to take any chances," the blonde blurted out. "I mean ... who wants to camp on the beach anyway? That's weird. You can drink on the beach, sure, but camp? Blech."

"Shut up!" Thalia snapped.

Luster simply kept blathering. "We asked Alastair about it, but he denied everything. He said things were right on schedule and it was going to be amazing. Other people, those who were more familiar with the island, said that what he promised was impossible. We didn't want to take any chances."

"I see." Galen pursed his lips. "I'm guessing that you kept promoting the festival even after you found out it was going to be a disaster. Even though you knew you were spouting lies, you kept it up, right?"

"We didn't have a choice," Luster whined. "We don't get paid until after the event. It's a good chunk of money, but it's contingent on saying what a wonderful time we had after the fact."

"Which is why you actually had to come to the island at all," I surmised. "He set it up so you would have no choice in the matter."

"Pretty much," Thalia agreed. "I did think it was going to be a good festival, though. Even though I knew it wouldn't be what he pitched, I thought it would be a good time. I didn't know it would turn out like this, that the people down there would be so miserable."

"I don't think you cared," Galen countered. "What are you going to do about payment now that Alastair is missing? I mean ... he's taken off and all that money is gone. You did all this for nothing."

Thalia narrowed her eyes. "Wait ... you didn't mention that."

"I told you Alastair was missing."

"Yeah, but I just assumed that meant he was hiding from you because he knew you would try to arrest him for being a big phony fraud. I didn't realize that meant we wouldn't get paid."

"Well, I can guarantee you're not getting paid. He's gone."

"He's probably just at that cabin he mentioned," Luster countered. "He said it was remote and he went there to think. That's probably where he is now. Have you looked there?"

Galen worked his jaw. "Alastair owns a mansion," he said finally. "Why would he be hanging out at a cabin when he's got a mansion?"

Luster shrugged. "I don't know. He said it was a therapeutic place. He mentioned it in passing only once. He called it Copper Hollow or something."

I watched for Galen's reaction. "Does that name mean anything to you?"

"Not Copper Hollow, but Cooper's Hollow." Galen was grim as he stood. "Are you sure he said he had a cabin there?"

Luster solemnly nodded. "He said that's where he went to unwind and invited me to go there with him. He was kind of gross, and I knew what he wanted, so I said no."

"You were probably smart to do that," I said to her. "He's definitely gross ... and a loser." I focused on Galen. "I've never heard of Cooper's Hollow. I thought there was only one city on the island."

"It's not a city. It's a little village. Originally it was a fishing village. Now it's just a ramshackle place where people hang out ... and live ... and farm ... and drink."

"So let's go there." I moved to his side. "If there's a chance he's out there we have to go."

"We definitely have to go," he agreed. "The thing is, we can't go at night."

"Why not?"

He risked a glance at Thalia and Luster and shook his head. Whatever he had to say couldn't be relayed in front of them. "We just can't. It'll take hours to get out there." He looked at the clock on the wall and did some calculations. "We'll have to wait until tomorrow. We'll be cutting it too close if we leave now."

He was acting strange. "But ... I don't understand."

"I'll explain later." He grabbed my hand and started dragging me away. "Thank you for the information, ladies. We'll be in touch."

"Wait," Luster called out. "You can buy me dinner if you want. You're not creepy like Alastair."

"I already have dinner plans," he replied. "Thanks for your time. You've been unbelievably helpful."

SEVENTEEN

I was still confused when Galen and I arrived at Lilac's bar for dinner. We swung by the beach long enough to check on things — it was rough out there and I felt bad for the people who'd spent thousands of dollars because they thought they were going to be able to hobnob with the witch and famous — and then stopped at the lighthouse to change clothes. Galen had officially taken over half my closet even though he had his own place. We no longer spent nights apart, which is how I wanted things, but I was starting to realize that we were so entrenched in each other's lives there was no escaping ... not that I wanted an escape. We did, however, need to define things.

"Hey," Lilac waved us toward a corner booth.

I smiled and waved back before heading in that direction, Galen on my heels. Once we sat, I focused on the menu rather than him ... something that apparently didn't sit very well.

"Why are you shutting me out?" he groused, his expression a mask of unhappiness.

"I'm not shutting you out," I argued. "You're shutting me out."

"I am not."

"You are. You won't tell me why Cooper's Hollow is a big deal. You also won't tell me why I didn't know Cooper's Hollow was a thing. You're definitely shutting me out."

The look he shot me was full of annoyance. "I am not. I told you I couldn't tell you about Cooper's Hollow in front of an audience. I meant it. I didn't say I couldn't tell you about it ever."

I folded my arms across my chest and waited. "We don't have an audience now."

For the first time in hours he cracked a smile. "Now I need to wait for an audience. I called Booker to join us. I want to wait until he's here."

Now I was really confused. "Why do we need Booker?"

"I need him to go with me to Cooper's Hollow tomorrow morning and there are a few things I need to talk to him about."

I waited for him to explain further. When he didn't, I decided it was time to push. "Are you going to tell me those things?"

"As soon as Booker gets here."

"Oh, geez." I rolled my neck and blew out a sigh. "Things are not going my way right now."

"Oh, no? From where I'm sitting you had a pretty good day. You invaded a seemingly powerful witch's mind and not only lived to tell the tale, but smacked her down. You had doughnuts. You got to spend the entire day with me. What's not to love about that day?"

My lips wanted to curve, but I fought the effort. "You won't tell me about Cooper's Hollow. That totally ruined my entire day."

Galen let loose an exaggerated eye roll. "Booker will be here in a few minutes. Give me room to breathe again until then, okay?"

I wanted to argue, but there didn't seem to be a point. He was going to do what he was going to do. Instead, I grabbed the specials menu from the center of the table and looked it over. "They have the steamer buckets you love so much."

"You love them, too," he pointed out.

"Yeah." I was noncommittal until his hand landed on top of mine and I lifted my eyes.

"I'm not keeping anything from you," he promised in a low voice. "I'll tell you about Cooper's Hollow. I'm simply tired and only want to go through it once. That's why I want to wait for Booker. I won't have the energy to romance you tonight if I expend too much talking."

That was enough to send me over the edge. I couldn't help feeling sympathetic to his plight. "I'm tired, too," I admitted. "I think it's making me a little cranky. I didn't mean to snap at you."

"I know." He squeezed my hand. "We've both had a long day. I didn't mean to snap at you either. The thing is, I love you. That means we're fairly tight ... and what's that saying? You always hurt the one you love. I didn't mean to be that guy today."

I went warm all over at the naked sentiment in his eyes ... and then a shadow moved in at my left and ruined things.

"You guys are officially the schmaltziest," Booker complained as he glanced between us. "I mean ... it's ridiculous."

For some reason, his reaction made me laugh, and that was enough to ease the tension. "You're just jealous," I countered, making room for him to sit next to me.

As if sensing trouble, Booker took a moment to study Galen's face and then took a step back instead. "Why don't you guys sit on the same side? I'll sit across from you. That way you can grope under the table and I'll be none the wiser."

I was about to argue with the idea when Galen happily shifted from his side of the table to mine.

"Thanks." Galen's grin was mischievous as he slipped his arm around my shoulders and regarded Booker. "You look beat, man. How are things on the beach?"

Booker glowered at him. "Things on the beach suck. I mean ... they really suck. Those people were sold a bill of goods and they're starting to figure it out."

"Shouldn't they have figured it out the first day?" I was confused. "I mean ... they were promised villas and there weren't even enough tents."

"Most of them thought this was going to be the trip of a lifetime," Booker explained. "They don't want to admit they were swindled out of a bunch of money on a crappy vacation, so they've been holding onto hope. That won't last much longer."

154

"What about Calliope?" Galen queried, moving his hand to the back of my neck so he could start rubbing away the tension pooling there. "She stayed the entire day, didn't she?"

"She did." Booker grimaced as he nodded. "She wasn't much help. She spent the entire time wheedling and crying. She went after each of your men in turn to find one who would let her escape. When that didn't work, she tried going after me."

"Hey, that might work out for you. As a guy who likes hooking up with women for a grand total of three dates, she might be right up your alley."

Booker's glare was withering. "Ha, ha. You've got one more day out there before things get really ugly. In fact, not even a full day. If things don't ease by nightfall tomorrow, they're going to start getting rowdy ... and not in a good way."

"Yeah. That's what I was worried about." Galen stroked his chin, thoughtful. "I have some things to catch you up on ... and then I have a favor to ask. The good thing for you is that it will get you off the beach. The bad thing is, well, it's at Cooper's Hollow."

Booker's eyebrows raised wildy. "Are you kidding me?"

"Nope." Galen was solemn. "I know we swore we would never return there, but it's come to my attention that Alastair might own a cabin on the land ... although I'm still not sure how that happened. Those women aren't exactly known for opening their arms to sleazy millionaires."

"What women?" I asked, my frustration coming out to play.

"Just a second." Galen held up a finger to still me and kept his focus on Booker. "I need to catch him up first."

They didn't always get along. Often, they were mired in competition. When it came to the big things, though, Booker and Galen were almost always in lockstep. I was coming to the conclusion that Booker was Galen's preferred form of backup for a big fight, and it was obvious they were both worried that's what we would face the next morning.

To give Booker time to consider the request, Galen told him about our day. He didn't leave anything out, including what happened between Bronwen and me. Booker seemed most intrigued by that tidbit.

"That's interesting, huh?" Mirth lurked in his eyes. "Our little Hadley is getting more powerful with every day that passes. Pretty soon she'll be the baddest entity on the island."

"Which is going to garner her attention she doesn't want," Galen replied coldly. "That'll attract the attention of the DDA."

Booker's smile slipped. "Yeah, well, I don't think you have much of a choice there. She's growing in leaps and bounds, and they're attracted to power. It's going to happen eventually."

"Yeah." Galen didn't look happy at the possibility, but he forced a smile for my benefit. "Whatever she did with Bronwen — and I'm not sure I fully understand it — but whatever it was, Bronwen was impressed. I think word is going to spread faster than we might like about Hadley's abilities."

"I think it's good that people fear her," Booker countered. "Her legend is already growing. You wouldn't believe how many people have come up to me to ask questions regarding what happened with the cupids."

Galen shifted, his body going tense. "What are they asking?"

"News has spread that she went out there alone," Booker replied simply. "People know that the rest of us were down for the count and she did everything herself. They're impressed."

I stirred. "That's not entirely true," I argued. "I went out there alone, but I joined with all of you for the big fight. We did it together."

"We did," Booker agreed. "You still went out there by yourself, and the amount of power you unleashed ... well ... it was impressive. A novice witch shouldn't be able to do what you did."

I looked to Galen for confirmation. When he didn't say anything, my stomach twisted. "You're saying I'm an oddity."

"No, sweetheart." Galen immediately started shaking his head. "You're strong. You're wonderful. Don't let what he's saying shake your confidence."

"I'm not trying to shake her confidence," Booker argued. "I'm saying that she's climbing the Moonstone Bay food chain pretty quickly. That's impressive."

"Well ... she's not ready to embrace that right now." Galen was firm. "Don't push her. She's had a big day."

That was true. A lot happened over the course of a few hours. I was still behind on one thing, though. "You still haven't told me about Cooper's Hollow," I reminded him. "You promised to do it once Booker joined us. He's here and I'm still in the dark."

My crabby response was enough to elicit a genuine smile from Galen. "You're sunshine and joy, Hadley. Truly."

Booker snorted. "I take it you haven't told her what to expect at Cooper's Hollow."

"No, and you understand why I need you with me, right?" Galen's gaze was pointed as it locked with Booker's "meh" stare. "It will be safer if we're together for this little excursion."

A sneaking suspicion nagged at the back of my brain. "Wait a second ... you're going to try to leave me here, aren't you? You're going to head out with Booker at the crack of dawn and leave me behind."

Galen slid his eyes to me. "What makes you say that?"

"You're obsessed with protecting me and whatever is happening out at this Cooper's Hollow has you agitated. You won't risk taking me with you if you're worked up like this. I know how your mind works."

"Well, that just goes to show you that you're not as smart as you think you are." He tweaked the end of my nose and grinned. "I do want you with me. In fact, you're going to be a key figure tomorrow morning."

"I am?" I couldn't keep up with what was happening. "Why am I a key figure?"

"Because Aurora likes you," Booker replied for him. "And, more importantly, Aurora was there when you took on the cupids. She saw what you can do. She'll have spread that story to her brethren, which means they'll be less likely to kick up a fuss when we invade their turf."

That's when things slid into place for me. "We're going to Aurora's village."

Galen nodded. "It's not technically another town. I know that's confusing. It's more a series of bungalows located between the beach and the river. They've taken over that part of the island — the sirens — and it's allowed because nobody wants to take them on."

I shifted on my seat as I considered what he was saying. "I thought the sirens hung out down here. I mean ... I always see Aurora down here. She and a few of the other sirens have been monitoring the water outside the festival for you."

"Aurora is the friendliest of the bunch, which boggles the mind, I'm sure. They don't like being too close to hordes of people. They prefer privacy."

"When the sirens first came to the island it wasn't bustling with people," Booker explained. "The part you know as the city was a quarter the size it is now — probably less — and it was full of pirates who spent their time carousing and drinking while avoiding the authorities."

"The sirens didn't like the authorities any more than the pirates did," Galen expanded. "They wanted a private spot. They picked the other side of the island, and the pirates and sirens came to an agreement. They avoided each other. As the city expanded, the sirens felt more and more invaded. They don't like it when people visit Cooper's Hollow."

"Are they going to attack us?" A knot formed in my stomach at the thought. "Are we going to have to fight?"

"Odds are they won't fight us," Galen reassured me quickly. "That would be a wasted effort. But if they're really crabby they might. Aurora will stand up for us to the best of her ability, but we might have to run."

I didn't like the sound of that. "Is that why we can't be there after dark? Because they might attack?"

He nodded. "I need to be able to see what's coming. Odds are we'll be perfectly fine. I just want to make sure that's the case. I want

Booker with me because he's another elemental and he's strong. The sirens respect him because he's helped a time or two."

"What if they have Alastair and don't want to give him up?" I asked.

"We'll have to decide what to do then. For now, we just need to confirm he's out there. If he is, odds are he's not leaving the island. Boats can't dock there. The current is too strong."

I learned something new every day on this island. "The sirens have helped us before," I persisted. "They've fought alongside us. Why is going out there tomorrow such a big deal?"

"There are two factions of sirens," Booker replied. "The ones who helped us when your reaper friend was flapping her mouth are the friendly ones. They want to join with the Moonstone Bay community. The others, the older faction, are the ones in charge, though. They like their privacy and they're not afraid to kill to maintain it."

Well, that was a sobering thought.

GALEN AND I WALKED ALONG THE beach on the way home, our fingers linked as we watched the ocean waves roll in. This part of the beach was off-limits to the festival attendees, but I could hear them carousing ... and they didn't sound as if they were having a bad time.

"Maybe Booker is wrong," I offered as we swung our hands. "Maybe things won't fall apart tomorrow."

"I hate to admit it, but Booker is rarely wrong about this sort of stuff." Galen's smile was grim. "We'll handle it when it occurs. Right now, the sirens are our biggest concern. Once we deal with them we'll figure out the festival stuff."

On a whim, I slowed my pace and fixed him with a serious stare. "I was thinking about something earlier. I know it might seem sudden, but ... I think it makes sense for us. If you believe it's a bad idea, you should tell me. I don't want to ruin this."

His expression was curious. "You're not going to ruin anything. Tell me what you're thinking."

"I thought of it when we were changing our clothes at the lighthouse. Every week you have to make a run to your place to get stuff and bring it to my place. That seems like a lot of effort when we spend every night together. Maybe ... um, maybe ... well ... I was thinking you might want to move into the lighthouse. There's plenty of room, and that way you wouldn't have to pick up stuff all the time. But ... you might think this is a horrible idea."

He chuckled as I babbled, his fingers gently moving to my hair to brush it from my face and stare into my eyes. "Do you want me to move in with you?"

"I wouldn't have asked if I didn't want it. The thing is, I don't know if that's too much for you. Maybe you need another space as your escape hatch, which I get. We haven't been together all that long. This feels right to me, though, and I just thought ... um ... don't stare at me." I lowered my eyes, mortified. "You think it's a bad idea, don't you?"

"No, I don't." He shifted his finger to my chin and tipped it up. "I've been considering the same thing. I didn't know how to broach the subject. I thought you would think it was too soon."

The invisible fist that had been squeezing my heart eased its icy grip. "Really?"

He nodded. "I would love to live with you." He swooped in and gave me a hard kiss. "I think it's a great idea. I don't want to be away from you."

This time the smile I graced him with was warm and welcoming. "Then ... we can do it?"

He nodded. "After we deal with this festival thing. We need to focus on that first."

"Totally."

He wrapped his arms around me and squeezed. "I think this is going to be good."

"Yeah." I let out a sigh. "Of course, I'll need to meet your mother before we move in together. That seems necessary before we do anything big like moving in together."

He groaned. "Ugh. You maneuvered me right into that one, didn't you?"

I ignored his tone. "Let's go home and celebrate our big life change

... and then get some sleep. The sirens await tomorrow and I want to be well rested for whatever comes."

"That sounds like a fine idea." This time the kiss he graced me with was softer. "I really do love you, Hadley."

"I love you, too."

"You're going to hate my mother, though. You've been warned."

I already suspected that was the case. Still, it was better to get it over with. Dragging it out wasn't going to help anyone.

EIGHTEEN

I was ready for action the next morning and dressed accordingly, including putting on a pair of black leather pants that I'd bought for a Halloween costume years ago. I could've still been giddy from the night before, but the look on Galen's and Booker's faces when I joined them in the kitchen were funny enough that it was worth whatever discomfort I would incur from wearing them in sweltering weather.

"All you're missing is a sharp, pointy stick," Booker commented as he sipped his coffee. It was so early the sun wasn't up, but Galen wanted to time our trip so we arrived at first light.

"Excuse me?" I arched an eyebrow, confused.

"You look like Buffy from that vampire slayer show."

That was just preposterous. "Buffy was blond. I am not. If anything, I'm Faith."

"Thanks for the clarification." Booker's gaze was speculative when he switched it to Galen. "Are you going to let her wear that?"

Galen looked caught. "She looks cute," he said finally.

"What does it matter what I'm wearing?" I demanded. "I think I look badass. They'll think twice about messing with me."

"Because of the pants?" Booker challenged.

"You have to look the part you feel," I replied airily, moving next to Galen so I could pour myself a mug of coffee. "I feel strong in these pants."

"You look strong," Galen commented. When I glanced up, I found he was staring at my rear end. When he realized I'd caught him, he straightened. "I mean ... you look like a total badass. The thing is, sweetheart, you're going to sweat to death in those things once we're out there. I don't think wilting because of the heat is the message you want to send."

He had a point. Still ... . "We'll be in air conditioning for the ride out there. How long are we really going to be out in the open?"

"You might be surprised. As much as I like the pants, they're not practical. Why don't you save them for a night when it's just the two of us? I know, how about the first night after I move in. That might be fun."

"You're moving in?" Booker's lips curved. "You guys aren't wasting any time, are you?"

"Hey, when you know, you know," Galen shot back. "It only makes sense. We spend every night together as it is. Why keep two places?"

"I'm not judging." Booker held up his hands in capitulation. "I simply find it curious. Just pretend I'm not here."

"If only," Galen muttered, shaking his head. He looked apologetic when his focus returned to me. "The pants are a bad idea. Why don't you change into something more ... um ... casual?"

"You were going to say 'normal,' weren't you?"

"Yes, but there's nothing abnormal about the way you look."

"*Whipped!*" Booker coughed into his hand.

Galen ignored him. "You look great. I want to hunker down and keep you here all day, but that's not an option."

He was adamant enough that I knew he meant business. "Fine," I sighed, "but you're ruining my badass rep by making me change into wimpy clothes. You've been warned."

"Thank you for the warning, baby. I'll regret the request for the next few hours. I can guarantee that."

Well, at least that was something.

. . .

I SAT IN THE BACKSEAT FOR THE ride to Cooper's Village. Booker's legs were longer, and he and Galen were talking strategy, something that felt out of place from what I knew about the sirens, but they were more knowledgeable on this issue so I let it be.

I was familiar with the road until we drove past Wesley's house, and then it branched to the left ... and turned rutted and rough. I was belted in, yet I bounced hard enough that my teeth clipped a few times.

"How does anyone get out here?" I complained when Galen took a particularly hairy turn. "If they've lived here for as long as you say, why haven't they have smoothed out the road?"

"That might encourage visitors," Galen replied, his eyes focused on the track in front of us. He didn't as much as meet my gaze in the rearview mirror. He was too intent. "They don't like visitors."

"But ... what about supplies? They must need supplies out here."

"People deliver, but they don't need much and they handle the bulk of their stuff on location. They have their own gardens, fish for protein, and cut down the trees for construction. They're very self-sufficient."

"And they're all women?" That was the part that really confused me. "There were men with Aurora that day when we were attacked, but you mentioned the women out here. You didn't say anything about the men. What's up with that?"

Booker snickered as Galen let out a long-suffering sigh.

"So curious today," Booker teased. "What's up with that?"

He was on my last nerve. "I'm just trying to figure out the intricacies of the island. This is my home now. I want to understand it so I'm not always the goof doing weird things."

"You're not a goof," Galen reassured me. "You're just ... new."

The way he said it made it sound as if that was bad. "Is that code for something?"

"It's code for being the most beautiful woman on the island."

Booker made gagging sounds as I rolled my eyes.

"That was laying it on a bit thick," I said. "Keep it up, though."

He laughed and then leaned forward. "We're coming up on Cooper's Hollow. Hadley, I need you to let me do the talking out here."

Booker snorted. "That should go over well."

Even though I was annoyed, I decided to show I was a mature individual. Instead of commenting, I blew a wet raspberry in his direction and turned to look out the window. I couldn't see anything. I was almost convinced this was an elaborate hoax ... but then the trees gave way to something I had never seen.

"Holy ... !" My mouth dropped open because I was in awe. "It's like *Swiss Family Robinson.*"

"Kind of," Galen agreed as the treehouses came into view. "This is the heart of the village. The cottages and cabins on the other side aren't this picturesque."

"And where do we think Alastair is?"

"That's what we're here to find out." Galen put his truck in park and killed the engine before glancing over his shoulder and snagging my gaze. "Remember that I'm the one doing the talking."

He was serious enough that I nodded, despite my agitation. "Yes, King Galen. You can do the talking while the lowly woman remains silent and demure."

"Oh, geez." He pinched the bridge of his nose. "This is going to be a thing, isn't it?"

"I guess we'll just have to wait and see."

I was anxious as I hopped out of the truck. The picturesque village featured houses built on tree branches and walkways between the houses. It was like a scene out of a movie ... and I had multiple movies from which to choose.

"Do they have Ewoks?" I asked after a beat as Galen joined me outside the vehicle.

He cast me a sidelong look. "Not last time I checked."

"Are they going to let me see inside of one of those cool treehouses?"

"No. I've never been inside and I've been out here at least thirty times over the years. They're very protective of their secrets."

That was disappointing. "Why do sirens — women of the sea — live in trees?"

Galen growled and then faked a smile. "You'll have to ask them ... but not today."

He was acting weird. "And why did you mention women and not men?"

"Because the men in this society are considered ... less. It's the women who rule."

Oh, well, that was interesting. "Maybe I should've been a siren. Then I could've bossed you around for a change."

"There's still time. Maybe they'll adopt you."

I could tell he was unsettled so I let it go and focused on the movement I saw beneath the trees. In short order, five women, all of them carrying dangerous-looking spears, approached us. I didn't recognize any of them, which was enough to make me feel nervous. Instinctively, I moved closer to Galen.

He slid me a sidelong look and an encouraging smile, and then focused on our hosts.

"Hello, Cordelia." He held his hands out in a conciliatory manner. "I apologize for interrupting your day, but something has come up that involves you guys and ... well ... I have a few questions."

I wasn't sure which woman was Cordelia until a devastatingly beautiful woman who looked to be in her forties stepped forward. She had long brown hair that hung well past her waist, and she wore what could loosely be described as a top. It barely covered anything, but she didn't look bothered to be on display despite outside guests.

"Galen." She bobbed her head and flashed her eyes toward Booker. "Cupid."

"It's good to see you, too," Booker drawled. He seemed much more relaxed than Galen, even though he hadn't been addressed by name. "It's been a long time."

"Not long enough," she countered, although there was very little bite to her words. When her eyes flicked to me I suddenly felt vulnerable, something I hated. "And this must be the new witch I've heard so much about."

"Hadley," I volunteered in a cracking voice. "Um ... Hadley Hunter. It's nice to meet you."

"And you. Aurora has spoken of you numerous times."

I wasn't sure if that was a good thing. "Oh, well ... great."

"Where is Aurora?" Galen asked, glancing around. "She might want to be present for this conversation."

"I'm in charge here," Cordelia reminded him. "Anything you have to say should be addressed to me."

"I wasn't suggesting otherwise. It's just ... we have a situation."

"As far as I can tell, you have numerous situations these days." Cordelia's eyes were back on me. "This one has been at the center of most of them. Is that the case again today?"

"Actually, it's not," Galen replied. "Hadley came with me because she's helping with the investigation. She was curious about Cooper's Hollow. I thought this might be the only chance for her to ever see it."

"Oh, if only that were true." Cordelia blew out a sigh and then gestured for us to come closer. "Let's sit in the shade. You can tell me why you're here and I'll decide if I want to help you. I probably won't, but you never know."

"That sounds great." Galen put his hand to the small of my back and prodded me forward. "You guys have been busy. Last time I was out here some of the walkways were in dire need of fixing."

"We came into some unexpected funds," Cordelia replied. "We're in the middle of a renovation."

"Well, it looks great."

We followed her to a bonfire area, numerous chairs spread around, and Galen made sure to position me between him and Booker. It was a conscious decision, something I was certain that Cordelia picked up on, but she didn't comment.

"So, we're looking for Alastair Herne," Galen started. "He's in some trouble."

"What sort of trouble?" a voice asked from the edge of the clearing. This was a voice I recognized, and I was happy to see Aurora slip through the trees. She was dressed for a change and I offered her a happy wave when I saw her.

For her part, Aurora merely smirked and shook her head. "Hadley. I wondered if you would ever make it out here."

"She's part of the team," Galen said simply. "As for Alastair, are you aware of what's going on with the Skyclad Festival?"

Aurora's grin turned mischievous. "A festival after my own heart. Who doesn't love naked dancing under the full moon? We've been monitoring the water as you requested. The attendees aren't exactly into swimming right now."

"I don't really care about that part," Galen said. "I'm most interested in the part where Alastair took gobs of money from unsuspecting people and then didn't follow through on certain promises. Well ... that and the murder."

Cordelia furrowed her brow. "I didn't hear about any murder."

"Salma Hershey. She was killed on the beach where the festival is taking place. It happened the night before all the guests arrived."

"And what does that have to do with Alastair?"

The way the woman asked the question made me suspicious. They definitely knew more about Alastair than they were letting on. Perhaps it had something to do with the money they came into. I wanted to ask about it, but Galen was determined to make himself the focus of the conversation ... so I let him.

"Alastair and Salma argued before she died. She knew that he was screwing over everyone."

"So ... he's a suspect?"

"He's our only suspect right now."

"That is ... troubling." Cordelia exchanged a look with Aurora, something unsaid passing between them. Finally, she sighed. "Alastair approached us about six weeks ago. He told tall tales about admiring our culture, blah, blah, blah. He offered us a great deal of money in exchange for ownership of one of the cabins on the outskirts of Cooper's Hollow."

"And you sold it to him?" Galen was incredulous. "That doesn't sound like you. Last time I checked, you guys hated outsiders."

"It was a great deal of money," Cordelia stressed.

"And we figured we would make him uncomfortable enough he

would never want to visit," Aurora volunteered, ignoring the scorching look Cordelia shot in her direction. "We were wrong."

"Does that mean he's here?" Galen shifted in his chair, eager. "Have you seen him?"

"I don't know that we can answer that," Cordelia hedged.

Aurora's expression darkened. "You can't protect him. We didn't agree to cover up his crimes when we sold him the cabin."

"Yes, but we don't allow outsiders on our land except under dire circumstances," Cordelia shot back. "That doesn't seem to be what we're dealing with here."

"If we don't work with Galen he'll have no choice but to encroach on our land. Isn't that worse than just telling him the truth?"

Cordelia let loose a heavy sigh, frustration evident. "I wish you would learn your place, Aurora. You shouldn't have spoken out of turn."

"I'm not sorry." Aurora was defiant. "I'm not even a little sorry. I didn't want to allow him out here to begin with. You made that decision. It's out of our hands now. We have to tell the truth. That's still who we are."

For a moment I thought Cordelia would argue with that assertion. Ultimately, she nodded. "You're right. Protecting him gets us nothing." Her eyes were stony when they landed on Galen. "He arrived in the middle of the night several days ago. He went straight to his cabin. We haven't seen him since."

"I need you to take me there." Galen appeared calm, but I could feel his anxiousness. "I'll take him into custody and we'll leave within five minutes. That's the best-case scenario for you."

"On that, you're not wrong. Aurora will show you the way." Cordelia got to her feet. "Don't make it a habit to come out here, Galen. Things will get ugly if you do."

"I try to stay off your land unless it's absolutely necessary. I felt this was necessary."

"Get your man ... and leave." Cordelia's eyes were heavy-lidded when she focused on Aurora. "We will talk later."

"I can't wait," Aurora muttered, her arms folded over her chest. She remained standing, rigid, until Cordelia disappeared from view, and then motioned to us. "This way. I knew allowing him out here would come back to bite us."

We followed Aurora, Galen linking his fingers with mine to keep me close. We walked a long way. It had to be close to half a mile. When we stopped outside of a nondescript cabin that had more in common with a shack than the awesome treehouses I saw in the center of Cooper's Hollow I was less than impressed.

"He paid you a boatload of money for this?" I asked, confused.

Aurora nodded. "I told Cordelia he was only doing it for a place to hide, but she didn't care. She saw dollar signs."

"And nobody has seen him since he arrived?" Booker asked.

"No. I think he knows better than trying to hang with us. He wouldn't be welcome."

Galen released my hand and moved closer to the cabin, his nose lifted in the air. As a shifter, he had an incredible sense of smell.

"What's going on?" I asked, instantly alert. His body had gone rigid.

"It's a dead body," Galen replied, his eyes shifting to Booker. "I don't think it's very fresh either."

Aurora furrowed her brow. "Are you saying Alastair is dead in there?"

"I'm saying someone is dead in there." Galen held up a finger to still me when I started forward. "I think it's best you stay here. We don't know what we'll find."

"I can handle dead bodies," I argued. "It's hardly the first time I've seen one."

"Just wait until Booker and I look first," he pleaded. "Please."

Grudgingly, I nodded, pouting as he and Booker headed toward the dilapidated building. They didn't bother knocking, instead throwing open the door and stepping inside. They disappeared from view, but were back within seconds, their faces drawn and pale.

"It's Alastair," Galen announced. "He's definitely dead ... he's been stabbed."

"Just like Salma," I noted.

He nodded, rubbing his forehead. "We need to get the medical examiner out here."

Aurora snorted. "Oh, Cordelia will love that."

"She'll have to live with it."

"Oh, she'll live with it." Aurora was grim. "And then I'll lord it over her forever that I was right and she was wrong."

NINETEEN

G alen did his best to keep me out of the cabin and away from the body, but he couldn't watch me every second so I managed to slip inside.

It was a mistake.

"Oh, geez." I almost went to my knees at the smell ... and the sight. Booker caught me under the arms and hauled me up and away, dragging me back through the open door.

"Are you trying to make Galen's head explode?" he complained as he moved me to the shade. "I'm serious. His head will just blow right off his neck if he knows you saw that."

"There's no need for exaggeration," I muttered as I rested my sweaty palms on my knees and tried to refrain from yakking all over the ground. I had a feeling the sirens, who were standing at the edge of the trees watching the medical examiner's team work, wouldn't like it. "Besides, I'm fine."

"You don't look fine." Booker pressed his hand to my forehead and then pulled it back. "Are you happy now? You saw the body. What did you learn from it?"

"That bugs can do things to the human body that I never imagined."

He arched an eyebrow, amusement lighting his features. "They can indeed. You need to stay out of there. There's nothing you can do inside."

"I thought maybe if I saw I might find a clue that Galen missed."

"Because he's such a crappy investigator?"

I balked. "No, because ... because ... ." Crap in a custard eclair. He had me and he knew it.

"I get that you want to be part of this." Booker was calm, rational. It made me want to punch him. "Galen has essentially made you his partner even though you're not a cop. I never thought I would see the day when a woman would tame him this way ... and so fast. I want to make fun of him for it, but I'm kind of jealous."

I straightened, flustered. I told myself that the sun beating down on me was the reason for my cheeks burning, but I was terrified it was something else.

"Not that way." Booker made a face when he registered my reaction. "I'm not jealous because he has you. I'm jealous because he's so happy."

"Oh." Whew. That made me feel marginally better. "You know, if you would actually spend time with a woman instead of running over them with your libido you might have a chance at happiness, too."

He laughed and shook his head. "I never thought it was anything I would want. Now ... I'm not so sure. Galen and I spent years competing with one another for the attention of women. It was a game to us."

"I don't want to hear this."

He ignored me. "I thought we would keep up that game until we were forty and then maybe — *maybe* — settle down. Then you came to the island and ruined our game. He settled down so much faster than I ever envisioned that I didn't realize the game was over until he was already on to another game."

Part of me felt sorry for him. He and Galen could pretend they disliked one another and only worked together out of necessity, but I knew better. They were close ... just in a really odd way. They relied on each other despite the sniping. If one of them was ever in trouble, the other came running. They simply pretended that wasn't the case.

The other part figured he could get his head out of his behind and find a woman to be kind to instead of run over.

"You'll get over it." I shifted my gaze to the back of the cabin, where Galen talked on his phone and paced. He didn't look happy. "Do you know who he's talking to?"

"One of his deputies. Things are deteriorating at the beach."

I pressed my eyes shut. That's not what I wanted to hear. "How bad?"

"I don't know the specifics. I heard punches are starting to be thrown ... and talk of sexual harassment."

I jerked my head in his direction, my heart pounding. "What kind of sexual harassment?"

"The verbal variety," he reassured me quickly. "I don't think it's progressed beyond that ... yet."

I didn't like the way he tacked on the last word. "We can't let it go beyond that."

"I think that's the problem he's having. He doesn't have enough men to patrol the beach."

"No, but ... the island is full of paranormals. We're talking strong magical beings. Can't he call in a few favors? Together, we should be able to keep the festival-goers in line."

He stared at me for a long time, and I was sure he was going to laugh and make fun of me. Instead, he rested his hand on my shoulder and called out to Galen, who looked annoyed at being interrupted.

"I have an idea," he said. "Actually, your girlfriend gave me the idea. She might be a genius after all."

"Of course she's a genius," Galen barked back. "What's the idea?"

BY THE TIME WE GOT BACK TO TOWN IT was well past lunchtime. My stomach was growling but we headed straight to the festival. Galen had to rein in the out-of-control people threatening the balance on the beach, and he was utilizing Booker's plan to do it.

"You stay close to me," he ordered when we reached the parking lot. "Don't go wandering off. These people have been stranded here for days. They're bound to be wound tight ... and you might make an enticing target."

"Because I'm your girlfriend and they think they can use me for leverage?"

"The people who would take you for that reason are a concern, but I can handle them. It's the others I'm worried about."

It took me a moment to grasp what he was saying, and when I did, I swallowed hard. "I didn't consider that. I'll stick close."

"Good." He flicked his eyes to Booker. "You keep an eye on her, too."

"She'll be fine." Booker was calm to the point of being annoying. "Nothing will happen to her. I told you my plan was golden."

"We'll just see, won't we?"

Galen strode across the beach with purpose, not stopping until he was directly next to one of his deputies. He plucked the megaphone out of the man's hand and headed for the stage that had been erected in the center of everything. He was so tall, his strides so long, I had to scramble to keep up with him. All around me I heard people complaining ... and they noticed when Galen arrived. He wasn't easy to ignore.

"What's happening?" Bronwen asked from the left. She sat in the shade of an umbrella with her fellow witches, appearing casual for all intents and purposes, and seemed amused at the way I jolted. "Hello, Hadley."

"Is that the witch you mind-blocked?" Booker asked, flashing a smile for the woman's benefit but following Galen's edict at the same time and keeping me close.

I nodded. "I think she might want to hurt me."

"You've already proved you can take her. I wouldn't worry about it."

"What's happening?" Bronwen repeated.

I merely shrugged and hurried after Galen. I didn't want to miss his announcement. It was bound to be epic.

"Did you find Alastair?" Calliope asked when we arrived at the stage. She stood on the bottom step, all decked out in a performance costume, looking eager for a break. "Are you going to drag him in front of the crowd and let them tear him limb from limb?"

I frowned at the question. "I don't think that's the sort of message we want to send for the health of the tourist industry."

"Oh, honey, the tourist industry on this island is officially dead," Thalia interjected. She was also hiding in the shade, although her cheeks were red enough that I figured she'd inadvertently missed a few spots with the sunscreen. "Once word gets out about this ... ."

"Things will be fine," Booker finished, slowing his pace long enough to look her up and down. She wore an ankle-length black skirt, a matching peasant top and an ebony scarf over her hair. "You know, if you wore something lighter in color you wouldn't be sweating your balls off."

Thalia shot him a withering look. "You show me yours and I'll show you mine."

"Don't tempt me, honey."

I wrinkled my nose as I watched the exchange. "Do you like her?" I asked as we closed in on Galen. "I mean ... are you attracted to her?"

Booker shrugged. "She has a certain something. I don't know how to identify it."

"She's grim."

"She definitely is, but sometimes the grim girls are freaks in bed."

My stomach twisted at what he was insinuating. "You're really gross."

"You're just saying that because you and Galen aren't freaks. If you'd loosen up a little bit you might find it's not such a bad trait to embrace."

"I'll have to take your word for it," I said dryly.

Theo Rafferty, one of Galen's newer deputies, was waiting for him when he reached the top of the stairs. "Hello, sir. Thank you for coming."

Galen almost looked amused by the young man's reaction. Almost. "Of course I came. I'm sorry it took me so long to get here.

We were on the other side of the island." As if suddenly remembering me, he turned and searched faces until he found me. "Come up here, please."

I did as instructed, but only because I wasn't in the mood for a fight.

"Stay up here and you should be fine," he said before turning back to Theo. "What do you have to report?"

Ever efficient, Theo pulled out his notebook and started reading off a list of infractions. "One Douglas Stickney, forty-three, punched Eden Jessup, forty-eight, in the mouth."

Anger coursed through me. "He hit a woman?"

"Eden Jessup is a man, ma'am."

"Oh."

Galen offered me a stern look. "Are you okay with a man hitting another man?"

Violence in general was offensive. Still, I was ready to go to war when I thought Eden was a woman. I couldn't muster as much enthusiasm now. "I'm good. Well, other than him calling me ma'am. I'm too young to be a ma'am."

"Duly noted." He put his hand on my back as a steadying presence and turned back to his deputy. "Continue. If Hadley interrupts again, keep calling her ma'am."

Theo smirked as I rolled my eyes. "Sir. Madeline Johnson, twenty-seven, stole a sleeping bag from Tina Marsters, fifty-one, which resulted in Ms. Marsters pulling her hair and yanking out a weave track ... although I'm not sure what that means.

"Melody Fisher, nineteen, was caught underage drinking," he continued. "Dakota Tomlinson, twenty-three, was caught supplying her with the liquor while trying to entice her into his tent. Todd Banks and Colin Jorgensen intervened and gave him two black eyes — one each — because they thought Miss Fisher was a minor."

As he continued to drone on, I started looking for a place to sit because the heat was getting to me. Galen grabbed my arm before I could sit cross-legged on the stage and pinned me to his side.

And still Theo went on ... and on ... and on. I was about to start whining about the length of his speech when he finally wrapped things up.

"That's everything?" Galen asked.

"Oh, don't ask him that," I muttered.

"That's everything, sir," Theo replied, kicking his heels together in some sort of weird salute.

"Thank you for being so diligent." Galen's smile was kind as he gripped the megaphone and moved to the center of the stage. He looked official, annoyed, a little tired ... and altogether sexy. I liked seeing him in charge.

"Hello," he called out to get the crowd's attention, waiting until the chatter died down to continue. "My name is Galen Blackwood. I'm the sheriff of Moonstone Bay."

"Then perhaps you should arrest yourself," a male voice called out. "You're the reason we're suffering out here. You're the reason we're dying."

Galen maintained his cool veneer. "Did someone die? I must've missed that."

"Probably because you haven't been here," another voice called out, this one female. "I haven't seen you around since this started. It must be nice to have somewhere to go, out of this heat."

I wanted to stand up for him, yell at the woman to shut her mouth, but I knew he would frown upon that. He liked to appear professional, and a shrieking girlfriend was pretty far from professional.

"I care about what's happening here," Galen countered. "The thing is, this isn't the only thing happening on the island."

"So, you're saying we're not a priority?" Thalia called out. "That's ... lovely."

I pinned her with a dark look. "Aren't you one of the lucky ones with a hotel room?" I blurted out.

Thalia's eyes went wide as at least twenty sets of accusatory eyes lasered on her. "No. I ... no. Don't look at me," she barked at those staring. "We're suffering here and they're not doing a thing about it."

A murmur went through the crowd and I found myself excessively nervous.

"What would you have us do?" Galen asked reasonably, his voice echoing much louder than anything Thalia could manage thanks to the megaphone. "We didn't arrange this festival. That honor goes to Alastair Herne and Calliope."

At the bottom of the steps, Calliope hunched her shoulders and found something fascinating to stare at on the ground.

"They took your money, promised you something that didn't exist and created this fiasco," he continued. "I have no control over anything that's happened here. The island's political leaders are in the same boat. We're trying to clean up this mess, do the best we can, but we're in a pickle.

"The ship can't return to pick you up for days yet. We can't command a plane to land and take you away. All of our hotels are booked. We're doing the best that we can."

"So bring out Alastair Herne," another man called out. "If we can't beat you to a pulp, give us Herne."

"I wish I could do that. I honestly do. The thing is — and this is the reason I wasn't on the beach first thing this morning — he's dead."

A ripple went through the crowd, a low murmur, and — I swear this is true — I heard a hiss of hate. Were people actually acknowledging their delight that he was dead or was I simply hearing that in my head? I couldn't be sure, but the noise was enough to cause me to take an inadvertent step back.

I smacked into Booker as I was trying to tune out the noise. He slipped an arm around my shoulder to offer me a bit of solace. Worry etched across his handsome face and the look he pinned me with was quizzical.

"What's wrong?"

That was a very good question. "I don't ... ."

I heard it again. It sounded like a huge snake, the sort that you might find in a nightmare ... or a Harry Potter movie. Someone — or, rather, multiple someones — was enjoying the news regarding Alastair's death.

Good.

He had it coming.

If anyone deserved it, he was the guy.

I only wish I could've been there to help whoever did it.

I wonder who it was. Was it someone here?

They don't know it's me.

My eyes snapped open at the last voice as I searched the crowd, desperate to find a face to match the words. I couldn't ascertain if the voice was male or female ... and nobody looked as if they were relishing Alastair's death. On the outside, everyone was the picture of sadness and regret.

On the inside, though, there was something dark festering in the underbelly of one of these people.

"The killer is here," I murmured.

"What?" Booker's eyebrows hiked high. "What do you mean? Do you know who it is?"

I shook my head. "No, but ... I hear him – or her."

"How?"

"I don't know. I ... ."

The hissing started again, this time more intense. I heard overlapping voices in my head. It started as five, easily grew to twenty, and then I became overwhelmed when fifty voices joined the din.

They were going to fight. They were already out of hand. There was no way Galen would be able to rein them in.

I'm still not sure how it happened or how I knew it was going to happen, but my inner danger alarm pinged. It didn't warn me that trouble was coming in my direction, though. It screamed for me to help Galen.

I was already moving before the alarm finished sounding. I grabbed his arm and gave him a vicious yank away from the crowd. Surprise was reflected in his eyes, and then anger. I didn't care. I tugged with everything I had, put a little magic behind it, and managed to pull him to the ground.

A shot rang out. A huge hole had been blown into the stage directly where he'd stood talking to the crowd.

I could only see it for a moment, and then his arms went over my head as he plastered his body over mine as a shield.

"Shots fired! Shots fired!"

It was Theo yelling, and I wanted to shake him. Was he kidding? Could anyone not see that?

"Keep your head down," Galen ordered in my ear, his arm over my head. "The cavalry is coming."

"The cavalry is here," Booker countered. He was on his knees directly next to us, his eyes on the water. "Look out. Here they come."

I jerked my head out from under Galen's arm so I could see the sirens rushing from the water, spears in hand. There had to be at least one-hundred of them, and they were screaming orders, high-pitched demands ripping through the air.

We were plunged into absolute chaos.

TWENTY

*G*alen was heavy on my back and I heard him whispering that it was going to be okay. There was no fear coursing through me — something I would have to think about later. I was more curious than anything else. The second I removed Galen as a target, terror had been replaced by curiosity.

I wasn't certain that was necessarily a good thing.

"I want to see." I moved Galen's arm from around my head and peered out, my eyes going wide when I saw Aurora taking down two belligerent men. She had a spear in one hand. She used the blunt end to corral the festival-goers. There was some sort of shell in her other hand.

"What is that?"

"Hide your head," Galen ordered, trying to shove me under him again.

I was having none of that. "I'm fine." I continued to struggle with him. "The danger is gone."

Galen pulled back slightly to look me in the face, his expression reflecting bafflement. "What do you mean?"

"The danger is gone," I repeated. "I want to see what the sirens are doing."

"But ... ." He didn't continue to try to wrestle me down, instead rolling off and eyeing the crowd with overt disgust. He rubbed his chin, and when he turned back to me I saw something other than worry reflected back. "How do you know that?"

"Know what?" I was having trouble keeping up on the conversation, mostly because I was determined to see the sirens at work. They looked to be scarily efficient, and because they weren't coming after me I was amused.

"How do you know the danger is gone?" Booker queried, shifting closer to us.

I shrugged, noncommittal. "I don't know. I just know. The same way I knew that Galen was in trouble."

"And that's why you intervened." Booker turned his gaze to Galen. "She's getting strong fast. I think she saved your life. That means you'll have to dote on her all night. I see seafood and endless massages in her future."

Galen barked out a harsh laugh, but he didn't seem amused as much as awestruck. "I think you might be right," he said after a beat, his thumb grazing my cheek. "You saved me."

Until that very moment I hadn't really considered it. I only knew Galen was in trouble and acted accordingly. If I'd stopped to think about what could've happened before acting, things might've been very different. Fear could've very easily paralyzed me. It didn't, and we were safe. That was the only thing that mattered.

"You're okay, right?" I instinctively began checking him for wounds, my hands busy as they moved over his shoulders and back. "You didn't get winged, did you?"

"I'm okay." He grabbed my wrists to force me to stop feeling him up. "I'm okay. More importantly, you're okay."

"How is it that I'm more important?"

"Because I said so." He swooped in and gave me a quick kiss before shaking his head and turning to the ongoing melee. The sirens had made quick work of most of the problem attendees. There were only a few still being chased about. "I have to handle this."

"I'll go with you." I moved to dust off the seat of my shorts, but he stopped me with a firm head shake.

"Stay here with Booker," he insisted. "This is my job. You've already done yours."

"But ... ."

"No." He pressed his finger to my lips and offered up a rueful smile. "If you're a very good girl, I'll take you to whatever restaurant you want for dinner tonight and you can order eight pounds of crab legs. I just ... for now ... I need you to stay here with Booker. I can only worry about one thing at a time and you'll take precedence if you're out there."

He was being so reasonable all I could do was agree. "Okay, but I'm going to hold you to the crab legs thing."

"I have absolutely no doubt."

IT TOOK ALMOST TWO HOURS TO GET things under control at the beach. The sirens were efficient to the point of being freaky, but they were still woefully outnumbered by the festival attendees. Still, to their credit, they managed to subdue the crowd ... although the question about who fired the gun was still up in the air.

"Do you think it was our killer?" I asked Galen as we made our way into Lilac's bar. Despite his offer to take me to a fancy restaurant, I requested a place where I was comfortable instead. He seemed to understand my weariness and agreed, but promised to make the fancy dinner a reality at some point after our current crisis was handled.

"I honestly don't know." Galen's hand landed at the center of my back as he prodded me toward our favorite table. Before I could slide into my side of the booth and get comfortable, he wrapped his arms around me and tugged me close. "You did really well today."

I absorbed his warmth for a beat and then pulled back. "Was there ever any doubt?"

His eyes twinkled as he slipped a strand of my dark hair behind an ear. I'd caught a glimpse of my reflection in the mirror behind the bar as we entered and I looked as if I'd been trapped inside a wind tunnel a good portion of the day. I'd decided to embrace it as a purposeful fashion choice rather than fret about it.

"Let's just say that I've always known you could do impossible things," he said quietly. "You're developing so fast." He turned rueful. "Don't leave me behind as you rush forward. We're still a team."

I sensed this was a true moment of melancholy, so I wrapped my hands around his wrists and squeezed. "I can't leave you behind. You might think I'm leaping ahead right now, but I'm always trying to keep up with you. We're going to be okay."

"Yeah." He cupped my face and gave me a soft kiss before resting his forehead on mine. "It could've been a much different day. Things worked out, so I'm not going to dwell on it."

We remained like that for a full ten seconds, separating only when Lilac pushed her way between us and inclined her head toward the booth. "This is an eating establishment. If you guys plan on doing anything else, I'll need a special license ... which I don't have time to get."

Galen snorted and released my hand before sliding into his side of the booth. He looked tired, as if he could sleep for forty-eight hours straight, but he also looked exhilarated. Things were under control on the beach, which meant his biggest worry had been put to rest. On top of that, he was alive ... thanks to me. It was a good day all around.

"I saved Galen's life today," I announced as I got comfortable.

Lilac arched an eyebrow. "Oh, yeah? Is this some new sex game you guys have developed? If so, I'm not in the mood."

"No. I mean I *really* saved his life. Someone had a gun at the festival and was aiming it at him."

"Seriously?" Lilac's sunny blond hair looked to be a shade redder than normal, which gave me pause. "When did this happen?"

"Almost two hours ago," Galen replied, cocking his head to the side as he regarded her. I couldn't help but wonder if he saw the same thing I did. "How has your day been going?"

"It's sucked wide, but that's hardly important given what you guys have been through," Lilac countered, nudging me with her knee to get me to slide over so she could settle beside me. "Tell me what happened."

Galen did just that, relating everything in a calm and concise manner. When he was finished, Lilac was flabbergasted ... but not for the reasons I expected.

"You tapped the sirens?" She was incredulous. "How did that happen?"

"They're looking for money," Galen replied, his hand finding mine on top of the table. He was feeling tactile this afternoon, which was fine with me because I was feeling the same. What happened on the stage had the potential to plague me with nightmares, though I was hopeful I would be so exhausted I would simply drop off and be dead to the world.

"They're always looking for money," Lilac noted. "Still, you must've been pretty persuasive."

"I said they could use whatever means they felt necessary as long as nobody died. I also said that if they had to use deadly force I wouldn't hold it against them."

"So you were all over the place." Lilac snickered. "Wow. I can't believe the sirens are running the show."

"I think that's another reason they agreed to it," Galen admitted. "Booker came up with the idea. I was leery about it at first, but seeing the way they whipped that crowd into shape I'm thinking they can hold it together until the festival ends."

"Won't they be expensive?"

He nodded. "Yeah, but I have discretionary funds allocated from the DDA for emergency manpower. I get a set amount every year and rarely make a dent in it. This year, I'm digging in."

"Hey, you have to do what you have to do." Lilac flicked her eyes to me. "So you're the big hero. I bet that means you guys will be celebrating tonight."

"Actually, we're celebrating something else. We're moving in together."

Lilac's eyes widened. "No way. You really are having a big week."

I waited for her to say something else. When she didn't, I was naturally suspicious. "Aren't you going to comment about how fast we're moving? That seems to be the point of interest for everyone else."

"And by 'everyone else,' she means Booker," Galen drawled.

"Oh, ignore Booker." Lilac offered up a haphazard wave. "He's persnickety because he's at a crossroads in his life. He's feeling rootless and can't decide what he wants to do, so he makes everybody miserable in the process."

"I know," I said. "He mentioned that this morning. He said Galen was his touchstone and he always thought they would keep competing for women until they were in their forties and then settle down. The fact that Galen did it so fast is ruffling his feathers."

"He mentioned that?" Galen preened as he leaned back in his seat, his feet coming to rest on either side of mine. "That's ... awful. Did he sound jealous?"

I shot him a quelling look. "I don't think now is the time to focus on that."

"It's always the time to focus on that," Galen countered. "I've had a long day. I almost died. I should be able to get my jollies wherever I want."

He had a point. "Fine. Knock yourself out." I grabbed the specials menu from the center of the table and studied it. "I want a double order of the crab legs."

"Double?" Lilac's amusement was on full display. "Are you going to make Galen roll you out of here?"

"No, but I am going to make him pay."

Lilac looked to Galen for confirmation and he nodded. "Today, she gets whatever she wants. She swooped in like a baller and saved my life. I think, at the very least, that merits some crab legs."

"I wouldn't disagree." Lilac got to her feet on a sigh as several women in the back corner of the bar called out to her, demanding drinks. "Did I mention I hate witches?" she growled. "Present company excluded of course." Her expression turned apologetic, but only briefly. "These crazy bats can't get off my island fast enough."

This time I was certain that the red in Lilac's hair had ratcheted up a notch. I glanced to Galen to see if he noticed, but he simply offered a small shake of his head. The message was clear. Now was not the time to mention the phenomenon.

Once Lilac set off with the drink orders, Galen and I settled into comfortable silence. It was obvious we were both exhausted after a long day — both physically and emotionally — and it was nice to be with someone who didn't need constant entertainment.

Perhaps thinking the same thing, he flipped my hand over and tracked his fingers across the palm, his eyes briefly shutting. I smiled at the sensuous way his fingers roamed the lines on my hand and opened my mouth to suggest we get the crab legs to go. That's when I caught sight of a familiar face.

"Isn't that the medical examiner?"

Galen's eyes snapped open and he jerked his head in the direction I indicated. The man standing in the doorway looked as if he felt out of place, his eyes busy as they bounced between faces. When he finally caught sight of Galen, he straightened and waved ... and then headed in our direction.

"Ugh. I hope this doesn't take long," Galen muttered, squeezing my hand before releasing it.

He needed rest, I realized. He was putting on a good show, but the adrenaline burst from earlier was starting to flag. He was the sort of man who needed downtime to decompress, and I had no doubt that's what he was craving now. I would find a way to get it for him.

"Hey, Steve." He bobbed his head in greeting as the man arrived at the edge of our table. "I don't know if you guys have been properly introduced. Hadley Hunter, this is Steve West. He's one of the assistant pathologists at the medical examiner's office."

I smiled at him because it seemed the thing to do. "It's nice to meet you."

"You, too." Steve took a moment to look me up and down — I had no idea what he was thinking — and then grabbed a chair from a neighboring table so he could sit at the end without crowding us. He focused his full attention on Galen. "I have some news for you."

"Is this good or bad news?" Galen looked grim. "If it's bad news, you might want to hold off until tomorrow. It will be easier for me to absorb it then."

"I don't know that it's good or bad news. It's just news."

"Oh, well, lay it on me." He winked at me and tapped his feet on top of mine under the table. It was a companionable move, which I appreciated. I still felt the overwhelming urge to take care of him.

"We've managed to match the wounds on Salma Hershey's body to an athame," Steve started. "Before you ask, we're sure. There was an odd notch on the blade that made a distinctive mark."

Galen's forehead wrinkled. "You found the exact murder weapon? How?"

"We didn't find the exact murder weapon. Or, well, at least we don't think we have. The athame in question is sold at three different stores on the island. It's one of the kitschy pieces we sell to tourists."

"And they all have the same notch?" I asked.

Steve briefly glanced at me, not bothering to hide the momentary flash of annoyance. Still, he answered the question. "It's a product of the design."

"Do we know if the athame was purchased recently?" Galen asked.

"No. I don't have answers for you on that front. I figure that's your job."

Galen rolled his eyes and nodded, his hand going to the back of his neck to rub at the tension I was certain was pooling there. "Well, at least we know what sort of weapon to look for."

"I sent a photocopy of the athame to your email. There's more." Steve paused for dramatic effect. "The same athame that killed Salma Hershey was used to take out Alastair Herne ... and it looks as if the murders were committed within three hours of each other."

I did the math in my head. "That probably means Salma died on the beach first, maybe after she argued with Alastair. He took off because he knew people were about to find out about his duplicity, and someone must've followed him."

"That makes the most sense," Galen agreed. "Except for one thing."

"The sirens," I surmised. I'd been wondering about that myself. "How did someone get on their property without them noticing?"

"That's also your job to figure out," Steve said as he stood, his eyes briefly traveling to the group of witches in the corner. He seemed to like what he saw. "I need to get going. My wife has dinner waiting for me and she hates it when I'm late."

I gaped. "You're married?"

Steve didn't respond, instead waving to Galen and turning on his heel and stalking toward the door. He took the time to glance back at the witches ... twice ... before disappearing.

"I can't believe he's married and was checking out those women that way," I complained as Galen chuckled at my outrage. "I'm serious. If you ever check out women like that while we're together I'll tie something you're very fond of into a knot ... and, yeah, I'll let you use your imagination as to what that is."

Galen's smile never wavered. "I guess it's good that you're all I want, huh?"

I went warm all over. "Yeah."

He held my gaze for an extended beat. "How do you feel about getting the crab legs to go and eating at home?"

I was already moving to scramble out of the booth. "You read my mind."

"Funny how that happens, huh?"

TWENTY-ONE

Galen didn't last long once we got back to the lighthouse. He put up a good effort, and demanded romance before starting the second half of our day, but he passed out on the couch before he could follow through on any of it, including eating his late lunch.

I packed away the extra food for later, put a blanket over him while kissing his forehead and then escaped. I left a note so he wouldn't worry, but I knew he would be down for at least two hours. He slept hard, but always woke rejuvenated. I figured it was a shifter thing. Either way, the morning and afternoon excitement had taken it out of him and he needed quiet, so that's what I gave him.

I didn't have a specific destination in mind when I left the lighthouse. I considered heading back to the beach to see how the sirens were doing with festival security. I very much doubted things would get out of hand again quite so soon, so instead I headed toward June's hotel.

I had no idea what drew me there. My brain told me it was a bad idea because I was likely to run into Bronwen. Her group had scattered once the sirens had shown up, and I was fairly certain they had only one place to retreat to. I wasn't fearful of her as much as curious, though, and that was one of the reasons I set the hotel as my destination.

Bronwen was alone on the patio, a large book open on the table in front of her. She seemed intent, as if she was reading about one of life's great mysteries. I took the opportunity to study her, and found that despite everything that had happened I wanted to like her. It was an odd feeling.

"Don't just stand there and gape, Hadley," she said without looking up from the book. "It's rude ... though I don't think you're much bothered by that prospect."

I huffed out a sigh and shuffled my feet against the concrete. "How did you know I was here?"

"You have a certain presence. Also, you're casting a recognizable shadow."

Oh, well, so much for her using her witchy powers to detect me. "I guess I should get better at this spying thing, huh?" I offered her a smile when she finally looked up, and slipped into the chair across from her. "What are you doing?"

"Why don't you invade my mind like you usually do and find out?"

I wanted to act annoyed and argue with her, but she wasn't wrong. "I didn't mean to do that."

"Really?" Bronwen leaned back in her chair. In this light, I could see the fine lines in her face much better. She was much older than I'd originally guessed, although she'd preserved herself ridiculously well ... which I found intriguing.

"Really." I refused to back down. "It was an accident."

"You also need to work on your lying while you're practicing to be a better spy," she said dryly. "I don't believe a word of what you just said. You've already admitted you were playing a game on the docks, testing out your new powers. That's the reason I didn't slap you harder that afternoon. I understand about curiosity.

"What you did yesterday is completely different," she continued. "You went rooting around my head with an express purpose, though I've yet to figure out what that purpose was. I thought I had the upper hand and was going to teach you a lesson, but you thought otherwise ... and you turned out to be right."

"I don't think it's a case of right or wrong," I countered. "I just ... thought I saw something between you and June. It seemed weird and I went digging. I was wrong, but sometimes I can't stop myself from being an idiot."

Bronwen's lips curved into an easy smile. "I think we've all been there. Still, not everything in this world is your business."

"It is when I'm trying to find a murderer."

"And do you believe I'm a murderer?"

"Probably not, but I have no reason to rule you out. You had as much reason as anyone to hate Alastair. He stole your idea ... and apparently millions of dollars that could've been yours. That has to be a hard pill to swallow."

"And now that he's dead you think I somehow tracked him down and killed him? How did I manage that? When was he killed? Where? How? I might be able to help you rule me out as a suspect if I have access to more information."

"Fair enough. He died the night before you arrived on the island."

She cocked an amused eyebrow. "And you think I somehow managed to teleport here from the cruise ship and kill him? I think you're giving me more credit than I deserve."

"I don't know. Can witches teleport?"

"Not usually."

"Can they fly on brooms? That sounds kind of fun."

Her expression turned pinched. "You don't know anything about being a witch, do you?"

The question felt as if it should've been insulting, but I couldn't figure out exactly how. Still, I shifted on my chair, uncomfortable. "I ... well ... I know some things."

Her grin only widened. "What do you know?"

"I know that I cast a protection spell yesterday, but I'm still not sure how I did it. I know that at the festival earlier today there was a warning in my head telling me Galen was in danger and I reacted on instinct. I also know that I can feel power coursing through my veins.

"Intellectually, I know it must've been there before I moved to Moonstone Bay, but I think I would've noticed if it were, so I'm starting to wonder if the island is the key to my magic. I haven't brought that up to anyone, because I don't want to look like an idiot."

Bronwen's countenance was calm. "I asked June about you after that first day on the docks. I was curious enough to dig a little. She was reticent about sharing information, but she did mention that you weren't raised on the island and are a recent transplant."

"That's not really a secret."

"No, but it is interesting. You just said you believe the island gives you power. You're an adult, have been for a long time, and yet you're just coming into your magic now. I think it could be several different things, but you haven't asked so I'm leery of volunteering my opinion in case you take it the wrong way."

"Why would you be leery about that?"

"Because you're powerful enough to kill me if you choose. You wouldn't even have to get up from that chair to do it."

My mouth went dry. "What?"

"Oh, don't pretend you can't feel that magic zipping through your veins. You're cocky, but I guess you have a right to be. You're also fearful, but you go above and beyond to hide that."

"Now who is invading whose mind?" I grumbled, rubbing my forehead.

She chortled, delighted. "Oh, you're very funny. June has grown fond of you. I tend to trust her judgment, even if you do have a few rude characteristics."

"To be fair, I don't even know what's considered rude in the witch world," I admitted. "I feel as if I'm constantly behind and trying to catch up on that front."

"I wouldn't worry. You're already so far advanced compared to others of our kind that you're towering over us. Still, I understand what you're saying. Power without understanding is a terrifying thing. Have you considered asking your boyfriend?"

I shifted on the chair, suddenly anxious to look anywhere but her eyes. "Galen and I talk all the time."

"Not about this you don't. Why?"

"I don't know. We just ... don't. He's the sheriff. He usually has a lot on his plate."

"In a town the size of Moonstone Bay, I have my doubts. Still, I don't care what you say. He would want to help you any way that he can. I've seen the way he looks at you, and you him. Why is it, do you think, that your instincts took over and demanded you protect him this afternoon?"

That was a very good question. "I don't know. I just figured that it happened because he was in danger and I was meant to help. It probably would've happened with anyone."

She shook her head. "I don't believe that. Your bond with him is profound. You've known each other only a few months, so that's fairly impressive. You were alerted to the danger to him specifically. You weren't alerted to what was going to happen to Salma and Alastair, right? No. This was a unique situation and you acted accordingly."

"Yeah, well ... ." I rubbed my chin as the door to the hotel opened to allow June entrance to the patio. She carried a tray with a pitcher of iced tea on it. Her smile was warm and welcoming when she saw me.

"I thought I heard your voice, Hadley. I grabbed an extra glass just in case. I'm glad you stopped by. Bronwen informed me of what you did at the festival this afternoon. I'm quite impressed. You saved one of my boys, and I'll forever be thankful."

My cheeks colored under the praise. "I'm kind of fond of him, too. It wasn't a big deal ... how did you know about it?"

Bronwen smiled. "I was there. Remember?"

"Oh, right. Then why did you let me go on about it like an idiot?"

"Because you crack me up when you babble."

Well, that was good to know.

"It was a big deal," June countered, her eyes filling with concern as she looked me over. "What seems to be troubling you? I would've thought you and Galen would be sewed together this afternoon. Did something happen?"

"He's napping." I saw no reason to lie. "After we got away from the beach, his energy level dropped to almost nothing and he passed out on the couch five minutes after we got home. He had big plans to romance me and everything, but they never came to fruition."

June snorted out a laugh. "That's just like him. He was always a big napper, even as a kid. Booker gave him endless grief about it."

"I think Booker and Galen enjoy giving each other grief because that's how they express their friendship."

"Figured that out, have you?" June winked as she poured me a glass of iced tea. "Both those boys are big talkers. True, they've gotten into the occasional scrap. I maintain that if they'd been left to their own devices rather than pitted against one another as children they would be the best of friends now."

"What makes you think they aren't?" I was serious. "They're friends. They just pretend they aren't. When one of them needs something, they immediately go to the other. Sure, they both complain and cry about it, but they still do it. If that's not friendship, I don't know what is."

"That's a very good point. I'm glad Galen is getting the rest that he needs. I'm surprised you left him, though. Bronwen said you basically jumped in front of a bullet for him."

I shot the witch in question a dubious look. "Um ... no. That's not what happened at all. I sensed trouble and dragged him to the ground, where he proceeded to roll on top of me and cover my head like I was a small child."

"You can't fault his instincts," June chided. "He loves you. He did the only thing he could think to do."

"And I did the only thing I could do. We're figuring things out. On the personal front, despite a few arguments here and there, we're good. It's the witchy front that I'm doubtful on, as your friend has figured out."

"She was trying to get inside my head because she sensed we were keeping something from her yesterday," Bronwen volunteered, her gaze pointed. "She's the curious sort and went digging for information. Unfortunately, she thinks what we're hiding has to do with Alastair's death."

The chuckle June let loose was dry. "Oh, you're hilarious, Hadley.

You should've just asked instead of invading her head. I would've told you."

"Told me what?" I was practically salivating at the notion that a secret was about to be revealed. "What's the big deal? Are you two working together? Oh, geez, June, you didn't kill Alastair, did you? I know you think he's a jerk, but Galen won't appreciate having to cover up a murder for you."

June's lips quirked as she shook her head. "We haven't committed a murder. Er, well, at least not together. We've been separated for a few years, so I guess anything is possible where she's concerned."

Bronwen snorted. "Nice. I'm glad to hear you have such a high opinion of me."

I narrowed my eyes as I watched their interaction. Something was definitely off about the way they conversed. If I didn't know better ... . Realization dawned on me. "You guys are a couple."

June's eyes sparked with mirth at my surprise. "It took you long enough to figure it out, though I don't know that I would say we're a couple. It's more that we used to be a couple and we're debating whether we want to be a couple again."

I was dumbfounded. "But ... you're so much older than her."

The merriment leaked out of June's eyes. "I'm not that old. I still have a lot of life left to live."

"And she's not that much older than me," Bronwen added. "Ten years is nothing in the grand scheme of things."

I tossed the idea around in my head ... and then started shaking it. "No, I'm sorry. You must be at least twenty years apart ... and forty is a better estimation. I mean, I don't want to be insulting or anything, but you looked a good ten years younger the other day on the docks. It must've been a trick of the lighting. I thought you were in your twenties that day. Now, though, you can't be out of your forties."

"I'm in my late sixties," Bronwen countered.

"You are not."

"But I am."

"No way." I looked to June for answers. "She's just messing with me, right?"

197

June hesitated, unsure how to answer. Ultimately, Bronwen did it for her.

"It's glamour," Bronwen explained, waving her hand over her face. When it passed by a second time, I gasped because the woman sitting before me looked nothing like the one I'd been introduced to. The lines I'd seen in her face were ten times more pronounced and there were wisps of gray in her eyebrows.

"I don't understand." My voice raspy. "How did you manage this?"

"Bronwen and I have known each other for thirty years," June explained. "We dated for a time, but she wanted to see the world and wasn't content staying on Moonstone Bay. I could never leave my father's hotel. You know that. We went our separate ways without bitter feelings.

"Through the years, we've spent time together, but usually only a few weeks here or there," she continued. "One of the reasons Bronwen wanted to stay at my hotel on this trip is because she's thinking of making a move back. A permanent move back. We're trying to ... figure things out."

I had so many questions. "You said you had a crush on Wesley." My tone was accusatory. "You said that, like, three days ago. How can you have a crush on Wesley — something I brought up to May because I wanted to work it out — if you're a lesbian?"

Instead of being offended by the question, June let out a hearty laugh. "I'm more than one thing. I like both men and women. It's simply who I am. That said, you shouldn't have gone after your grandmother that way. She and Wesley are soul mates. They belong together. He was never going to leave her, despite her being a ghost, and you put her in an awkward position."

I frowned. "I was just trying to help."

"I know you were, my dear." She patted my hand in a conciliatory manner. "The thing is, your grandfather's love life is none of your concern. My love life isn't either. You'll have to worry about your own love life and stay out of the business of others if you hope to have a chance on this island."

"Whatever." I was feeling grouchy. "I still can't believe I didn't realize you were bi-sexual ... or however it is you refer to yourself." Something niggled at the back of my brain. "Galen knows, doesn't he?"

"It's not exactly a secret."

"Does he know about your relationship with Bronwen?"

June hesitated before answering. "I don't believe so. She visited a few times when he and Booker were children, but I was careful to keep them separate from my personal life. It's not that I was embarrassed or anything, mind you, but they both had difficult mothers and I didn't want to encourage either of those women to limit my access to their sons. Those boys needed a steadying influence, and that's what I provided."

I couldn't argue with that. "Yeah, well ... ." I pursed my lips and glanced between their faces. Bronwen now looked like the woman I'd seen on the docks, her glamour firmly in place. "I forgive you from hiding it from me." I rubbed my hands together and focused on Bronwen. "As payment, I want to learn to do that."

"It took me a very long time to perfect," she countered. "It's a skill you can't learn in one day."

"Just teach me the basics ... and tell me why you do it. I mean, I can see changing your appearance because you're on a covert mission and want to hide your identity, but ... long haul? It has to be exhausting to keep it up for hours upon hours, day after day."

"It *is* exhausting," Bronwen agreed. "Why do you think I'm considering moving back here? I want a chance at a relaxing life again, and this is the best place I know to get it. As for why I do it, vanity and money. I give paying customers the face they expect to see. It all depends on them."

Ah, well, that made sense. "It's still a cool trick. Show me."

"Okay, but you need to practice before you take it out for a test drive. That's very important."

"Sure." I waved my hand impatiently. "What do I have to do?"

TWENTY-TWO

I spent an hour under Bronwen's tutelage. She wasn't always patient. She snapped at me a few times for getting ahead of myself, and when the glamours I tried turned out to be abject failures, I realized she was right. I enjoyed rushing headlong into things and despised taking the time to learn them properly. That was something I would have to get over.

I hadn't heard from Galen, so I figured he was still sleeping. His injuries weeks ago had healed quickly, but I'd wondered if they would eventually catch up with him. He talked big, puffed out his chest and flexed his muscles, but he was still human. I figured the sleep would do him good.

It left me with nothing to do and nowhere to go. If I returned to the lighthouse, I would wake him. He wouldn't allow himself to fall asleep a second time. That meant I had to find something else to do with my time, and it was only when I was passing in front of Lilac's bar that I got an idea.

"Do you want to go on a spying mission with me?" I wasted little time and launched straight into my spiel when I caught her at the bar. "You've been living here the past few days and need a break — the red roots of your hair agree — and I think some fresh air would do you good."

Lilac continued shaking a martini as she eyed me. "You want to spy on someone? Who?"

"The people on the beach."

"Why? They're all miserable. I should know. I've been waiting on them for days."

"I don't think they're all miserable. I'm sure a lot of them are. One of those miserable people took a shot at my boyfriend today. I would like to figure out which one."

"Can we kill him or her when we discover the culprit?"

I was uncomfortable with the bloodthirsty question. "I was kind of thinking we would just hand him over to Galen."

"Wuss." She barked out the single word, but her expression had lightened a bit. "You know what? I think that's a fabulous idea. Let me finish this order and tell the other bartenders we're heading out."

"Great. It won't be an issue if you leave them alone, will it?" I didn't want to be responsible for Lilac's business falling apart because I was bored.

"They're professionals and I pay them well. They can handle it. Give me five minutes."

TRUE TO HER WORD, LILAC AND I WERE on the sidewalk and heading to the beach within the promised five minutes. She sucked in an extended breath the second we were outside, and I could tell she was trying to calm herself.

"I'm guessing you've had it up to here with witches?"

"Not all witches," she countered. "I don't hate you or anything. I just ... big groups of them have always made me nervous."

"Is that a demon thing?"

She held out her hands and shrugged. "I don't know. Maybe. I think it's more that I don't like it when people are plotting against me because of what I am. I get the feeling that all the people visiting this island are plotting against me."

"That's kind of paranoid."

"Yeah. I can't help it. They make my skin crawl."

A quick look at her profile told me she wasn't exaggerating. "Why do you think that is? And ... wait ... I don't make your skin crawl, do I?"

The look she shot me was full of annoyance. "Would I be spending time with you — voluntarily, I might add — if you made my skin crawl?"

"Probably not, but you're a nice person. You don't like to upset people unless they've really got it coming. I could see you trying to spare my feelings."

She snorted. "You aren't the sort who would want her feelings spared and I'm not the type of person who wants a friendship built on lies." She shot me a reassuring look. "We're solid, Hadley. You don't have to worry about that."

"Good." I was relieved. "You're kind of my best friend on the island, so that would've been a total bummer."

She snickered and shook her head. "You're kind of my best friend, too."

We lapsed into amiable silence. She was the first to break it.

"How are things with Galen? You guys moving in together is a big step. Are you excited?"

"I think it's going to be good. But Booker kind of irritated me when he said that it was fast."

"I told you to ignore Booker. He's not a good judge of relationships. Besides, I think he's going through an existential life crisis or something."

"Oh, yeah?" I was amused at the prospect.

"He and his mother aren't speaking right now because of what happened with the cupids. I think he told himself he always wanted that, but the reality is more difficult for him to deal with than he envisioned. He doesn't have Galen to annoy and he's not keen on making new friends. I think there was a hot minute when he considered pursuing you because you're not attracted to him simply because of those cupid pheromones, but he realizes that's a lost cause. You and

Galen bonded so quickly that it was over before anyone else got a chance to stick a toe in the water."

And that right there was one of the things bothering me. "Do you think we bonded too fast? I mean ... do you think the way things are between us burns too bright to last for a long time? I'm a little worried he's going to lose interest in a few weeks or something."

She slowed her pace. "Are you really worried about that?"

"Do you think I'm being ridiculous?"

"Um ... yeah. Galen is over the moon for you. That won't change. You obviously feel the same way about him. There's no rule about how fast people should fall in love. Sometimes you just know."

I cast her a sidelong look. "What about you? Do you want to find someone to be with?"

She bobbed her head without hesitation. "Absolutely. But finding someone to put up with this isn't easy." She gestured toward her hair, which looked redder than normal under the sun. "The truth is, ever since I unleashed my demon powers to help protect the reapers I've been having a bit more trouble reining them back in."

That was news to me, though in hindsight it really shouldn't have been. Her hair had been vacillating between red and blond for weeks and I'd been a little worried ... and also a little too nervous to question her on it. I was a witch, somehow powerful even though I wasn't sure how I'd gotten there. Her demon powers were a sight to behold, though, and I had no doubt she could take me out if she put her mind to it.

"Is there anything I can do to help?"

"I just need a stretch of quiet time. On this island, though, that doesn't seem to be a possibility lately." Her gaze drifted to the bodies milling on the beach. "I just hate those stupid witches."

I tried to contain my laughter ... and failed miserably. I was laughing so hard by the time that Aurora joined us that I had to struggle to catch my breath.

"Do I even want to know what you guys find so funny?" the siren asked as she glanced between us, her gaze lingering on Lilac's hair. "Who pissed you off?"

"She hates witches," I volunteered as I recovered, rubbing my hands over my shorts and straightening. "She wants to kill them all."

"You and me both," Aurora lamented. "These idiots ... well ... you would think after the tenth time I prod you with a spear that you would stop doing the stupid thing that made me prod you. Not so with these people."

The words had a sobering effect on me. "How are things? You haven't found anyone trying to hide a gun, have you?"

Aurora shook her head. "No, and we've been looking. What happened earlier was ... ugly. Right now, we're keeping up constant patrols. If we see a group that looks like it's going to get out of hand we immediately go over and break them up. It seems to be working so far."

"But how long can you keep it up?"

Aurora shrugged. "We've split up into groups so we can take shifts. We should be okay for a few days. Galen said he'd have everyone off the island before that's an issue."

Which brought up another problem. "Once these people are allowed to leave we'll lose our shot at catching a killer. Galen will deny it, of course, say we'll continue pushing, but he knows as well as I do that his chances are pretty much nil once we lose track of these people."

"Do you have any firm suspects?" Aurora challenged. "I mean ... it was my understanding that you believed Alastair was guilty of killing Salma, which is why you tracked him to Cooper's Hollow. He's been dead almost as long, though, which means you have no suspects."

"That's true. I'm more interested in how someone managed to cross your boundaries without you knowing, kill a man, and then sneak away without anyone seeing as much as the hint of a shadow. What's up with that?"

Aurora's eyes darkened. "I don't know, but Cordelia isn't happy. She's demanding a committee investigate how it went down. Someone will pay for that mistake. There should be no way someone can cross our borders without us knowing."

"Even if they came in from the ocean?"

"Especially if they came in from that direction. We know the water better than anyone. We would've known if someone was in it."

"Then ... whoever it was had to approach by land, and it's a haul to get out there. It seems to me you would've heard a vehicle, even if they parked down the road a bit. There are no lights and yet you couldn't see without having headlights on. Someone should've seen something."

"Are you suggesting we have a mole in our group?" Aurora looked distinctly uncomfortable at the prospect. "How would that even occur? It's not like our people hang out in Moonstone Bay to make friends with a killer."

"You're in Moonstone Bay quite a bit," I argued, realizing my mistake too late. "Not that I think you're a killer or anything. I mean ... you're definitely not a killer. I was suggesting that perhaps one of your people manages to get into town more often than you realize. I don't think you're a killer."

"Stop babbling, Hadley," Aurora ordered, earning a perfunctory head bob from me. "I know you don't think that I'm a killer, though I have killed multiple times. I simply haven't done it in this fashion. As for someone managing to get into town without anyone noticing, I have my doubts. As you said, I'm in town all the time, and Cordelia never has trouble finding out about my trips."

"Does she get angry at you for them?"

Aurora's shrug was noncommittal. "Cordelia is a woman trying to keep a dying community together."

I was taken aback. "What do you mean? How are you dying?"

"Not in the literal sense," she replied on a dry chuckle. "We're simply at a crossroads. Those who prefer a new way of living now outnumber those who enjoy the old ways. Cordelia is hanging on by her fingernails. They will snap eventually."

"What will you do when it happens?"

"Figure things out, as I always do." Aurora's eyes narrowed and fixed on a spot over my shoulder. "Do you know them?"

I looked behind me, frowning when I caught sight of Luster and Thalia. They stood together under a large palm tree, their heads bent together. "Yeah. They're two of the witches that Alastair paid to be here. Supposedly they realized that things were going to go south but had no choice to attend if they wanted the money Alastair promised."

"I very much doubt they'll get that money now," Aurora noted, straightening when she realized the witches were heading in our direction. "I wonder what they want."

"I don't know, but I'll do the talking." I laughed at myself when I realized what I'd said. "Maybe Galen and I are spending a little too much time together."

"You're fine." Lilac planted her hands on her hips as she stared at Thalia. "She was in my bar yesterday, and she wasn't pleasant. I don't like her." Lilac's hair darkened, causing me to take an inadvertent step back. She wasn't kidding when she said she didn't like the witches. Perhaps it was a bad idea to bring her here after all.

"I've got this." I strode forward and fixed Thalia with what I hoped was a pleasant look. "I see you still have your head. You must not have ticked off the sirens too badly."

The look she shot back was withering. "Where is your boyfriend?"

"He's otherwise detained. Is there something I can help you with?"

"I seriously doubt it," Thalia replied with a sneer. "As far as I can tell, you're not good for anything. I want to talk to the sheriff. Now ... where is he?"

My temper ratcheted up a notch. "He has other things to deal with. The sirens are in charge out here now. If you have a problem, take it up with them."

"Or keep your mouth shut," Aurora countered, smirking when Thalia gave her some serious side-eye.

"Did you find out where the sheriff is?" Luster asked as she joined the group. As usual, she looked absolutely clueless. "My skin is starting to chafe under this sun. We need to find him."

"She says he's otherwise engaged," Thalia replied, jabbing a judgmental finger at me. "I think she's full of it. She just doesn't want us to spend time with him because she's territorial."

"He is all kinds of yummy," Luster enthused. "Do you think he's taken?"

Thalia pinned her with a hateful glare. "This is why we don't spend more time together. You always ask why I can't stand you. This is why." She threw up her hands. "Did I not just refer to the sheriff as her boyfriend? That means he's with her."

"Oh." It took Luster longer than it should've to catch up. "I didn't even think about that. I guess it makes sense. That's why they've been holding hands a few of the times I talked to them."

"And probably why he rolled on top of her to keep her from being hit by a stray bullet," Thalia added.

"I don't know." Luster's gaze was keen as it roamed my face. "I don't think she's his type."

Lilac cleared her throat. "How do you know what his type is?"

"Because I've seen him. He's so dark that he would look better with a blonde. Like me." She smiled serenely. "Do you know where he is, by the way? We really need to talk to him."

I ran my tongue over my teeth to refrain from saying anything biting. While I debated how to respond, Lilac jumped in.

"She already told you that he's busy doing other stuff," the demonic bartender snapped, her temper on full display. "Do you not understand the meaning of those words? He's not here. If you have a problem, take it up with the sirens."

"Why don't you mind your own business?" Thalia suggested, attitude on full display. "This has nothing to do with you. When we need a watered-down drink we know who to call."

"My drinks are not watered down," Lilac hissed.

"Please. That gin and tonic I ordered was eight bucks and it was all ice and tonic. You run a scam at that bar of yours, lady, and you should be ashamed of yourself. In fact ... ." Thalia didn't get a chance to finish what she was going to say.

Lilac's hair turned a violent shade of red a split instant before her hand ignited in blue flames. She was reaching for Thalia's throat when I reacted, putting my hands up and grabbing her wrist to keep it away from the wide-eyed witch as Lilac began muttering.

"What the heck?" Luster squeaked and scurried to leave.

Thalia remained rooted to her spot.

"My drinks are not watered down," Lilac snapped. "And I've had it with you stupid witches." Her other hand glowed hot with blue flames that she pointed directly at Thalia.

I reacted out of instinct, calling on my own magic and pointing it at her wrists. The power I called careened into Lilac's wrists, forcing them up so the bolt of deadly fire that she sent toward Thalia soared over the woman's head and landed sizzling in the water about thirty feet away.

For a moment I was relieved. It was over and everybody was safe.

Then I risked a glance at Lilac and found her glowering at me ... and I realized we were nowhere near done.

"You shouldn't have done that," Aurora cackled. "Now she's going to kill you."

TWENTY-THREE

*L*ilac's eyes were pits of molten lava.

I swallowed hard and took a deliberate step away from her.

There was a moment when it felt as if we were in a movie and Lilac was creating her own wind tunnel, the strands of usually blond hair going crimson as they whipped about without help from the outside elements.

Then, she took a deliberate breath and exhaled heavily, her hair tone drifting down. Her roots were still red, but I sensed the immediate urgency had passed.

"What were you thinking?" Aurora asked in a low voice.

I found she was staring at me.

"What do you mean?" I balked. "I was saving Thalia."

For her part, the grim witch had distanced herself from our trio and was trying to make herself small behind some palm trees. She kept darting her head out to stare in our direction and then tucking it back in when she made eye contact with one of us. I didn't blame her for being afraid. Lilac's temper was a thing to behold.

"You shouldn't have gotten between her and Lilac," Aurora chided. "Don't you understand that Lilac could've incinerated you?"

I spared a glance for the normally amiable bartender and found her staring at the sand, clenching and unclenching her hands, and sucking in even breaths. It was clearly a calming technique.

"She wouldn't have hurt me," I said finally. Even though Lilac was clearly struggling, I believed that to be true. "This is my fault. I shouldn't have dragged her out here. She told me she was fed up with the witches."

"Then you definitely should've left her alone," Aurora agreed. Her gaze was curious as she looked Lilac up and down. "You look better."

Lilac let loose a hollow laugh. "Than what?" Her voice was shaky but I was relieved to hear the familiar humor rippling under the surface.

"Than you did right before it happened," Aurora replied bluntly. "It was clear you were going to go there in those last seconds. Your face and hair turned red, your eyes did that lizard thing they're prone to when you lose it. The only thing you were missing was a tail and horns."

I was taken aback. "Wait ... she has a tail and horns?"

Aurora bobbed her head. "They only come out right before she goes nuclear. I've seen them twice ... and never seen the people she was talking to at the time she lost it ever again. It's fun."

Lilac made an exasperated sound deep in her throat. "Don't listen to her. She's messing with you."

I narrowed my eyes and glared at Aurora. "Are you seriously messing with me?"

She snorted. "Yes, because you're an easy mark. It's often impossible for me not to mess with you."

"I don't have horns and a tail," Lilac replied calmly. This time when she stretched out her hands they stayed that way. "The eyes do go lizard-like, though. I'm not sure why. I guess because the original demons were more serpentine."

I tried to picture that. "That's kind of freaky, huh?"

"Yeah." She licked her lips and slowly lifted her eyes to hold mine. There wasn't a hint of lizard in them now. "I'm sorry."

"You don't have to apologize." I meant it. "I just ... I was worried. I thought you might set her on fire. If that happened, I would either have to lie to Galen or watch you go to jail ... and I'm pretty sure I'm incapable of lying to Galen."

"You just need to practice more," Aurora countered, patting my arm. "You're probably good at it and simply don't realize it."

I stared at her for a long moment. "When was the last time you had a significant other?"

She pursed her lips, considering. "What year is it again?"

I arched an eyebrow and turned back to Lilac. "It's really okay. I wasn't afraid."

"You should've been." Lilac was matter-of-fact. "Seriously, you should've been afraid. I could've hurt you, Hadley."

I opened my mouth to reassure her that I wasn't afraid of that possibility, but my attention was drawn by a flurry of activity. Striding in our direction from the parking lot was Galen. His hair was a mess from his nap and his eyes were clouded with fury.

"He doesn't look happy," Aurora noted. "Perhaps I should ... ." She moved to skedaddle in the opposite direction, but a stern finger from Galen stopped her in her tracks.

"Don't even think about it," he warned, not stopping until he was directly in front of me. His gaze was keen as he looked me up and down. "Are you okay?"

I nodded dumbly. "Why? What have you heard?"

He scowled. "I'm going to give you a quick hug because I was worried, and then we're going to get to business. Part of that business is going to include me yelling at you."

I should've seen that coming. "Before you even consider that, you should know that I was never in any danger."

Aurora snorted. "I thought you said you couldn't lie to him."

Galen's eyes darkened. "I want someone to tell me the entire story. I don't want embellishments. I don't want smoothed edges. I want to know exactly what happened."

I opened my mouth to respond, but he extended a warning finger. "Not you."

"Then how about me?" Thalia volunteered, stepping from behind the trees. Apparently she had found her courage ... now that the sheriff had shown up to lambast us all.

"And what do you have to do with this?" Galen asked blankly.

"I'm the witch who was attacked for no good reason."

I rolled my eyes and growled. "No good reason? You verbally assaulted my boyfriend and talked down to Lilac. You're lucky your entrails are still on the inside at this point."

"She's not wrong," Aurora said cheerfully as she took one of the abandoned canvas chairs to our left. The people who had been sitting in them before Lilac lost her temper disappeared pretty quickly in the aftermath of the argument.

Galen shot the oddly exuberant siren a quelling look. "I know you get off on it when people jump headfirst into fights, but this is not the time."

Aurora's response was an extended tongue and loud raspberry. "You're not the boss of me."

"You're on my payroll, which makes me the boss of you."

Aurora looked as if she was going to argue the point, but snapped her mouth shut and opted to study the end of her spear. Galen kept his eyes on her for an extended beat and then turned to me.

"Here comes your hug." He pulled me close, burying his face in my hair for a moment and inhaling deeply. It was a nice moment. Then he pushed me back and his eyes filled with icy anger. "Why did you leave the lighthouse?"

That wasn't the question I was expecting. "Why does that matter?"

"Because I thought you were with me." He looked angrier than I expected. "I didn't mean to fall asleep."

His reaction was enough to set my teeth on edge. "You needed the rest. I ... ."

"Hold up." Thalia was obviously feeling bolder. She was all brashness and bossiness when she stepped forward. "You said he was busy with work, that he was investigating murders. That was apparently a lie."

Uh-oh. I pressed my lips together and sent a silent apology to Galen.

"She said he was otherwise engaged and he was," Aurora shot back. "Why must you be so difficult? What does it matter if he took two hours' downtime? The guy has been working his tail off for you people since this entire mess started. Give him a break."

"He's the sheriff." Thalia refused to let it go. "He's supposed to be handling this situation, not sleeping on the job."

Luster, who had decided to join the party, cleared her throat to garner attention. "If you're tired, you should try some homeopathic sleep remedies. I have a few if you're interested. They're guaranteed to knock you out for eight hours and have you rising without any ill effects."

"I'm good," Galen said dryly. "Thanks, though. As for you ... ." His expression was hard to read when he pinned Thalia with a look. "If you have trouble with the way I'm handling things you're more than welcome to take it up with the township board."

Aurora and Lilac made twin sounds of delight at the prospect, causing Thalia's eyes to darken.

"I don't think it's unreasonable to demand movement on this situation," Thalia countered, readjusting her tone and planting her hands on her hips. "You guys act as if you're the injured parties here, but we're the ones who were lied to and stolen from."

She wasn't wrong, but her attitude bothered me. "You're staying at one of the hotels," I reminded her. "You seem to be better off than the people stuck on this beach. Why are you the one speaking for them? You're not exactly suffering."

I was gratified when a low murmur went through the crowd.

"She has a point," a voice said. It was hard to tell if it was male or female. "Why is she getting us all riled up when she doesn't even have a tent out here?"

The look Thalia shot me was full of venom, which made me want to crow. I wisely held it together.

"None of this matters." Galen's voice was strong as it lifted over the group. "We didn't plan for this to happen. The individual who set the wheels in motion on this is dead. We don't know what happened to him — or Salma, for that matter — but we're chasing leads."

"You mean you're napping," Thalia groused.

I scorched her with a glare right out of Lilac's demon playbook. "I just saved your life not ten minutes ago. You might not want to repay that kindness in this way."

"Hadley, it's fine," Galen offered, absently waving his hand. "I've had worse accusations thrown at me over the years ... and I was taking a nap."

A nap he desperately needed. Even though he'd been dragged to a witch fight in the middle of the beach, probably getting woken in the process before he was ready, he had more color to his cheeks and his eyes were more alert. That was a win in my book.

"You needed the nap." I was insistent. "It's been a long day and you didn't sleep all that well last night."

"Neither did you, but you didn't nap with me," he pointed out. "Why is that? I was worried when I woke up and you weren't there."

"I left a note," I protested.

"Which I found on my way out, after I'd already gotten a call to wake me up."

I was confused. "A call about me? If so, you made it here in record time."

"Actually, the call wasn't about you. Once I realized you were gone, I knew exactly where you'd headed."

"You know that Lilac almost killed her, right?" Aurora asked. "She almost liquefied her right here on the beach."

Lilac made a choking sound as I glared at the amused siren.

"She didn't almost kill me," I countered, heaving out a weighty sigh. "Stop saying that. You'll give her a complex."

"I already have a complex." To my utter surprise, Lilac was calm. Where I expected to find apology, I found relaxation ... that had apparently taken over when I wasn't looking. "I did lose my temper. I've been living on the edge for days. It was only a matter of time ... and Aurora is right that I shouldn't have come down here with you.

"The good news is, I blew my stack and nobody died," she continued, amusement lighting her features. "That might not have always been a possibility. It was today because Hadley intervened. The mouthy and pouty witch is still alive — although I'm not certain anyone would miss her if she was gone — and we're right back where we started. Nobody was harmed, so no crime was committed."

Galen's eyebrows drew together. "Wait ... I think I'm missing part of the story. When I was arriving in the parking lot I was told Hadley saved one witch from being attacked by another. Are you saying you were the attacking witch?"

"I'm not a witch, but I was the one ready to attack." Lilac turned sheepish. "I can't help it. These witches have been driving me crazy."

"I'm with you there." Galen's hand was heavy on my back. "That doesn't mean you can attack them for no reason."

"I know that."

"She didn't really attack them," I interjected. "It's more that she ... vented." I thought about it a second and immediately warmed to the idea. "Yeah, she vented. It's like walking into a room and screaming out your frustration. It's a good coping mechanism."

"Oh, yeah?" Galen studied my face for a moment, and even though he was clearly determined to stay angry I was convinced his lips wanted to curve into a smile.

I nodded, solemn. "I recommend venting as often as possible."

"Then I guess we have that to look forward to later tonight," he said. "I'm going to vent all over you."

That wasn't exactly my idea of a good time, but it was better than the alternative. "Fine. Are we done here?"

"No." He was incredulous. "I need to issue some warnings. First, you can't vent on the witches, Lilac. If you need to vent, take it some-place private and attack the trees or something."

Lilac nodded without hesitation. "For the record, I feel ten times better now that I've vented. You have absolutely nothing to worry about."

"I'm thrilled that's the case." He turned his eyes to Thalia. "What-ever problem you need solved, take it up with the sirens. May I suggest this one right here?" He patted Aurora's shoulder and earned a dark glare for his efforts. "I think she'd be a good sounding board for you."

"I need someone with actual power in this town," Thalia countered. "You're the sheriff. You're at the top of the food chain."

"Oddly, that's not the case. Either way, I have two murders to worry about. Your wants and needs are secondary. If you need help, there are sirens and deputies on this beach at all times. Go to them."

"But ... ."

"No." Galen shook his finger. "I really do have more important things to deal with." He swiveled to face me. "Which brings me to you."

The words were spoken with humor, but they sent a chill down my spine. "I'm not going to apologize for leaving," I insisted. "You needed to rest and I was keyed up. I knew if I stayed that my energy would wake you, and that's not what was best for you. I refuse to apologize."

"Besides," Lilac added. "She's an adult. I think she's allowed to leave the house whenever she feels like it."

"Not when there's a murderer on the loose," Galen countered. "I want her to be safe, and I refuse to apologize for that."

"Then I guess you'll have to come to a compromise," Lilac said. "Like, for example, Hadley can make an effort to understand that Galen is only a bossy brute because he loves her. Galen can make an effort to understand that Hadley is a curious soul who can't always control her impulses. If you put your heads together, I'm sure you'll come up with something."

"Thank you for acting as our therapist," Galen said dryly, shaking his head and focusing on me. "I'm not angry. Well, I'm not angry with you. Not really. You didn't do anything."

"If you're not angry with me, who are you angry with?" I was genuinely curious. "Is it Thalia? She's still standing over there staring. You can vent on her if you want ... but not in a sexy way."

This time he couldn't stop himself from grinning. "I'll keep that in mind." He leaned over and pressed a hard kiss to my forehead. "I'm angry with myself. I don't know why I passed out that way. I'm usually more aware of my surroundings. I was so out of it someone could've come into the lighthouse and taken you right out from under my nose and I wouldn't even have stirred."

I pressed my hand to his forehead. "You're not warm."

"No," he agreed. "I'm still building up my stamina since ... well, since the cupids." He turned acquiescent when my eyes narrowed. "Don't give me grief. I've felt mostly fine since then. I've been a little more tired than usual, but once the full moon hits and I shift, I swear I'll be good as new. You don't have to get worked up."

I wasn't so certain. "I'm going to vent all over you later. You're supposed to tell me when you're sick. I think that should be one of those rules that can't be broken."

"I'm not sick. I'm just ... a little tired."

"Is that like being a little pregnant?" Aurora queried. "I'm just asking for a friend."

"I'm fine," he reassured me. "I feel a lot better after the nap, recharged even."

"That's good, but we're still going to talk," I argued. "You have to tell me when something is wrong."

"Fine. Then you have to tell me when you're sneaking out of the lighthouse, but only if there's a murderer on the loose because I don't want to set unfair rules."

"Fine." My temper flashed. "I agree to your terms."

"Oh, so sweet." He extended his hand. "Should we shake on it?"

I choked on a laugh, which only made me more agitated. I didn't want to encourage this sort of behavior, but he was so darned cute. "Sure. Why not?" I shook his hand and wasn't surprised when he pulled me into his arms for another hug. He kissed my neck and then released me, turning serious. "So ... I didn't come down here because I heard you almost got yourself killed helping Lilac vent. I really did get a call that had nothing to do with this situation."

I'd almost forgotten about that. "Who was it?"

"Bradley Hopper, from the bank."

The name meant nothing to me. "And what did he say?"

"I asked him to check on a few things for me before we left for Cooper's Hollow," Galen replied. "I sent him an email, which he responded to, but I forgot to check. He got worried when he didn't hear back and called me. He found some interesting information."

"Well, don't keep us in suspense," Aurora drawled. "What information did he dig up?"

Galen didn't as much as pause for dramatic effect. He was too excited. "All of Alastair's accounts have been emptied. All of them. There's not a dime left."

Surprise smacked through my stomach lining and caused me to jolt. "How is that possible?"

"I don't know, but they're tracking the money. I have to get over there. I thought you might want to come."

"Do I?" I eagerly stepped in his direction. "Does this mean we're not fighting?"

"We're not fighting," he agreed, "but I reserve the right to vent later if it becomes necessary."

"That sounds more than fair ... as long as I have the same option."

"I think you should just let it go. I'm really the only one with a reason to be upset."

"Yeah, that's not the way this works."

"Fair enough."

TWENTY-FOUR

*B*radley Hopper looked like a typical banker. He wore an expensive suit, slicked-back hair, and boasted what could only be described as a villain's mustache. It actually curled at the corners, and I could not stop myself from staring.

"This is Hadley," Galen said by way of introduction. "She's helping me on my investigation."

Bradley nodded at me in a perfunctory manner. I couldn't tell if he accepted the information at face value or was merely playing along.

"It's nice to meet you, Ms. Hunter. I've heard all about you, of course." He extended his hand. "I'm familiar with your grandfather. I understand the two of you have been spending some time together."

"We have." I took the chair Galen gestured toward. "He's a great grandfather. He bought me a golf cart." It seemed a lame thing to say, but I was feeling out of my depth.

"Yes, I know. He used our facility to procure financing to purchase it." He beamed at me before turning to Galen. "I don't have much other than what we discussed on the phone. It's going to take us a bit of time to track what I've already told you."

"I understand." Galen sat next to me and crossed his feet at the ankles. "I still need some information."

"Like what?"

"For starters, when was the money transferred?"

"Why is that important?"

"Because Alastair is dead and if the money was transferred before then, he might've done it. If it was transferred after ... ."

"Ah." Bradley bobbed his head in understanding. "I get it. Let me look. Um ... let's see. The first account was emptied two days ago at ... nine in the morning. The other accounts followed suit within the hour."

I glanced at Galen, thoughtful. "He was already dead at that point."

"He was," Galen agreed. "How was the money transferred?"

"The normal way."

Galen bit his bottom lip. I could tell he was struggling to maintain his temper. "No, I mean was it done in person or online?"

"Oh." Realization dawned on Bradley's face. "It was done online. Whoever did it knew the passwords to his accounts. There's no reason to believe it wasn't him."

"Except he was dead at the time," I pointed out.

"Yes, well, there is that." Bradley looked distinctly uncomfortable. "Perhaps he asked his attorney to do it for him, or a financial advisor."

"Do you know who he was working with as a financial advisor?" Galen asked.

"It think it was Dirk Bradshaw at the office on Main Street, but I'm not certain."

"Okay." Galen took a moment to contemplate that and then pushed himself to a standing position. "We need to know where that money went. I've got the prosecutor working with a judge to issue a warrant to freeze those funds."

"How can they do that when the funds are gone?" I asked.

"We should be able to follow the trail of money and freeze them wherever they land," Galen replied. "I guess that might prove difficult if the money has been moved offshore or to a foreign bank, but we'll cross that bridge when we come to it."

"Sure. Where are we going now?"

"Dirk's office. We should be able to get there just before closing."

"Lead the way."

He smiled. "You don't have to come if you don't want to. I know this probably isn't your idea of fun."

"I'm fine. I like learning things. Besides, once we're done I expect you to buy dinner, so it's not as if I won't be getting anything out of the deal."

"There is that." He prodded me toward the door and looked back to Bradley. "Find that money. I want it done today."

"I'm working on it."

"Work faster. This is important."

DIRK BRADSHAW WAS MUCH MORE laid back than Bradley. In fact, he wore plaid shorts and a Hawaiian shirt. His back was to us, but the bell over his office door signified our arrival and he spoke before looking.

"I apologize, but it's too late in the day to see clients," he supplied. "I'll be back tomorrow morning, bright and early." When he turned and saw who was waiting for him, his face fell. "Oh, you're going to make me stay, aren't you?"

Galen nodded without hesitation. "I most certainly am. We have business to discuss."

"But I don't want to." Dirk sounded like a whiny fourteen-year-old, which had me biting back a smile. "I have plans with the guys from the real estate office. We're going to head down to Lilac's bar, get drunk and see if we can pick up desperate witches. It's all we've talked about all day."

Galen's eyes flashed with amusement, but he didn't back down. "Hopefully I won't take up too much of your time. The sooner you stop arguing and start helping, the faster this will be over."

"Oh, man. Fine." He flopped in the chair behind the desk and fixed Galen with a petulant glare. "What do you want? Last time I offered to help you invest that huge trust fund of yours you turned me down."

"I don't pay any attention to that trust fund and you know it."

Galen was calm as he sat. "I'm here about Alastair. I heard he might be a client of yours."

"Alastair?" Dirk furrowed his brow. "Why do you want to know about him? Unless ... are you going to arrest him for what's going on down at the beach? If so, I have to tell you that's a mistake. That's not how to get him to cooperate."

The way Galen shifted on his chair told me he was uncomfortable. It was obvious Dirk hadn't heard about his client's death.

"That's not why I'm here," Galen countered. "In fact ... um ... this is going to be difficult for you to hear. I assumed you already knew. I apologize in advance for how this is going to sound, but ... Alastair is dead. He has been since the night before the festival started."

All the color drained from Dirk's face. "No way."

"He was out at one of the cabins at Cooper's Hollow. He'd locked himself away — probably because he knew I would eventually come looking for him. We found his body."

"I can't believe it." All thoughts of escaping gone, Dirk slumped back in his chair. "How did he die?"

"Badly. He was stabbed multiple times ... with the same knife that took out Salma Hershey."

Dirk's mouth dropped open as he absorbed the news. "You're kidding. I assumed that was some sort of sexual thing, like she had a date and it went wrong or something. I didn't realize she was involved in this Skyclad Festival."

"She was acting as an influencer," Galen volunteered.

"I don't know what that means." Dirk drew his eyebrows together. "Is that like a silencer on a gun or something?"

Galen's chuckle was hollow. "No. Basically she accepted goods and money to praise things on the internet. That was her job."

"That's not a job."

"I happen to agree with you. That doesn't mean it's not a thing." He shot me a sly look upon using my words and continued. "Apparently she was aware that Alastair was running a huge scam. The thing is ... I don't understand why he would go to these lengths to steal money. He was rich. Obscenely rich. Why would he do this? I'm hoping you can answer that question."

Dirk straightened in his chair and I didn't miss the way he gripped his hands together. "Well ... you know I can't release financial information to you until I get clearance from a judge." His eyes traveled to the clock on the wall. "And that's not going to happen today."

"You could tell me off the record."

"And risk losing everything I've built if my other clients find out." Dirk shook his head. "You know I can't do that, Galen. I need you to get a warrant. Once you have that, I'll gladly sit down and talk to you ... and I think it will be an enlightening conversation. But I have to follow the rules."

Galen looked as if he was about to argue but then changed tack. "Fine. You should know that we just came from the bank. All of the money in Alastair's accounts is gone. It's been transferred to other accounts. They're working to track it, but ... it might take some time."

Dirk rubbed his chin, thoughtful. "I don't know what to tell you. I can't share his financial information — even though he's dead — without a warrant. That's simply how it works."

"Then I'll get a warrant." Galen pushed himself to a standing position. "I'll be back tomorrow morning. Be ready."

"I'll be ready." Dirk walked us to the door. "I really do wish I could tell you. Ethically, though, it's a violation."

"I get it," Galen replied. "That doesn't mean I'm happy about it. Have fun with your witches, but make sure you're here on time. We need to find answers and fast. And I'm guessing you'll have some interesting information."

"I think you'll definitely be interested. I still intend to chase the witches, but I don't plan to stay out late. I'm going for the needy ones, so I think it will be over fast."

"That's nothing to brag about," I offered, earning a chuckle from Galen.

"I'm sorry I didn't get to meet you under different circumstances," Dirk volunteered. "I hear you're all kinds of fun, which might explain how you managed to snag our illustrious sheriff so fast."

"I am all kinds of fun."

"I bet you are."

INSTEAD OF TAKING ME TO A RESTAURANT FOR dinner, Galen surprised me when we stopped at the grocery store long enough for him to disappear inside and return with a picnic basket. He smiled when he registered my surprise and handed it to me before climbing behind the wheel.

"No peeking."

"Why not?" Now that he told me I couldn't look, I had an over-whelming urge to pry open the lid and dig deep.

"Because I said so." He navigated his truck through town, bypassing the festival beach and giving it only a passing glance before pulling down a familiar street. I knew where he was going before the destination popped into view.

"Why are we going to the cemetery?"

"Because we haven't been there in weeks."

"But you don't like the cemetery." That was an understatement. Galen absolutely hated the cemetery. I, on the other hand, was oddly drawn to it. That could have something to do with the fact that someone — nobody knew who — had cursed the property so the inhabitants crawled out of their graves and wandered the property nightly. Sure, they were dangerous zombies and walls had to be erected to keep them in, but they were still there, just hanging out. One of those zombies was the mother I'd never met. After I first discovered the truth about the cemetery, I spent hours every night watching her through the observation window built into the fence. I couldn't help myself.

"That's not true," he countered as he pulled onto the street in front of the cemetery and parked, killing the engine and smoothly turning to me. "I don't hate the cemetery. I find it fascinating, just like you. The difference is, I don't want you wasting your life pondering the dead when you could be focusing on the living ... namely me."

The answer was meant to be flirty and deep at the same time, and it made me smile. "You're not so bad to focus on. We don't have to come here."

"It's been two weeks," he repeated. "While I don't think it's healthy for you to be here every night, I also don't think there's anything wrong with the occasional visit. I'm worried that you stopped coming to appease me."

"But ... that's not true. I didn't make a conscious choice to stop coming. It's more that things happened and I was distracted. I always meant to come back, but between you getting hurt and us deciding to be gooey and in love for a few weeks, that was one of the easier things to give up."

"And I get that." He slipped a strand of hair behind my ear. "I don't want you to change who you are. It occurred to me today when I snapped at you for sneaking out of the lighthouse that it wasn't fair. I wasn't really angry with you. I need you to know that."

"No, you're angry with yourself for needing more than twenty minutes to recover," I surmised. "I already figured that out. You're the big, strong protector and if you're not at one-hundred percent you somehow think that diminishes you.

"For the record, that's man thinking, and it's ridiculous," I continued. "I can't change the way your brain works and I really don't want to. You're perfect the way you are. Needing a few weeks to recover doesn't make you weak."

"I am mostly recovered," he reassured me. "The long trip out to Cooper's Hollow and spending so much time in the sun today took it out of me, though. When you mix that with the adrenaline rush from the shooting, well ... I just needed a nap."

I smiled. "And you got it. Now you're recharged and ready for a picnic."

"I am." He reached over and snagged the basket. "I'll take this. You grab the blanket from behind the seat."

"You act as if you don't trust me not to peek," I grumbled as I pushed open the passenger-side door.

"I don't." He strolled to the front of the truck and waited for me. "Come on. I think we need some bonding time."

"If we get any more bonded they'll have to pry us apart with a crowbar."

"I don't think that would work." He linked his fingers with mine. "I just want some quiet time. I think we're guaranteed the witches won't look for us here. All I want is you and me for the next two hours."

"A different way to recharge."

His grin was slow and seductive. "Exactly."

WE SPREAD THE BLANKET, gorged on sandwiches and potato salad, and then he pulled a box from inside the basket. I'd caught sight of the box as he was unpacking the food, but he'd refused to let me see inside ... until now.

"Gimme." I held out my hands expectantly, earning a laugh from him.

"Say please."

"Please."

"Give me some love, too." He tapped his cheek for emphasis.

I rolled my eyes, but only for form's sake. When my lips brushed against his stubbled cheek he caught me by the back of the head and shifted so our mouths mashed together. It was a playful move ... and it left me breathless.

"What's in the box?" I whispered as we stared into each other's eyes, causing him to laugh.

"Go ahead and open it." He handed it over.

I tore into it with the finesse of a two-year-old discovering wrapping paper for the first time, gaping in open delight when I saw what was inside. It was a small cake, a perfect representation of the lighthouse on it. The water was blue frosting, a full moon in the sky. And there, standing in front of the building, were small figures clearly meant to represent him and me.

"We didn't really get a chance to celebrate moving in together," he started. "I just thought we should do something to mark the occasion."

I had no idea why, but tears started pricking the backs of my eyes. "It's really cool. We need a photo of it before we eat it."

He patted his phone, which was resting on the blanket. "I already have that covered. It's chocolate cake with a salted caramel ribbon through it."

My mouth watered at the prospect. "Oh, yum."

He dipped his finger in the frosting at the edge of the cake and held it toward my mouth. "I thought something sweet for my sweetie was necessary tonight. We've both earned a bit of a mental break."

I laughed at his earnest expression. "That was a step too far."

"I know, but ... it's the truth."

I licked the frosting and leaned close. "I love you."

"I love you." He leaned in and kissed me with everything he had. I sank into the kiss, enjoying the way his arms automatically went around me. As much as I wanted the cake, this was nice, too.

And then I heard it. The whispering was back.

She thinks she's so special. I'll show her special.

She needs to keep her nose out of other people's business.

Why do they always have to be together? If I could just separate them.

I jerked back my head and stared into the bushes to our left. There was no rustling or shadows. But I felt evil permeating the air, and the source was close.

"What is it?" Galen asked, instantly alert.

"Someone's watching us."

He didn't ask how I knew. He didn't request more details. He stood, pulling me with him.

"We'll go together." He was firm. "I'm not splitting up from you at this cemetery again, not after what happened with the incubus."

I nodded without hesitation. "We'll go together."

"Stick close ... and have that magic you've become so good at ready in case we need it."

He didn't have to ask. I was already prepared for a battle. "Let's do this."

TWENTY-FIVE

Galen's legs were longer than mine and he was sprinting before I realized it. I couldn't keep up and almost stumbled, giving him a push to keep going when he looked over his shoulder.

"I can't keep up. Go."

"No." He immediately started shaking his head as a twig snapped in the underbrush ahead of us. The look of longing on his face when he turned back in that direction would've been comical under different circumstances. He was like a dog kept from chasing the Frisbee that was obviously thrown for him.

"You have to go." I was insistent when I pushed him this time. "I'll be right behind you. Don't worry. I just can't run as fast as you."

The sound of another twig breaking, this time deeper in the trees, helped him make up his mind. "Don't die on me," he barked as he took off. It was obvious he was torn, but if this was our only chance to catch the bad guy he didn't want to miss out.

I followed him, but he was athletic and vaulted over a bench at one point. I, of course, had to go around it. Had I tried to jump it I would've fallen on my face. By the time I hit the trail, he was out of sight.

I pulled up short, cocking my head as I tried to listen for the sound of footsteps. It wasn't easy given the way the wind rustled the leaves. Despite his size — and he was a big guy — Galen was light on his feet. I couldn't hear the echo of his footsteps and was reticent to keep going in case we couldn't find each other.

I sucked in a breath, stared for another full minute, and then turned on my heel to head back to the picnic blanket. That's where he would look for me if he lost track of his quarry. If he didn't, he would still return to update me on taking someone into custody.

Everything was exactly as we left it, and I dropped to a sitting position. As much as I wanted to dig into the cake — I'm a stress eater and could've inhaled the entire thing in ten minutes — I knew I had to wait. It was a celebratory cake. It wouldn't be much of a celebration if Galen didn't even get a bite.

To protect it, as much as give me something to do with my hands, I put the box back together and gathered the leftover wrappers and containers from our sandwiches and potato salad. When he still wasn't back, I let myself start imagining the worst. I like to think I'm an optimist, but as a realist I recognize that pessimism smacks me across the face at least three times a day.

I was feeling low, worried to the point of distraction, when the whispering started again.

She's alone.

Why is she alone?

Where is the sheriff?

Is he still out there?

Should I move on her?

Because the questions were driving me crazy — and making my palms sweat — I heaved out a breath and lifted my chin.

"I know you're out there." I didn't make a move to seek out the source of the chatter. I wasn't dumb enough to let whoever it was draw me into the foliage, where he or she could attack and I might not even see it coming. "I don't know who you are. I don't know why you've done all of this. But we will find you."

She thinks she's going to find me?

How did she know I was here?

Perhaps she's as powerful as the others have been whispering.

I furrowed my brow and glanced from left to right. Something occurred to me as I was listening, and now that I'd gotten the notion in my head it was hard to dislodge.

"I know there's more than one of you."

That did it. The whispers started in earnest.

She knows. We have to kill her.

Now isn't the time. The sheriff is coming. He's almost here. We have to run.

We can't just leave her. She knows.

She knows nothing. She's only guessing.

"I'm doing more than guessing," I called out, hoping to unnerve the voices. "I can hear you. Every thought you have, every word you try to whisper, I can hear you."

The silence that followed was deafening. Then, clear as dawn on a cloudless day, one of the voices spoke. Of course, it was only in my head, but I felt the malevolent fury laced through the words.

We're not afraid of you.

"You should be. I'm coming for you. All of us are coming for you."

We'll be waiting.

I thought about pushing harder, trying to bait the voices to attack, but they were gone. I could feel it the second they disappeared. Less than a minute later, Galen burst through the bushes. He was sweating profusely, there was a scratch on his cheek, and he gasped for breath.

"You're okay." He looked so relieved as he leaned over to rest his hands on his knees that my heart gave a little tug. "I was worried when I realized you were no longer behind me. Where did I lose you?"

"When you jumped the bench. Not all of us were track stars."

He smiled. "I could catch him ... or her. I guess it could be a her. It was weird. I thought I heard noises from two different directions. I think whoever it was tried to throw me off the scent. They were good at it, because I couldn't find a trail."

"I don't think that we're dealing with one genius," I countered. "I think we're dealing with at least two people."

"Why do you say that?"

"I can hear voices ... and they're talking to one another. I mean ... like in their heads. I think that's the way they communicate. I somehow picked up on it because of what I can do."

"Well ... that's interesting." He didn't put up much argument as he moved back to the blanket. "Do you think they're gone?"

I nodded. "I know they are. They knew you were coming back and took off. I thought about trying to track them down but figured it was safer to stay here."

"It definitely was." He swooped in and gave me a soft kiss, his hand pushing my hair from my forehead so he could study my face. "Well, if they're gone we won't find them tonight. It will be weird to stay here after that."

"You've got that right."

The smile he sent me was genuine. "How about we take the cake home and eat it in bed?"

"Now that sounds like the highlight of my day."

"I thought you would like that."

GALEN WAS STILL ASLEEP WHEN I woke the next morning. Usually he was up a good twenty minutes before me. He would then proceed to stare until I woke up. At first I thought it was creepy, but it didn't take long for me to get used to it. This morning, however, I was thrown when I realized he was still down for the count when I opened my eyes.

To make sure he got as much sleep as he needed, I left him in bed and padded out of the bedroom. I didn't bother changing my clothes — a shower could wait — but did brush my teeth before hitting the kitchen for coffee. I found my ghostly grandmother trying to load the dishwasher. Her hands were ethereal, so she had to constantly practice, and sometimes she didn't have as much luck as other times. That didn't stop her from trying, of course.

"You're finally up." May's eyes flashed with impatience as she turned to me. "You left a mess in the kitchen."

She was finicky in a lot of ways — something I found endlessly amusing — but my mind was too weary to mess with her today. "I'm sorry. It's been a long couple of days." I added water to the coffee machine and set it to percolate. "I'll do the dishes in a bit."

May's eyes widened when she got a better look at me. "You don't look as if you feel very well, dear. Are you sick?"

"No. I just didn't sleep well. I kept having these weird dreams. I could hear voices but didn't know who they belonged to, and when I went looking all I found were these giant snakes. It was ridiculously creepy."

Instead of commiserating with me, May looked amused.

"It's not funny," I groused, moving around her to grab the glasses from the sink and shove them in the dishwasher. If she was going to continue looking at me that way I was going to have to get the chores done before I started contemplating breakfast. "I'm tired ... and a little cranky."

"I can see that." May's smile was so wide it almost encompassed her entire face. "Late night with Galen?"

"Yes, but not for the reasons you think." I did my best to ignore the horrified look on May's face when she realized I was shoving the glasses in without rinsing them. "It's a dishwasher," I reminded her. "It's supposed to wash dishes. There's no reason to do it twice."

May rolled her eyes. "It's more sanitary."

"Well, I'm not in the mood to be sanitary." I finished loading the dishes and rinsed my hands before adding detergent and pressing the button. "Something has been happening to me."

"If this is about the games you've been playing with Galen, I'm sorry, but I can't listen. You may be an adult, but I'm still your grand-mother. As adorable as you two are, there are still lines that shouldn't be crossed."

The look I shot her was withering. "Listen, I'm never going to want to talk to you about my sex life. You needn't worry about that. I wasn't talking about Galen. Things between us are good."

"Is that why there's frosting all over the upstairs sheets?"

My cheeks burned under her careful scrutiny. "He bought cake last night. We were celebrating."

"Oh, yeah? What?"

It was probably best this came out when Galen wasn't around to bear witness. "He's going to move in here. Once this investigation is settled and we have our murderer behind bars, we've decided to live together."

Instead of chiding me — as I suspected most grandmothers would under similar circumstances — May chuckled. "I figured that was coming. You two practically live on top of each other as it is. It's not practical to keep a second place when you want to spend all of your time together."

I was flabbergasted. "Aren't you supposed to give me a lecture about giving the milk away for free or something? I seem to remember my college friends getting that diatribe when they tried to live with boyfriends."

"You're an adult."

"I know."

"You're allowed to live with your boyfriend." May looked absolutely delighted. "You two belong together. I've seen the way you look at one another. This is good."

I was relieved ... though I wouldn't have minded the lecture. I never got one when she was living. Once, even though she was now dead, might've been nice for my memory book. Still, I wasn't about to complain. "Thank you."

"You're welcome." She made a show of trying to pat my hand, but all I felt was a soft fluttering. "If Galen isn't the reason you didn't sleep, what's the problem?"

I sank onto one of the open stools and rested my elbows on the counter. "It's a long story."

"I'm dead. I have nothing but time."

"That's true." I grinned and then launched into the tale. It had been days since we'd touched base. She wasn't even aware that Alastair had gone to that great scammers convention in the sky. When I was finished, she seemed more concerned than surprised.

"I knew you would be powerful. I think I always knew that. You're manifesting so fast, though, I don't know what to think."

"I don't either. Some of it's fun. Like, yesterday, one of the witches staying at the Cabana Clutch hotel with June showed me how to conduct glamour spells. I'm not very good at them yet, but she said I caught on faster than most. And I did make myself look like Beyoncé. Sort of. She's a performer, by the way. She's awesome."

"I know who Beyoncé is."

"Just checking."

"And I'm thrilled you're learning new skills," May insisted. "You're a strong girl, Hadley. You're going to be an amazing witch. You just need to make sure that you don't get ahead of yourself. Eventually, your powers will be something you can always rely on. You're so new at this that you can't yet put your faith in them because you're not always aware of exactly how you're doing something at any given time."

"I'm well aware that I'm capable of confusing myself." I rolled my neck and blew out a sigh. "I don't know what to make out of any of it. It's giving me a headache, so I've decided to think about something else ... at least for the time being."

"That's a good thought. Think about Galen."

"Actually, I was thinking about June. Did you know she was a lesbian?"

May was good at covering her emotions most days, but she couldn't quite shutter fast enough this time. I didn't miss the mischievous grin that flitted across her face before she shut it down.

"You did know!" I couldn't hide my annoyance. "Why didn't you say something? I mentioned I wanted to set her up with Wesley and everything."

"I told you that wouldn't work."

"Yeah, but ... I thought you were just saying that because you wanted to keep Wesley for yourself. Not that there's anything wrong with that, of course. I just ... well ... I don't want him to be lonely."

"And you think I do?" May turned stern. "Listen here, young lady, I'm not in charge of Wesley. I wasn't his boss in life and I'm certainly not his keeper in death. I love him with my whole heart. I always have. If I thought there was a chance he might move on with someone else and find some modicum of happiness I would leave him to it. But I don't think that's possible."

"Because he feels the same way about you?"

May nodded. "Sometimes people mate for life. Wesley and I were those sorts of people ... even though we often needed breathing room from one another. We did the absolute best we could. We're still doing that."

"Yeah." I felt mildly guilty for intruding in their relationship. "It's just ... I didn't want June to be lonely either. It turns out that I was barking up the wrong tree. She and Bronwen have some sort of long-term relationship."

"She and Bronwen?" Galen stepped into the doorway, bare-chested, and ran a hand through his disheveled hair. He looked as if he'd slept hard. "Are you kidding me? Bronwen looks like she could be her granddaughter."

"I told you already she was using glamours. We talked about it at the cemetery. You were more interested in the food."

"Yeah, but ... ." He trailed off.

"Bronwen is in her late sixties," I offered.

Galen immediately started shaking his head as he headed for the coffee pot. "No, she's not. There's no way. She's in her twenties."

"It turns out that's part of the glamour thing she does. She showed me how to do it yesterday, but I'm not good at it yet. My Beyoncé is pathetic."

He slid me a sidelong look and I could tell the potential for fun wasn't lost on him. "We'll get back to that," he said after a beat. "I don't understand. The woman we saw at the docks was young. I've seen her several times since and she was young those times."

"It's a mask. I thought I noticed her looking more tired some days, as if she hadn't slept well. Turns out she doesn't always apply the glamour uniformly. She says it takes a lot of power to do it. She gave me some lessons."

"That sounds fun." He slipped a strand of hair behind my ear as he moved to stand by the stool. "I think we need to have some ground rules if you're going to run around making yourself look like someone else. Like ... no trying to fool me. You can mess with everyone else, but not me."

I thought about arguing — the power was a new toy I wanted to practice with — but I understood his worry. "I will only put on a glamour around you if we're both aware."

"Thank you." He kissed my forehead and went back to the coffee machine. "As for June, I knew she was into women ... and men, but mostly women. She didn't talk about it when we were kids, but Booker and I were fairly certain that was the case. She dated men throughout the years, but I'm pretty sure that was to get people off her case."

"Well, it doesn't seem fair that she would have to do that," I said. "I don't know whether things are going to work out with her and Bronwen. They don't seem to know either despite being in contact off and on for years. June is the sort of person who knows exactly who she is. Bronwen seems to be three different people."

"And they all have different faces," he muttered, shaking his head. "Well, I don't know what to make of it. I just want June happy. If she wants to spend her golden years with this Bronwen person, it's none of my business. I'll stand behind her no matter what."

He was good that way. Still ... . "You could've told me she was a lesbian so I didn't look like such an idiot when I tried to set her up with Wesley."

"I happen to like it when you look like an idiot. Besides, it wasn't my secret to tell."

And he had another point. "I'm still annoyed."

"I'll make you breakfast this morning to make up for it. After that, we need to hop in the shower and get going. Dirk should have the warrant by nine, which means I want to be there five minutes later to start grilling him."

"Right." I'd almost forgotten. "I want pancakes and juice."

"I think that can be arranged." He gave me another kiss, this one softer.

"I think I'm going to like this cohabitation thing if I get a home-cooked breakfast out of you a few times a week."

"Right back at you."

TWENTY-SIX

*D*irk was indeed waiting for us, and he looked none the worse for wear after his witch hunt the previous evening.

"Did you get lucky?" I asked as Galen and I reclaimed the same chairs we'd sat in the previous day.

His smile was benign. "A gentleman never kisses and tells. How would you feel if our esteemed sheriff told everyone in town about the time he spent with you?"

"I believe that memo has already been sent. He's kind of a big talker."

Galen's smile was indulgent. "I am," he agreed. "I'm a little curious, too."

"I did meet a striking lady who was in dire need of being soothed," Dirk replied. "She's very upset about the festival falling apart. Apparently none of the things they were promised have come to fruition ... but she's still hopeful that some big circle ritual they have planned will be held under the full moon tonight."

"I forgot it was the full moon." I glanced toward Galen. He generally gave me plenty of notice when it came to the phases of the moon. He could shift whenever the mood struck, and I'd seen him do it a time or two, but he mostly considered it a solitary endeavor. The full moon was his favorite night. "I guess I lost track."

"It doesn't matter," Galen supplied. "I'm pretty sure I'll have to stick close to the festival. They leave the day after tomorrow. I'm running out of time."

"Which is why you're here," Dirk noted, tapping on his keyboard. "The warrant came through first thing this morning. What is it that you want to know?"

"First, what did Alastair's finances look like?" Galen started. "I mean ... we know he had money. How much money are we talking about?"

"Well, it's probably considerably less than you might imagine. He was almost completely wiped out in the stock market crash of 2008. Even before then he wasn't doing all that well. He made a series of risky investments, which is why he came to me in the first place."

"Are you saying he was broke?"

"No. He wasn't rich, though. He was bleeding money. I would say he's worth about one million dollars."

"That's a lot of money," I argued, my mind busy. "Most people — especially people his age — could stretch that to last."

"Except Alastair wasn't most people," Dirk explained. "He was a man used to being able to spend whatever he wanted. That, of course, was the problem."

"I would've thought the Herne family was worth more than that," Galen argued. "I mean ... have you seen that house? The house alone has to be worth six million."

"Eight million, actually, but it's underwater." Dirk steepled his fingers and let out a sigh. "Alastair would freak out if he knew I was telling you this. He's dead, so it doesn't matter, but he's probably rolling over in his grave."

"He's not in a grave yet," I offered. "You're safe."

The smile Dirk shot me was devoid of amusement. "Yes, well ... here we go." He tapped his keyboard again. "Alastair inherited at a young age. He was nineteen at the time, which is long before you or I came along on the scene, Galen, but I have the full history here.

"His father, Cornwall Herne, was something of a miser. He amassed the bulk of the family's fortune, although his father did provide seed money ... as did his grandfather and great-grandfather. The Hernes were well-to-do and known throughout the island ... but Cornwall wanted more.

"He leveraged the entire Herne fortune to buy four cargo ships," he continued. "Those ships were the only vessels bringing items on or off Moonstone Bay for a good forty years. Since the people on the island were fairly well off, he could basically name his price ... and he got it."

"Why didn't the other residents simply buy their own ships?" I asked. "I mean, like you said, they were rich."

"It was a hassle, and until people stopped trying to land at Cooper's Hollow it was dangerous. You wouldn't believe how many shipwrecks there are out there. People claim the water is haunted by ghosts."

"It's true," Galen confirmed when I looked to him. "The waters on that side of the island are treacherous. There's a reason the sirens claimed it for themselves ... and we gladly gave it to them. They don't need boats and it's best to keep any sort of vessel away from that area. The sirens handle that themselves."

"Right." Dirk nodded. "Once the shipping channels were firmly mapped out, that allowed competition to come in and the Hernes lost their grip on what had been, up until then, a cash cow. Cornwall was smart, and he moved on to the next thing, which was construction."

"For a long time, the Hernes were responsible for everything built on Moonstone Bay," Galen explained. "That's why so many of the buildings look alike."

"Cornwall was brutal when it came to business," Dirk added. "He had a horrible reputation. He was mean to his wife and wasn't very kind to his only son."

"So Alastair learned to be a turd from his father," I mused. "That's ... interesting. I hope I don't inherit that trait from my father."

"You're fine," Galen reassured me. "Go on, Dirk."

"Alastair was a young man when his father disappeared while on a kayaking trip around the island," the financial advisor volunteered.

"Cornwall was known to keep in shape, and kayaking was one of his favorite endeavors. He wasn't afraid to visit Cooper's Hollow, and even though he'd been warned about the currents there, he kept going ... and that's where he disappeared one day.

"His kayak was found in pieces," he continued. "It had shattered against the rocks out there. His body was never found. Lost at sea ... ."

I opened my mouth, but Galen shook his head before I could ask my question.

"It wasn't a shark shifter," he guaranteed. "Don't let your head go there."

"Fine." I folded my arms over my chest and pouted. "I'm totally going to see a shark shifter one day. Just you wait."

"I'm keeping my fingers crossed for you." Galen's gaze was heavy on Dirk. "I've heard the stories about Cornwall. Nobody liked him, but everybody respected him."

"Pretty much," Dirk agreed. "When Alastair inherited the family fortune, his mother was bypassed. Cornwall was a stingy bastard, and as I said, cruel to his wife. She received one-hundred grand and was sent on her way."

I shifted on my chair, dumbfounded. "By Alastair? Are you saying Alastair did that to his own mother?"

"He was always a jerk," Galen answered for Dirk. "There's a reason everyone on this island has a bad Alastair story."

"Unfortunately, Galen is correct," Dirk confirmed. "Alastair basically kicked his mother out of his house and sent her to the mainland. My understanding is that she had to get a job."

"Well, there's nothing wrong with working, but ... that's low." I shook my head. "I can't believe he'd do that to his own mother."

Galen reached over and snagged my hand, giving it a squeeze. It was a silent acknowledgment that he knew what was really bothering me. Some of us would give anything to actually have a single memory of our mother. Alastair threw his mother out as if she were trash.

Dirk cleared his throat to get our attention, refraining from commenting on the private moment. "When Alastair inherited his father's estate it was worth almost one-hundred million dollars."

I let out a low whistle. "Wow. Are you saying that didn't make him one of the richest people on the island?"

"Unfortunately no," Galen answered. "I told you that this place is crawling with old money ... and old ideals. Alastair is only the tip of the iceberg."

"And, unlike his father, Alastair couldn't hold on to the money," Dirk added. "Every generation of Herne took the money they'd been bequeathed upon the death of their father and built on it. But all of that came to a screeching halt with Alastair.

"He didn't even try to add to the family coffers," he continued. "From the first moment that money landed in his lap, he started spending ... and he never stopped."

"I don't understand how he burned through one-hundred million dollars," I said. "I mean ... how is that even possible?"

"Not all of it was his fault," Dirk reassured me. "Some of it was the changing times. For starters, we live on an island. We don't have endless land to build on. I think Cornwall assumed the city would keep growing until it ingested the entire island. That's not what the DDA wanted, and it's certainly not what the other factions — including the sirens — wanted."

Galen flicked his eyes to me. "There would've been a war," he explained, "if the city tried to move too far out. The other creatures who live in the woods and hills — and, yes, even the volcano — would've put up a fight. At some point, and I'm not entirely sure when, but at some point boundaries were drawn and we've stuck to them ever since."

"The boundaries weren't drawn until after Cornwall died, so he had no idea it was coming," Dirk offered. "I have to assume that Cornwall would've had another plan in place before he died if he'd seen the writing on the wall. Alastair wasn't driven enough to follow in his father's footsteps.

"You see, he always wanted the easy way out," he continued. "Cornwall had a solid financial advisor, but he took seven percent. Cornwall considered that the price of doing business. Alastair wanted someone cheaper."

"I'm betting someone cheaper didn't have the same knowledge base as the expensive guy," I noted.

"Exactly." Dirk grinned at me, and this time it was legitimate. "It started with bad returns on investments. Then it turned into outright losses. The guy Alastair hired embezzled money. The funds dwindled fast given the money that he was shelling out for the upkeep of that house and the yacht he insisted on buying and never using. He even bought a private jet, but he couldn't keep it on the island so it was stored in a hangar on the mainland. He spent money he didn't need to spend ... and it started to drain him."

"And now he's down to one million?" Galen, stuck on that number, shook his head. "I don't want to tell you your business, but that can't possibly be right. My understanding is that Alastair shelled out millions of his own money on this festival. He expected to make ten times that back, but he did put the initial funds out there."

"Did he?" Dirk cocked his head. "He hasn't touched his accounts with me in a week. I don't know for certain what he had in the bank, but I can guess. He had about five-hundred thousand invested through our funds. It's locked up tight and can't be drawn for another ten years if he wants the full worth of the account returned to him. He chose a very high-risk investment, and that comes with strings attached."

"But ... I heard him say it," Galen protested. "I heard ... ." Slowly, he turned his gaze to me. "You were right."

I wasn't expecting the quick shift. "I was right about what?"

"That first night, after Alastair and I argued on the beach, you asked me why he would host this festival if he didn't need the money. I shot you down and said it must be a prestige thing, but you were right. If I'd chased the information then, maybe none of this would've happened."

I hated it when he doubted himself. "You couldn't have known. I'm confused about how Alastair managed to fund this entire thing if he didn't have any money."

"What did he fund?" Dirk challenged. "The Porta-Potties belong to the city. The brochures were paid for on Calliope's credit card. I know because I heard him arranging the deal. The tents were fronted to him by the Bentley brothers, who assumed they would be getting paid after the event. Alastair convinced them that would be the way to go because they could just figure in the resale value on the tents after the fact.

"The food trucks were secured on credit cards, bills that I'm certain will never be paid now," he continued. "The entertainment, such as it is, isn't scheduled to be paid until afterward. What does that leave?"

"His influencers," I automatically answered. "He paid a bunch of people to hype the festival online. Surely they had to be paid upfront."

"No." Galen, thoughtful, shook his head. "The day Cissy and the others were in my office to answer questions they said they weren't supposed to be paid until after the festival."

Now that he mentioned it, I sort of remembered it as well. "Wow. This thing was a scam from beginning to end."

"But how do all the pieces fit together?" Galen's frustration came out to play. "Did Alastair have any business dealings with Salma that you were aware of, Dirk?"

"No. I don't think he would've necessarily told me if he did, but I never saw her name on any of the festival contracts."

"I just can't figure it out." Galen rubbed the back of his neck and got up to pace. "Salma knew the entire thing was a fraud and was trying to shake down Alastair. The information you just gave us makes him an even more likely suspect in her death because he couldn't afford to pay the hush money she demanded.

"The problem is, Salma and Alastair were killed within a few hours of each other, and with the same knife," he continued. "That indicates we have one killer."

"Two voices, though," I murmured, more to myself than him.

Slowly, he tracked his gaze to me. "Yeah, but one of those voices didn't belong to Alastair. He's gone. Unless ... you don't think you're starting to hear ghosts, do you?"

"Other than May you mean?"

He turned sheepish. "That was a stupid thing to say. Of course you hear ghosts. I hear them, too. When they want to be seen on this island, they're seen."

Something occurred to me. "Is it not that way in other places?"

"Actually, no," Dirk replied. "Only those with a specific gift can communicate with ghosts in most places. It's rare. This island, however, has never been normal. It's littered with ghosts, spirits that are stronger than in most places, and everybody who wants to see them can."

I filed that away to think about later and returned to the problem at hand. "We have to break it down in the simplest terms. Who would want Salma dead? Who would want Alastair dead? We have to look at them separately. I think that's the only way we'll figure this out."

Galen's grin was quick. "You're starting to think like an investigator. Maybe I really will add you to my team. I mean ... you didn't run headlong into danger last night. You did the smart thing. I agree about tearing apart everything we know and starting from scratch. We're obviously missing something."

"Do you need anything else from me?" Dirk asked. "If not, there's a pretty witch waiting for me at Lilac's bar."

I checked the clock on the wall. "It's not even noon."

"I have to go home and freshen up."

"I think we can take it from here," Galen said dryly, shaking his head as he stood. "I do have one more question. I know you're not Alastair's lawyer, but do you happen to know what happens to his estate in the event of his death?"

Dirk hesitated, and then nodded. "I do. I didn't have anything to do with that situation, but I heard him on the phone with his attorney once. He was arguing about setting up his will. As it stands, his mother will inherit everything because he had no children ... at least to my knowledge."

"That's because I'm certain no one could stand having sex with him despite the money," I muttered. "It would kind of be poetic if his mother inherited after all, huh?" I smirked. "Now that might be enough to have him rolling over in his grave."

"Except it won't be nearly as much as she would've gotten when Cornwall died," Dirk pointed out.

"No, but you said he had five-hundred grand in an investment and more money in the bank … ," I trailed off, something niggling the back of my brain. "Galen, didn't the bank tell you how much of his money went missing when we met there?"

Galen shifted his eyes to me, conflicted. "I … no. They did not. They just said multiple accounts were drained and they weren't sure where the money went."

"If it was only a couple-hundred thousand dollars rather than the millions everybody was expecting, wouldn't they have mentioned it? I mean … Bradley seems like a pretty diligent, if annoying, guy."

"That's a very good point." Galen rubbed his chin, considering. "I think we have to head back to the bank. Apparently I wasn't as wily as I should've been."

"Can I ask the questions this time?"

He held my gaze for an extended beat and then nodded. "I think you've earned it."

"Yay!" I clapped my hands and did a little dance. "I finally get to do the grilling. This is going to be great."

Galen laughed as he moved his hand to the small of my back. "Let's not get ahead of ourselves, okay?"

I ignored him. "Can I threaten him with hard time if he doesn't come up with the right answers?"

"Oh, geez." He blew out a sigh. "Your head is going to be huge by the end of the day if we solve this thing."

"You have no idea."

TWENTY-SEVEN

*G*alen was thoughtful when we reached his truck. I could tell his mind was working at a fantastic rate. The only thing I couldn't figure out was what he was thinking.

"You have something, don't you?"

"What?" He stirred and glanced at me as he maneuvered his truck onto the main road. We had only four blocks to go. We could've walked, but if we needed to make it someplace fast it was best to keep the truck with us.

"You have something," I repeated. "You think you know who did this."

"I don't." He vehemently shook his head. "I just ... the money is something to consider. Maybe he was killed because he didn't have as much money as he pretended and that offended someone. I don't know why, but that's sticking in my head right now."

I wasn't sure what to make of the statement. "But ... why Salma?"

"That's the other thing." He licked his lips and focused on the practically non-existent traffic. "What if he killed Salma and somebody else killed him?"

I'd considered that possibility but ultimately discarded it. "I think the odds of having two killers are slim."

"You're the one who said we're dealing with a team," he reminded me. "You can't back off that now."

He had a point. "Let me rephrase that," I started. "I don't think it's possible to have two killers with separate motives. That's what we would have in your scenario. Alastair would've killed Salma to cover up his financial misdeeds and someone would've killed Alastair because ... why?"

"Maybe it's all about the money. Or maybe it's about the festival. Maybe our killer stumbled across Alastair and Salma on the beach, witnessed what he did, and realized it was all a sham."

"And then followed him to Cooper's Hollow, where he was hiding out, and managed to take his own knife to kill him with?" I challenged.

"Ugh. That is a tough detail to navigate around." He grinned as he pulled into the bank parking lot. "You really are turning into quite the little investigative thinker, baby. I'm impressed."

I rolled my eyes. "Don't be impressed until we figure this out. I think we're close. We're just missing one piece that will make the whole picture make sense."

"Well, we'd better find it soon because we're running out of time. The first ship to take these people away docks tomorrow. So far we've managed to stave off any bloodshed ... but I don't know if our luck will hold."

I considered that statement as I hopped out of the truck and crossed to the front to join him. "Whoever did this had access to the athame and a gun. You can't take a gun on a cruise ship, right?"

He shook his head. "Not usually. You can on a plane as long as it's packed in stowed luggage. Maybe we should be giving a hard look at the people who flew in."

"It has to be someone who arrived the day before the festival started. That's when Salma was killed. That's when Alastair went missing off the beach and fled to Cooper's Hollow. The sirens said he showed up alone. That means he either killed Salma and fled or someone else waited until right after he took off to take out Salma and then chased him."

"According to you, we have a team," he reminded me for the second time. "They could've split up. One could've stayed with Salma on the beach and the other could've followed Alastair."

"Except the same knife was used."

"Good point ... but that particular athame is available at multiple stores on the island. Maybe our killers bought them together because they knew they might need more than one weapon."

"That would stick out, right? I mean ... if two people went into one of the stores and bought athames together — before the start of the festival — that would have to stand out to the clerks."

"You know, that's a very good point." He ran his hand over my hair to smooth it. "I'm going to send out a deputy to question the sellers. We might get lucky."

"See. I'm more than a pretty face."

He smirked and gave me a quick kiss. "So much more. Come on. We need to talk to Bradley. I — or rather, you — have some serious questions about the money."

"You've got that right."

INSTEAD OF WELCOMING US WARMLY, Bradley looked agitated when Galen pushed his way into his office.

"I don't believe we had an appointment," Bradley groused, shaking his head. "I'm busy here, Galen."

"We're all busy," Galen countered, waiting until I was seated before joining me. "I'm investigating two murders, which I think takes precedence over whatever it is that you're doing."

"Last time I checked I was helping you investigate those murders," Bradley countered. "Isn't that why I've been working overtime to track Alastair's funds?"

"Yes, but now I have more questions about Alastair's money. For example, how much went missing?"

"Excuse me?" Bradley's eyebrows migrated up his forehead. "I don't understand what you're asking."

I cleared my throat to get Galen's attention. When he turned, I pinned him with an expectant look. "You said I could ask the questions."

He sighed and nodded. "So I did." His gaze shifted back to Bradley. "Hadley will be taking over from here."

"And I'm looking forward to it," I said, leaning forward. "We're not asking about the amount of money just to be nosy. It's important, because it's come to our attention that Alastair wasn't nearly as rich as he pretended to be."

"And how rich did he pretend to be?" Bradley asked. "Do you know how much money he supposedly had?"

"I know that he put on a show that wasn't exactly true," I replied, unruffled by his tone. He clearly didn't like being questioned by someone who didn't have a badge to back up her position. He would just have to get over it. "I know that he inherited a huge amount of money from his father and blew through almost all of it."

"That's a slight exaggeration," Bradley hedged. "He certainly wasn't as well off at the end as he was at the beginning, but he was still one of our premier customers."

"How much money?" Galen prodded. "It's important, Bradley. We're not going to leave without the information."

"Yes, well ... he had multiple accounts. The money was spread through various money market, checking and savings accounts. I would have to add it up."

"Do that," Galen instructed. "We'll wait."

Bradley looked between us for a moment before rolling his eyes and going to work on his computer. "This is highly irregular," he complained.

I ignored him and tapped Galen's hand. "You were supposed to let me ask the questions," I whined.

"You did ask the questions."

"You let me ask one question and then took over the conversation."

"Yes, well, I'm a control freak. I can't help myself. You weren't asking the questions fast enough."

"That's not fair."

"Life isn't fair."

"I expect a gift of some sort — perhaps a massage — once this is all over with to make up for it."

"I'm positive I can make that happen, but maybe not tonight. If we can sew this up before darkness falls ... ."

He left it hanging and I knew what was bothering him. "You need to run under the full moon."

He hesitated before answering. "I need to shift," he confirmed finally. "If I can run for a bit in my wolf form I'll be completely back to normal after ... well ... after that whole cupid thing."

"You're still upset about that." It didn't take a genius to figure that out. "I'm sorry. You got hurt because of me."

"That's not true." He wagged a finger. "I was hurt because they were jerks and idiots and they wanted to get their hands on that seal. We didn't realize May had it until it was already too late. That's not on you."

"You wouldn't have been hurt if you weren't dating me."

"Well, sometimes the pain is worth it." He snagged my hand and squeezed it. "Don't blame yourself. You did things exactly right that night. You're coming into your own, my little witch. I like seeing it ... even if the growing pains aren't always comfortable."

"Yeah, but ... ." I decided to drop it. We weren't going to come to a meeting of the minds on the subject so it was a wasted effort. "You need to run to recharge and completely heal. So, we'll make it happen. Whether we find our killers or not, you're heading out."

"We'll see." He turned back to Bradley, who was watching us expectantly. "Do you have our number?"

"I do." Bradley wrinkled his nose. "I was waiting for you two to stop talking to one another long enough for me to get a word in edgewise."

"We're done now," Galen reassured him.

"For now," I added. "We're going to fight about him shifting later, whether he likes it or not."

Galen growled, but otherwise didn't acknowledge that I'd spoken. "What do you have for us?"

"He transferred a total of fifty-million dollars from six accounts,"

251

Bradley replied without hesitation. "Er, well, since you say he was dead at the time of the transfers, I guess it's fair to say that someone else transferred the money."

I was taken aback. "But how is that possible? Dirk said he only had about a million total, and five-hundred thousand of that was tied up until a certain time."

"That's what Alastair had until the last month," Bradley said. "In the past few weeks, his net worth had grown tremendously."

"To the tune of fifty-million in two weeks?" Galen's eyes flashed. "Did no one think to question where that money was coming from?"

"I ... no." Bradley held out his hands and shrugged. "It's not bank policy to demand a history of the source of money. We simply accepted the deposits, which is all we're required to do."

"Can you trace where the money came from?"

"We can, but that will take a lot of time and resources. There were at least five-thousand transactions coming in within a four-week period. Some of those are still pending."

"I don't understand." Galen looked to me. "Do you understand what he's saying?"

Actually, I did. "The money that was moved was the festival money." I rubbed my forehead as I tried to do the math. "You said that some people paid ten grand and others twenty grand. He claimed he put millions in beforehand, but that's not true. I think Calliope handled most of the outgoing money. She thought she was going to get a split of the profits, but he never intended for that to be the case. We're dealing with five-thousand people at ten to twenty grand a pop. That could easily amount to fifty-million dollars."

"Un-freaking-believable." Galen looked to the ceiling. "Fifty million is definitely worth killing for."

"But who killed for it? And, more importantly, how did they get out to Cooper's Hollow to kill him without the sirens noticing?"

"That right there is a good question." Galen pressed his lips together and shook his head. "I don't even know where to start looking."

That made two of us.

.   .   .

WE RETURNED TO GALEN'S OFFICE. He wanted to brainstorm and I wasn't keen to be left behind. After several hours of watching him pace, which was starting to get on my nerves, I excused myself.

"Where are you going?" he asked, suddenly suspicious.

"I need some air."

"You're not going to find trouble, are you?"

"No." I tried to push down my annoyance at the fact that he would even suggest that, but it was difficult. "I'm going to get some air ... because you're sucking up all that we have available in this room. Then I'm going to buy some water, and maybe swing by Lilac's bar to get us lunch before returning. Unless you have a problem with me trying to take care of you, that is."

His expression softened. "I'm sorry. I'm just ... worried. Whoever it is we're dealing with — two people apparently — knows who you are. They weren't following me last night. They were following you. I just want you to be safe."

And because I knew that was true, the leading edge of my irritation with him dulled. "I know. But it's broad daylight and I'll be sticking to the main drag. We're not making any progress right now, and all we're doing is annoying one another. I think a thirty-minute break will do us both good."

He caught the front of my shirt before I could make it to the door and pulled me close to give me a kiss. "I'm sorry. I'm just frustrated. I feel so close ... and yet so far away. This isn't your fault."

"I know." I patted his arm. "It's not your fault either. I don't think either of us is used to this much together time."

"Are you second-guessing your invitation for me to move in with you?"

"No." I adamantly shook my head. "We'll be fine on that front. It's no different than how we already live, except you won't have to make runs to grab clothes and other stuff from your place. I think the difference is how much time we've been working together."

"We've worked together before."

"We have, but not quite this much. I think, going forward, we need to balance better. We're both going to have needs that have to be fulfilled. To make sure that happens, we need to be honest with one another ... and with ourselves. This will only work if we're both willing to compromise, which I think we are."

"We are." He gently pushed my hair from my face. "I'm sorry I've been irritating you with the pacing. I can't help myself. That's how I think."

"I know. I'm sorry I've been irritating you with the sighing. That's how I think."

"I only like it when you sigh with happiness."

"Good to know." I gave him a quick kiss. "I'll pick up lunch for both of us after I get my air and then we can get back to it."

"That sounds like a plan." He offered me a half-wave as he went back to his desk. "If you're going to be more than an hour text me so I don't worry."

"No problem. That I can do."

THE FEW MINUTES OF SOLITUDE DID ME A world of good. I was starting to feel a bit sheepish about the way I left. The true problem was that Galen and I both liked being in charge. We weren't good at ceding the top spot in the investigative pecking order. We were going to have to come to a meeting of the minds about that at some point. For now, we were fine feeling our way around. We'd done remarkably well so far. I didn't expect that to change.

I walked around the block four times, until I felt calm, and then I headed for Lilac's bar. On a whim, I decided to take the long way, which just so happened to circle past the cemetery. I honestly had no idea why I wanted to go during the day — it's not as if the zombies were out and about when the sun was out — but something called me in that direction.

I returned to the spot where Galen and I had our picnic, taking a moment to look in every direction before focusing on a set of thick bushes. It was here that I was convinced the voices from the previous evening had been hiding.

I picked my way around the bushes, not stopping until I was on the other side. Sure enough, I found that whoever had been out here had a clear view of the spot Galen and I had been sitting in. Had I decided to make a move at the time, I probably could've discovered who we were dealing with relatively quickly. Galen might've talked big about me doing the right thing, but I was starting to doubt myself. This would already be over if I'd ignited my courage and chased the voices.

I couldn't go back and change things, but I was kicking myself.

I circled the area several times, no idea what I was looking for. Shoe prints? Maybe, but I was fairly certain that only worked in movies. A psychic image? That would be better, but would it be accurate? Galen had brought up the very real possibility that I might see what I want to see when trying to read the minds of those I know. The same could be true when looking for a killer. I might see someone who I already disliked, which could possibly taint the process.

I heaved out a sigh after my fifth circle. There was nothing here. I was reasonably assured of that. I was about to leave when the glint of something tangled in one of the bush branches caught my attention and I leaned forward.

There, nestled in the green boughs, was a silver chain. I grabbed it without thinking, only kicking myself after. The odds of Galen being able to get prints on something as delicate as the chain I was dragging out were slim, though, so I tamped down my guilt.

By the time I removed the item, I realized it was a silver necklace ... and there was a charm dangling from it. It was a moon, and I knew exactly where I'd seen it before.

I straightened quickly, my breath clogging in my throat. When I turned, I found Thalia watching me with flat eyes. There was something different about her, something deadly. And when she spoke, I realized that at least part of the puzzle was coming together.

"You shouldn't have come back here," she growled. "Now you've made things all the more difficult."

I thought it would be difficult to find my voice. I was wrong. "I could say the same for you."

"Except you're the one who is going to die."

"Oh, yeah? I guess you're going to have to prove that."

"Gladly."

TWENTY-EIGHT

"*A*ren't you at least going to try to run?" Thalia looked puzzled by my reaction.

"No." This was the best possible place for this showdown ... though I would've appreciated a little backup. I had no doubt I could take Thalia. It might be a brutal fight, but I was determined to win.

"You're not very smart." She clucked her tongue and shook her head. "I believe that's mine." She indicated the necklace I held. "I didn't even realize it was gone until this morning. I figured I should find it before someone discovered it. A small detail, but a detail nonetheless."

"I think I'll hang on to it," I countered, shoving the necklace in my pocket and looking her up and down. She was dressed completely in black again and her countenance was even paler than usual. "I'm confused about why you've done this. All of this. It makes no sense. Did you even know Alastair, other than the money he paid you to be here, that is?"

"I knew Alastair better than most," she countered. "He simply didn't realize it. I had to lead him — and hard — to me when I learned of the festival. I figured it was my only chance to get back what was mine."

"And what is that? What do you think he owed you?"

"Everything he took." Thalia was blasé as she shifted her eyes to the east. There were footsteps approaching and for a second I was excited at the prospect. Then I was filled with dread.

"Whoever that is doesn't need to be involved in this," I warned, my voice low. "We can just pretend things are fine and once they're gone we'll start pulling hair or whatever it is you want to do."

"I don't think that will be necessary." Thalia's eyes flashed with impatience when the bushes gave way to allow entrance to yet another witch. I almost gasped when I saw who it was, but in hindsight, it made sense. Well ... sort of.

"You didn't have to leave me behind," Luster complained, her sunny hair glinting in the peek-a-boo lighting. "I said I was going with you. I had to go to the bathroom first. You know how those lines are ... at least if you want a decent Porta-Potty."

I swallowed hard as I glanced between faces. "You're working this together." There was no reason for me to be so surprised, and yet I couldn't shake the doubt creeping in. This wasn't right. How could this possibly have happened? "I knew there were two of you, but I didn't see this coming."

"I wouldn't get too upset about it," Thalia said dryly. "You weren't meant to figure it out. There's a reason we are the way we are."

"Yeah." Luster looked more amused than bothered to find me with Thalia. "You weren't supposed to find out. We put on a good show in public so people don't realize we're a team. It's always been this way with us."

"Always?" I cocked an eyebrow. "How long have you been doing stuff like this?"

"For a bit," Thalia replied, raising her chin. "I need my necklace back. You can't keep it. Besides, where you're going, you won't need it."

She sounded sure of herself. And, honestly, I wasn't as comfortable taking two of them on as I had been when it was only Thalia. Still, there was no reason to panic. I had to stretch out this interaction until I came up with a plan.

"I think I'm going to hang on to it for now, but I am curious about why you want it so badly," I admitted, my eyes traveling to the necklace Luster wore around her neck. It was a match to Thalia's, except it was a sun. The charms almost looked as if they fit together, like one of those old "best friends forever" necklaces young girls got when they were in middle school. "I'm curious about a lot of things."

"I'm sure you are." Thalia's voice was laden with contempt. "But we're not here to bond. This isn't some *Scooby-Doo* moment."

"I'm not giving you the necklace." I was firm. "As for the *Scooby-Doo* moment, why not play the game? You're going to kill me, right? That's the only play you have. Why not at least tell me why I'm dying before you carry out the deed?"

"That seems fair," Luster said pragmatically. "It's not as if we don't have time. The ritual isn't until tonight. She's the last thing we have to take care of."

And there it was again. Ritual. It was the second time I'd heard it today. "What ritual are you planning?"

"It's none of your concern," Thalia snapped. "You don't need information. You're not part of this. If you'd stayed away and minded your own business you wouldn't be dying today. This is on you, and there's a lesson in there about poking into things you ought not poke into."

"Fair enough, but I still want to know." I kept my eyes on both of them in case one tried to move on me. I expected Thalia to be the one to attack, but I'd underestimated Luster before and I wasn't keen on the idea of doing it again. "Luster will tell me. She wants to share the information."

The blonde perked up when I singled her out. "I do think it's only fair, Thalia. Besides, I kind of want to see her face." Luster's cutesy grin evaporated into an evil grimace. "What is it you want to know?"

"Well, for starters, why kill Alastair?"

"Money," Luster replied without missing a beat. "He had it and we wanted it."

That was simple enough. "And Salma?"

"An accident," Luster hedged, shifting from one foot to the other. She looked genuinely uncomfortable. "We didn't want to have to do it. We didn't even know her. We didn't have a choice. We were going after Alastair — he was supposed to die on the beach to make things easier — but she came back after they finished arguing. We thought she'd left, but she returned."

"We had a choice to make," Thalia volunteered, giving in and joining the conversation. "We could've tried to take them both out on the beach, but there was every chance one of them would get away under those conditions ... and we couldn't risk that. Besides, we didn't want Alastair to see us coming."

"So you took out Salma first."

Thalia nodded. "It was quick, but then we second-guessed ourselves. We didn't want it to look like a professional hit."

"Thalia made me go back and stab her another six times even though we were well on our way to leaving." Luster jutted out her lower lip into a pout. "She thought it was better if the cops believed it was a crime of passion."

"That was good," I offered. "We did wonder about that at the start. The problem is, Salma wasn't seeing anyone and fights over internet gigs don't generally push friends to murder. Still, it was a nice attempt."

"It was great," Thalia countered. "You didn't have any idea it was us until right now. Don't pretend otherwise."

I wanted to argue the point, but she wasn't wrong. "I didn't suspect you," I admitted. "I had no reason to believe it was you. I still don't understand why you went after Alastair. I mean ... money is great and all, but is it really worth murdering?"

"I guess that depends on your point of view," Thalia countered darkly. "From my point of view, it was definitely worth it ... especially after what he did."

"Are you talking about stealing the Skyclad Festival money? I know he promised to pay you guys, but ... how much could he have possibly absconded with? How much did he promise you in return for the publicity and your presence?"

"Twenty-grand each, but that's neither here nor there," Thalia fired back. "He owed us, but it was a debt that could never be repaid."

"I don't understand. You'll have to spell it out for me."

"And why would we want to do that?" Thalia sneered. "You've been nothing but a pain in our behinds since the start. You and your stupid boyfriend. Oh, and the cupid ... and the demon ... and those filthy sirens. There's a reason they were supposed to be kept on the other side of the island. Why did you invite them to this side?"

I drew my eyebrows together, flummoxed. She seemed to know a lot about an island she was visiting for the very first time. How was that possible? There was something very important that I was missing here.

"You're from Moonstone Bay, aren't you?" I asked finally, going for it. "You're familiar with the political climate and inner workings of the island. The only way that's possible is if you spent a great deal of time here."

Instead of congratulating me, Thalia made an incredulous face. "It took you long enough. Did you really think all of this was over some stupid festival? The festival was simply a way for us to get close to him. I mean ... really."

Something about the way she talked made me grit my teeth. "How did you cross the boundaries at Cooper's Hollow without the sirens knowing?"

If Thalia was surprised at the sudden shift in topic she didn't show it. "It wasn't difficult. All I had to do was mask our scents and cast an invisibility spell. I've done it before. In fact, I've done it on their land before."

"When?"

"When Cornwall had to die, of course. You didn't think I was going to put up with the way he treated us forever, did you?"

I worked my jaw, the possibilities she was spinning too numerous to absorb. "You're Alastair's mother. I ... don't remember hearing your name, but you're her."

"How is that possible?" Thalia asked with a blank face. "I'm obviously younger than him."

I thought of Bronwen. "It's a glamour. You're hiding your age with a glamour spell ... and you came after Alastair because he stole your

AMANDA M. LEE

inheritance. Obviously it was an inheritance you thought you deserved, because you killed your husband to get it."

I took a moment to let the rest of it fill my mind. "What a bitter disappointment it must've been for you," I continued. "You went through the trouble to learn the magic you needed to hide yourself, risked your life by crossing the sirens' land, and managed to kill your husband without anyone finding out. And then you didn't inherit."

Thalia scowled. "I probably should've expected that, but I didn't. I knew he was cruel, but to be that cruel? Had I known, I would've arranged for Alastair and his father to have an accident together. But at that time I was still trying to mold him into a decent human being. What a waste of time that turned out to be."

I couldn't help but agree with her. "I was told you were essentially banished back to the mainland and had to get a job."

She nodded. "That's true. When you go from living in the lap of luxury to trying to make a small amount of money stretch for the rest of your life, it's not easy. I had to get work as a party planner, if you can believe that. I mean ... what a loathsome job."

"I know a lot of people who like parties," I offered. "It doesn't sound so bad."

She ignored me. Now that she'd told me most of her story she obviously had every intention of telling me the rest. "It was mindless work. It gave me plenty of time to plan, though, and perfect my craft. Do you know that Alastair never once bothered to visit me? Not once. We're talking decades upon decades, and all the while he was dithering away the money his father left him. He didn't even have a family to support. He wasted it all on boats and watches. He spent it on unnecessary home improvements and one-of-a-kind furniture he never even sat in. He basically flushed it down the toilet."

Now that she'd brought it up, I had another question. "Shouldn't you be dead ... or at least in a home or something?"

Thalia made a mocking face. "That was going to be my line to you."

"I'm serious. You're ... old. Alastair was in his late sixties, which would put you in your eighties. I guess maybe dead was a little harsh, but you certainly shouldn't be strong enough to run around this island killing people. I know a little something about glamour spells. You're still you underneath, so ... how are you doing it?"

"Who says it's a glamour spell?" Thalia shot back. "That was your theory, not mine."

"But ... ." Slowly, I shifted my gaze to Luster, who was watching me with overt glee ... and something akin to pity.

"She's still trying to figure it out," Luster noted. "She hasn't put that final piece together."

"She hasn't," Thalia agreed. "We've gone this far — even though I didn't want to — so I guess we might as well go the rest of the way. Because this is your show, I'll expect you to kill her. She'll put up a fight and it's too hot to sweat. That's one thing I always hated about this island. It's hot year-round."

"Yeah." Luster rubbed her hands together and focused on me. The order to kill me obviously didn't bother her, and part of me couldn't help but wonder if she was more dangerous than Thalia. There was something deranged about Luster ... and the cracks in her facade were starting to widen. "So, here's the thing: Nobody is using a spell to make themselves appear younger. We actually are younger."

"We?"

"Thalia and me." She flicked her finger between herself and the other woman. "Don't you understand yet? We're both Annie Herne."

My stomach clenched at the admission. I remembered something from a book I'd read in May's library not long after arriving. What stuck with me was the only explanation for what was happening.

"You split your soul," I rasped, my heart rate picking up a notch. "The only way to cheat death is to damage your soul. That's what wraiths do to carry on long after they should've passed. I know that from the reapers I've met. This, this is something else. It's a different spell. It requires an elixir."

"Very good." Luster grinned as she did a little dance. She was enjoying herself. "The elixir is made from the blood of a loved one you've murdered with a ceremonial athame. It was always a plan for me, er, us. Now we're an us but I still think as a me sometimes."

I looked at them even harder. "Annie Herne split her soul when she hit the mainland. She was obsessed with paying back her son and needed time to do it."

"Oh, this wasn't just because we wanted to pay back Alastair," Thalia reassured me. "Nobody wants to die. We were already making plans for this before Cornwall's death. This was always the endgame. Make no mistake about it. Where things got mucked up was Cornwall's will. We thought we would get everything ... and instead he left it to that little weasel."

"Even then we had hope that Alastair would do the right thing," Luster volunteered. "We thought he would offer to give us a sizeable amount of the money. But he didn't, and from that moment he was lost to us."

"He never really had a chance," I mused, clenching and unclenching my fists as things finally coalesced. "People complained he was a soulless jerk, but with a father like Cornwall and a mother like you he never really had a chance to be a better man."

"Perhaps. It hardly matters now." Thalia beamed at me. "We thought we'd missed our chance at the money when we realized Alastair had burned through it all. That was worth it alone to kill him. But when we realized what he was doing with the festival ... we saw a different chance."

"It wasn't nearly as much money, but we're not Alastair," Luster added. "We know the proper people to invest with. We can turn that fifty-million into a hundred-million."

"And live forever," Thalia enthused.

Standing there, together, they looked like opposite sides of a coin. One side was dark, the other light. That was probably by design, I realized. They were forever joined and forever annoyed with one another. That part probably wasn't planned, but it was simply a component of their new reality.

"Which of you took the shot at Galen?" I really wanted to know.

"Actually, that was neither of us. We did give one of those idiot warlocks a little push when we realized he had a gun on him," Thalia replied. "I was right there, almost next to you, when the gun went off.

We thought you would stop looking for us if you were mourning him. We didn't expect that idiot to miss."

I caused him to miss, I realized. I heard the whispers because Luster and Thalia were excited. They couldn't shutter because they were essentially sharing the same brain. That was a detriment to them, but one they clearly didn't recognize.

"So, this is the end game for you guys?" I blew out a sigh. "You've gotten everything you want."

"We have," Thalia agreed. "Now, when we end you, we'll finish things. Then we'll host a special ritual this evening, steal as much magic as we can from the other witches — and I don't think it will be much because there's very little real magic on that beach — and then we'll be on our way the next day. Nobody will be able to stop us, and I doubt your sheriff will even try because he'll be so distraught over losing you."

"It really is the best outcome," Luster agreed, shifting closer to me. "I want you to know I really wish we didn't have to kill you. Although ... you know what? I really don't like you. It's more that I wish we didn't have to devastate that handsome boyfriend of yours. I would like to give him a whirl, but it wouldn't be smart to stay behind, so we'll be leaving despite how handsome he is."

My stomach clutched at the words, and I found I wanted to do her great bodily harm. Instead, I fingered the moon charm in my pocket and ran the story through my head again. I knew these women were joined together. They shared the same soul, which was fragmented. They'd been separated into two people. What would happen if they were forced to join together again as one? Would that be enough to end them?

We were about to find out. It was the best move I had, perhaps the only one. "I have just one more question."

"Fine." Thalia linked her fingers in front of her and waited. "This will be the last bit of stalling we'll allow."

"Okay." I forced a bright smile. "Did it hurt when you separated yourself?"

"Yes." Thalia opted for honesty. "It hurt a great deal. We almost didn't survive. Shredding a soul is a painful process." She wrinkled her nose. "Is that really your final question?"

"Well, technically it has two parts."

"I figured. What's the second part?"

"Will it hurt if I shove you two back together again?"

Thalia snorted. "How do you plan to do that?"

"That's not possible," Luster added.

"Let's see." I lashed out with my magic, slamming a bolt of energy into Thalia's chest. She was caught off guard, and knocked end over end as she flew to the other side of the bushes. I could no longer see her, but it didn't matter. Luster was my biggest worry.

My left hand glowed green as I grabbed her shoulder and she cried out, stunned beyond measure. I heard her calling out to Thalia in her mind ... but there was no answer. I must've hurt Thalia more than I realized.

What do I do?

How do I respond?

It hurts.

Do something.

Where are you?

Why have you abandoned me now?

I funneled more energy into the magic, burning her in the process. She cried out, tried to wriggle away, but it was already too late. With my right hand, I lifted the moon charm I'd found on the bush and shoved it toward the sun counterpart. I had no idea if this was going to work, but I had to try.

Despite her pain, Luster registered what I was trying to do at the last second, turning her full attention to keeping the necklace pieces from joining.

She no longer had enough power.

I'm afraid.

Thalia didn't answer and I was beyond caring. I pressed the two pieces of the pendant together and poured as much energy as I could into sealing it. Luster screamed, her head snapping to the sky as energy poured out of her eyes. She looked like an otherworldly hell beast being drained by the sun up above.

I pushed as hard as I could, until I had nothing left. I dropped to my knees and watched as Luster fell backward and turned to ash. She was gone in an instant, leaving me with nothing but my thoughts.

They were dark.

TWENTY-NINE

*I*t was on shaky legs that I met Galen. When I called to tell him what happened, he initially thought I was messing with him. He cut me off when I started laying things out, though, and promised he was on his way.

He was fast.

"Hey." I forced a smile for his benefit, hoping I looked stronger than I felt. "Long time no see."

He immediately drew me to him and buried his face in my hair, inhaling deeply.

"I'm okay," I reassured him, patting his arm. "Really, I'm okay. Just a little tired."

He rubbed his cheek against mine and then pulled back. "You'll do anything to get me to shift tonight."

That was enough to elicit a genuine smile. "I want you back to one-hundred percent."

"I want the same for you." He pushed my hair out of my face and studied me. "You're tired, but you'll be okay."

"I can go to bed early while you're out running around after dark, howling at the moon."

"That sounds like a plan." He rubbed his hands up and down my arms and then turned to the body on the ground. Luster had turned to dust. Thalia had turned into an old woman, although she was very clearly dead. I wasn't quite sure what to make of the phenomenon. "I don't understand any of this."

I related the story to him again, this time without interruptions, and when I finished he was grim. "Well, that's one messed-up family."

"You think?"

He let loose a hollow laugh. "As long as you're okay; that's what I'm worried about most. They admitted everything?"

I nodded. "But they didn't shoot at you. That was some guy they influenced. I didn't catch a name. I had other things on my mind."

"That's okay. If they influenced him, he's likely no longer a threat."

"Yeah, well ... ." I dragged a hand through my hair. "What do we do now?"

"We call for the medical examiner."

"But ... how will we explain it? You don't have to take me in, do you?"

His eyes lit with amusement. "No, Hadley, you don't have to worry about that. Believe it or not, this isn't the first weird death we've had on the island. It happens all the time. I believe you've witnessed a few others."

"Yeah, but I'm not usually the one who causes the deaths."

He worked his jaw. "Is this a psychological thing? Do you need counseling or something?"

"I'm thinking a strong drink and a nap will do me."

"Then that's what you'll get." He gave me a quick kiss and then reached for his phone before breaking into a smile. "I really am considering adding you to my investigative team. You have a real knack for this."

"Running headlong into danger without realizing it?"

"That, too."

I CRASHED HARD, SKIPPING LUNCH AND the drink, and instead crawling into bed. Galen made sure to tuck me in before leaving to deal with the events of the afternoon. It was dark when I finally woke.

Galen would be out running, something he desperately needed, so I didn't kick up a fuss about being alone. I headed downstairs, looked over the scant offerings in the kitchen, and took a bag of salt-and-vinegar potato chips to the back patio. From there, I could hear the revelry down the beach. Apparently they were still whooping it up at the festival. It didn't sound as if anyone was dying, so I decided to take it as a win. They would be leaving the next day. We just had to get through the night.

"Hey." Galen appeared in the bushes to my right, causing me to jolt. He was dressed in simple running shorts, no shirt. His chest gleamed with sweat. The sight was enough to make my mouth dry.

"What are you doing here?" I looked around, expecting to see more shifters with him. He liked to run with a group of other wolves, something I didn't begrudge him but often wondered about. Were there women in this group? Did they all get naked together? Was there actual butt-sniffing? Yeah, my mind goes to weird places sometimes.

"What do you think I'm doing here?" He cut through the foliage to join me, his hand immediately going to my forehead. "You were warm earlier. I was a little worried. You seem to have cooled down now."

"You're shirtless. That makes me hot."

His smile was wolfish. "None of that talk until I'm sure you're feeling better." He nudged me to lean forward so he could climb on the lounger behind me. "You need better food than this. You haven't eaten since breakfast."

"We don't have anything. I'm not very good on the domestic front. You'll have to get used to that when we move in together."

"You're a whiz in the kitchen when it comes to breakfast." He snagged a chip and popped it into his mouth. "I'll call and have some food delivered. What do you want?"

"I'm fine."

"Well, I'm ravenous. I'm ordering something for myself. Do you want me to eat a lobster feast in front of you?"

That was a low blow. "Well, if you're going to order something ... ."

He chuckled and drew his phone from his pocket. He seemed in good spirits, and his color, which had never been truly bad, was back to what it should've been. "I'll text Lilac and have her send something down. Do you want dessert, too?" He didn't wait for my answer. "I'm guessing we both want dessert. I'll get cheesecake. That's one of your favorites."

I leaned back against his chest and sighed when his arms came around me. "Did she say how long?"

"Forty minutes."

"I guess we can survive until then."

"I think we can find something to distract ourselves." He kissed the nape of my neck, sending chills down my spine. "How are you feeling? Really."

"I'm fine. You don't have to worry about me. How are you feeling?"

"I'm absolutely perfect." He moved my hair from my neck and rested his chin on my shoulder. "I'm more worried about you. And I'm not the only one. Wesley was making noise about coming by, but I told him to wait until tomorrow."

"That's probably best. I don't want to put on real pants."

He glanced down at my sleep shorts and chuckled. "I happen to like your outfit."

"You like me in whatever outfit I happen to be in. I bet you'd like me in lederhosen."

"Put them on — and nothing else — and we'll see if you're right."

That sounded unlikely. "How about we just stick to as we are for right now?"

"Yeah." He was warm. I started absorbing the heat he gave off. It was nice. "Do you want to know what happened while you were sleeping?"

"I do."

"I figured. The medical examiner says that Annie — and we do have a positive identification — died of old age. There was nothing big wrong with her, but a lot of little things."

"I think it was the shock of being put back together."

"Probably. She was gone the instant it happened. I don't want you worrying about her suffering."

"Given what she did, I'm not sure she didn't deserve to suffer a little. Of course, Alastair deserved it, too. It sounds like Cornwall deserved whatever she did to him. The only one who didn't deserve it was Salma."

"She was in the wrong place at the wrong time," he agreed. "We can't go back and change that, so we have to move forward."

"I guess. What about the sirens? Did you tell them how Annie managed to cross their boundaries?"

"Yes, and they claim it's not possible."

"Are they just saying that because they don't want anyone else to try it?"

"That's a very good question. I'm not sure. It's worth some consideration, but later." He snuggled close. "Bradley has managed to track down most of the money. It will be returned to the festival-goers as soon as possible. They know it's going to take weeks, but they're in pretty good spirits."

"I hear them." My eyes drifted to the full moon. "Did you get enough running in?"

"It's almost midnight. I got more than enough."

I hadn't realized how late it was. "I'm glad. You didn't have to cut things short on my account. I would've been fine."

"I wanted to be with you." His answer was simple, but it warmed me to my core. "Once I was certain the healing took, I immediately separated to come back. There will be a full moon next month if I want to stay out later. You're all I want right now."

"That's kind of nice. It's also nice that Lilac is sending food so late."

"She's up ... and she's fine with it."

We lapsed into silence for a time.

"What's going on down at the festival?" I asked.

"Naked dancing under the full moon."

I laughed ... until I realized he wasn't joking. "You're serious?"

He nodded, grinning at my reaction. "I figured we could eat our late dinner and then take a walk down there to check it out."

"I'm not getting naked in public."

"Good. I don't want to have to kill anyone for staring at you."

"I don't want you to get naked in front of all those women either," I supplied. "I'm not sure I'm up to yanking a lot of hair."

"I thought we could just watch from the bluff. It might be fun. There might even be magic on display."

"Yeah. I'm up for it."

"I thought you might be." He kissed my neck again. "And then I thought we might start planning my move tomorrow. There are some things we have to set in motion."

"Including me meeting your mother."

He sighed, the sound long and drawn out. "You're not going to let this go, are you?"

"Nope. You can't have half the dresser until after I've laid eyes on her."

"She'll be difficult. I'm warning you now."

"I'll survive." I shifted so I could stare into his eyes. "Today proved I can survive almost anything, even if I'm alone and outnumbered."

"I would prefer that not happen again."

"I still want to meet your mother."

"Fine ... next week."

"I've heard that before. You said I was going to meet her a few weeks ago and then something came up. I want a concrete plan."

"Then we'll come up with that tomorrow, too."

"So ... lobster, naked dancing and plans to move in together. All in twenty-four hours. It's been a pretty good day after all."

"They're all going to be good days going forward. I promise you that."

Made in United States
North Haven, CT
14 February 2023

32550669R00168